Seduction

'I'll show you.' His teeth gleamed in the dimness. When he spoke again his voice was lowered. 'Lift your skirt up.'

I stared at him, my heart beginning to thump.

'Lift your skirt,' he repeated, leaning in ever so slightly. 'I want to see your thighs.'

I looked down at my legs. Sunlight shining through the little hexagonal holes in the blind lay in bright specks all over my white skirt.

'Show me.'

The table shielded me partially from the rest of the restaurant. I put my hands on the fabric and began to gather it slowly, revealing my knees. Why not? I asked myself. They were knees, that was all.

'Good. Now, all the way.'

Very slowly I pulled the skirt right up, almost to my crotch. I wasn't showing him anything he couldn't see on a poolside, I reasoned, but it wasn't the reasoning part of my mind that was in charge. The light-spots on my pale thighs were blinding white.

'Very good. Well done.' His voice sounded thicker. 'Now, do you feel that?'

I felt something all right: my knickers were full of heat and wetness, my clit was pulsing, and my entire lower body felt heavy and swollen. Marcus put out a hand very carefully and stroked his fingertips up my thigh. I bit my lip.

Look out for other Black Lace short fiction collections

Already published: *Wicked Words 1–10*, *Sex in the Office*, *Sex on Holiday*, *Sex and the Sports Club*, *Sex on the Move*, *Sex in Uniform*, *Sex in the Kitchen*, *Sex and Music*, *Sex and Shopping*, *Sex in Public*, *Sex with Strangers*, *Love on the Dark Side (Paranormal Erotica)*, *Lust at First Bite – Sexy Vampire Stories*.

Paranormal erotic romance novella collections:
Lust Bites
Possession
Magic and Desire
Enchanted

Seduction

A Black Lace short story collection

Edited by Lindsay Gordon

This book is a work of fiction.
In real life, make sure you practise safe, sane and consensual sex.

Published by Black Lace 2009

6 8 10 9 7 5

Honey Trap © Janine Ashbless; Rush © Gwen Masters; Malicious Intent © Sommer Marsden; Garden of Eden © Primula Bond; The Cicadas © Carrie Williams; The Rancher's Wife © Kristina Wright; Christmas Present © A.D.R. Forte; Not Knowing It © Charlotte Stein; Just One Night © Terri Pray; All for One © Rhiannon Leith; It's Got to Be Perfect © Portia Da Costa; The Shopping List © Shayla Kersten; Twelve Steps © Shada Royce

First published in Great Britain in 2009 by Black Lace, Virgin Books, Random House, 20 Vauxhall Bridge Road, London SW1V 2SA

www.black-lace-books.com
www.virginbooks.com
www.randomhouse.co.uk

Addresses for companies within The Random House Group Limited can be found at:
www.randomhouse.co.uk

The Random House Group Limited Reg. No. 954009

A CIP catalogue record for this book is available from the British Library

ISBN 9780352345103

The Random House Group Limited supports The Forest Stewardship Council (FSC®), the leading international forest certification organisation. Our books carrying the FSC label are printed on FSC® certified paper. FSC is the only forest certification scheme endorsed by the leading environmental organisations, including Greenpeace. Our paper procurement policy can be found at www.randomhouse.co.uk/environment

MIX
Paper from
responsible sources
FSC® C016897

Typeset by TW Typesetting, Plymouth, Devon
Printed in the UK by CPI Bookmarque, Croydon, CR0 4TD

Contents

Honey Trap
Janine Ashbless

If you stand at the right angle near a floodlight in the garden of the Royal Aqaba Hotel, and you happen to be wearing just the right sort of light cotton dress, then the light shines through the cloth revealing everything beneath it. I wasn't aware of the full significance of that at the time. It took me a few hours to even realise that it had happened.

Rhys had fetched pre-dinner drinks from the bar under the palm trees. I had a sunset-coloured cocktail in my hand as we wandered between the flowering shrubs, pausing every so often to admire the fish in the artificial rills winding at our feet. In a country where fresh water was precious, the hotel made a point of conspicuous consumption. The evening was just settling to a comfortable warmth after the baking heat of a day we'd spent mostly in the sea. We stopped in front of a floodlight and Rhys kissed me, snaking his hand about my waist.

'Are you enjoying it all?' he murmured.

'Of course I am.'

'And you still love me after all these years?'

'All these years?' Four years of marriage was hardly a lifetime. I grinned cheekily at him. 'Oh, I think so.'

'Good.' His gaze lifted from my face and I saw his eyes widen a little. 'Oh – Marcus. Evening.'

Turning, I saw a man leaning on the parapet of a little ornamental bridge. He nodded at us. 'Rhys.'

'Astrid, this is Marcus Stringer. I met him in the bar that first evening. Marcus, this is my wife Astrid.'

We made polite greetings. Rhys had made a slight tactical error in mentioning our first evening, since he'd annoyed the hell out of me then by insisting on going down to the bar for a drink when I'd wanted to roll him on the bed and mess up the clean sheets. I'd ended up spending a grumpy half-hour reading on my own, and he'd had to work with some vigour to make me forgive his thoughtlessness.

Marcus, it turned out, was an American, and I forgave Rhys even more because he had that whole George Clooney look, in spades. He was on his own that night, and I had no objections when Rhys invited him to join us at dinner.

'Are you holidaying by yourself, Marcus? Is your wife not here?' I asked as we flicked open our table napkins. I figured it would be acceptably gauche to ask right now; if I left it too long the question would look plain nosy.

He smiled. 'I'm not married.'

'Oh, right.' I reached for the table water.

'Allow me.' He took the carafe from my hand and began to pour into our glasses. 'No, I know I'd make such an appalling husband that I've decided to spare any woman the pain of finding it out for herself. Besides, I like to travel solo. You meet more people that way.'

My interest was piqued. 'Where've you been travelling, then?'

'Right round the Middle East. Yemen, Syria, Egypt – now here. Backpacking mostly, but I felt I needed to chill a bit by this stage.'

I felt my jaw drop. There just weren't that many American tourists in Arab countries at the moment: to find one with the guts to do it solo genuinely surprised me. 'Yemen?' I said, almost squeaking. 'Oh – I'd love to go there! What's it like?'

So dinner that night was eaten to the tune of a long interrogation about the countries Marcus had been to. Rhys mostly sat and listened, smiling faintly. Our new acquaintance wasn't even based in the States, it turned out; he worked for a German manufacturing company and constantly flew back and forth between its different European offices. I had a marvellous time vicariously indulging my wanderlust. Then the conversation turned to what we had been doing: Rhys's scuba-diving mostly. He'd become wildly enthusiastic over the last few days.

'Don't you dive?' Marcus asked me.

I pulled a face. 'Not really.'

'The idea was,' explained Rhys, setting an empty wine bottle aside, 'that we'd both get our PADI certificates before we came out here so we could do the coral reefs properly. But Astrid caught a cold the week we were booked in for the intensive course, and got an ear infection.'

'They wouldn't let me go down.'

'Of course not,' Marcus answered.

'So she missed out on the certification. She's been on the beginners' dive here, but it's not the same.'

'I don't even think I'm that keen any more,' I admitted. 'I mean, it's lovely on the coral and the fish are fantastic, but you know; there's only so much of it I'd want to do in a day. Unlike Rhys.'

'I'd stay down there all week; I really would.' Rhys sighed. 'But Astrid's getting itchy feet, I think. This isn't really the right place for a holiday if you're not interested in the beach or diving.'

'It's OK,' I reassured him. 'It's a change from the usual.'

'Well, would you have any interest in visiting a Roman ruin?' Marcus wondered. 'There's a wayside settlement they've just finished excavating about an hour out of town, on what used to be the Via Traiana Nova. I'm taking a taxi out there tomorrow. Would that be your sort of thing?'

My eyes widened. I love ambling about ruins trying to picture what it would have been like to live in such places. 'That would be great! Would you mind us joining you?'

'Not at all.' His eyes crinkled warmly.

Marcus left us after dessert and Rhys and I retired to work off the effects of the two bottles of wine. As we walked back through the gardens to our apartment I noticed a couple passing by one of the powerful uplighters that lit the façade of the hotel. For a moment her dress turned into a misty nimbus with the shape of her body perfectly outlined within. I caught my breath, wondering if the same thing had happened to me earlier in the evening. Then I checked myself, reassured. Rhys had been looking right at me as we stood in the gardens; if there had been anything untoward he would have noticed and done something about it.

I'm not used to drinking at dinner; it made me giddy and giggly that night. It seemed to put lead into Rhys's pencil though, and he chased me squealing across the bed, determined to spank my behind no matter how much I tried to *almost* thwart him. 'What did you think of Marcus, then?' he asked, pinning my wrists behind my back.

'He seemed a nice bloke.'

'Huh. Bet you liked him more than that. Bet you thought he was fit.' His hand descended sharply on my bottom and I squealed into the mattress.

'He was all right, I suppose,' I admitted. Rhys, I realised, was a bit jealous. 'For someone that old, anyway.'

'What are you, then – jail-bait?' But the conversation fell apart after that as we concentrated on spanking and fucking.

The next morning, though, despite having been all enthusiastic about our excursion while he'd had a few glasses of wine inside him, Rhys suddenly lost interest. 'Tell you what, love,' he said, eyeing the dive boats in the harbour with the gleaming eye of the fanatic, 'why don't you go out to this Roman thing with Marcus and enjoy yourself?'

'On my own?'

'You'll be fine with him. He's been all round the Middle East; you heard. He speaks a bit of Arabic, and knows what he's doing better than I would out there.'

That wasn't quite what I'd meant but I just frowned, a little hurt that Rhys found the reef more alluring than a day with me. I also felt, even though I didn't admit it to myself at the time, a tingle of pleasure. Marcus was attractive and interesting and had travelled all over the world. I was more than happy to spend a day in his company, even alone. Perhaps especially alone.

Marcus himself didn't seem exactly upset that it was just me, when we met in the hotel lobby. 'Your husband must be the trusting sort,' he remarked with a disarming twinkle. I chose to misunderstand him.

'Well, you're not in a position to kidnap me, are you?'

'Not really.' He cast an eye over my figure. 'Good choice of clothes.'

Because we were leaving the hotel I'd picked a summer dress with a long skirt and modest sleeves down to my elbows. Against the sun I'd brought a floppy-brimmed straw hat. 'I'm not daft,' I pointed out.

'You certainly aren't. But the way some tourists dress, you'd think they had no idea at all.'

We went out to meet our taxi driver. He spoke only a little English, but Marcus's combination of Arabic and French allowed them to carry on a trilingual discussion about the route and the timing. I left my travelling companion to it, trusting him to get everything sorted. With both of us in the back seat of the car we set out inland.

For someone so keen on foreign travel I paid remarkably little attention to the baking-dry scenery on that journey, because I was enjoying the conversation with Marcus too much. We had so much in common, in taste if not experience, that it was startling. We both enjoyed the same books, the same movies, the same music. When I mentioned attending the Glastonbury Festival we were united in preferring the fringe to the main stage events, and he insisted I ought to go to Burning Man one year soon – something I already held as an ambition.

It is, somehow, enormously flattering to see our own traits mirrored by someone else, as if it validates us.

But I was also beginning to get a handle on him; why this attractive, confident man should be 'appalling' husband material. It was there between the lines of his life-story; he'd been a volunteer worker in Botswana, spent a couple of years as a teacher and then a tourist guide in the Far East, and now bent his talent to making quick easy money from business positions that lasted no more than a year or two each before he moved on to the next faceless corporation. Marcus had a terminal case of itchy feet. Day-to-day life was hardly real. His career didn't interest him and he laughed at the thought of ambition; it was entirely about making enough money to fund his leisure travel. He just wasn't the sort who could settle down to family life. He would always be looking for new horizons, new experiences and – I rather suspected – new girlfriends. It didn't make me dislike him. It just made me grateful that Rhys and I could balance our own selves rather better. Marcus had a life I could admire, but not covet.

Then our conversation was interrupted by the driver. 'You are married?' he asked, looking at us in his rear-view mirror.

'Yes,' said Marcus without hesitation, laying his hand just above my knee and squeezing proprietorially. I was so surprised I couldn't react.

'Ah. How many children?'

'None yet.' Marcus didn't remove his hand. 'We only married this year. And you – how many children do you have?' The conversation spun away onto the driver's family and Marcus seemed entirely happy exchanging gossip, making up on the spot the occasional detail about our family life, while I tried not to swallow my tongue. All the time Marcus kept his hand on my thigh, his fingers warm through my cotton skirt. Only when the subject was exhausted did he sit back, casting me a conspiratorial smile.

I stared out of the window after that, disquieted by his behaviour – and by my reaction to it. The touch of his hand had sent a bolt of heat through my body and my sex was suffused with an uncomfortable warmth. But I didn't have long to worry about it, because we turned off the main road and down into a wind-scoured valley, tooting our horn as we pressed through a flock of goats, and finally reached a fenced-off collection of ruined walls beneath a cluster of cafés and souvenir stalls. There wasn't any time to worry as we ran the gauntlet of traders, paid for entry and finally slipped into the calm of the archaeological site.

'All right?' asked Marcus as we tramped down the concrete path.

I stopped. 'That was a bit presumptuous of you back then. About us being married.'

He looked amused. 'Would you rather be known as the sort of woman who's willing to share a taxi with two men she *isn't* related to?'

'Oh, I get why you did it, just . . .'

'Of course,' he added, not quite keeping a straight face, 'you are exactly that sort of woman.'

'Hey! That doesn't mean –'

'Of course it doesn't. I know that. Just because you'll let a strange man sit next to you and talk to you, doesn't mean you'll fuck him just because he wants it. You might fuck him if *you* wanted it, but that's the nuance that doesn't translate very easily: female choice.'

I bit my lip, taken aback. He held my eye. 'That was the

subject of my thesis at university,' I said, feeling oddly at sea. ' "Female Choice in Victorian Fiction".'

'Really?' His eyebrows rose appreciatively. 'There you are, then. You know what I'm talking about.'

'Yes . . .'

He held out a photo-guide he'd bought at the ticket office. He hadn't asked if I wanted it. 'Go for it, Astrid. We can take as long as you like.'

Accepting the book, it occurred to me that I hadn't challenged his assertion: *you might fuck him if you wanted it.* By then it was a bit too late.

We wandered around the place together, unhurried. It wasn't a big site, though it had a marketplace and a temple dedicated to Jupiter, a small theatre, some large houses designated vaguely as 'official residences' and a few *in situ* mosaics. I was just pleased to be out exploring. Some of the buildings had been partially restored and the head-high walls cast the only patches of shade. While I was examining the mosaics Marcus wandered off to poke around in some semi-roofed cellars. I decided the artwork depicted Leda and the Swan, though it was very worn. When I'd taken enough photos I had a look down a well shaft and then went to find Marcus again.

He was standing with his back to the shady side of a wall, his Panama hat in his hand, fanning himself lazily. He smiled as he saw me approach, then tilted his head, inspecting my shoulders. 'You've caught the sun, Astrid.'

I made a noise of dismay, reaching automatically for the tube of sunblock in my bag. I burn easily; it's something that comes with the carrot-coloured hair and the freckles and blue eyes.

'Let me do that.' He took the tube from my hand.

'Ah – I'm not sure that's a good idea.'

His smile was utterly disarming. 'Hey; we're a married couple, remember?'

'I don't think even married couples are supposed to touch each other in public.'

'Well.' He made a show of glancing around. 'Nobody's looking at the moment. Turn around and I'll do the back of your neck.'

I gave in. My neck and shoulders were already tight with the first inklings of sunburn. Marcus gathered my bobbed hair in his hand to bare the nape of my neck then squirted out blobs of sunblock. I bowed my head obediently, wishing my insides wouldn't squirm like that. The tug on my hair was subtly suggestive of erotic violence. The cream was deliciously cool and his fingers gentle, working in slow patient strokes to smear it over my shoulders and up to my hairline. It felt lovely. Rhys was always swift and businesslike when he did it; this was irreproachably gentle, but the effect on me was far less innocent. I pressed my lips together so as not to make any noise.

'OK. Let me do your face.'

I turned, flustered, as he let my hair fall back into place. 'I can do that.'

'Shush. Close your eyes or it'll sting.' He squirted little white pearls of suncream onto his fingertips, then stuffed the tube out of the way into his jeans. I stood, feeling horribly conflicted, as he dabbed the cream on my face. Then I closed my eyes. He stroked all over my face, both hands moving in symmetry, up to my forehead, thumbs down the line of my nose, massaging across my cheekbones. I felt all the breath go out of me. There was absolutely no mistaking it this time; this was a caress he was giving. His fingers stroked under the line of my jaw and I trembled with the effort of holding still. Then he just cupped my face. I opened my eyes slowly.

'You've got wonderful freckles,' he murmured, his eyes shining.

Slowly I pulled from his hands, trying to remember to breathe. 'Ah . . .'

'Shall we go sit in the shade? There's a wall at the back of the theatre and we'll be able to catch any breeze coming up the valley.'

'I'm a bit warm,' I admitted faintly, wondering if he would have kissed me if I'd kept my eyes closed. Wondering if I dared want him to.

We went and found his patch of shade, and sat side by side on the bare rock step, looking down the valley at the dried riverbed. All the trees looked dead. Two small boys were trudging after their goats in the mid-distance. We sipped our bottled water. I glanced sideways at Marcus, who was sitting with one leg bent up, his wrist resting on his knee, his bottle swinging from his hand. There was a faint, distant smile on his lips as he gazed out over the land, which provoked me. 'What are you thinking about?' I asked.

He answered without hurry and without looking at me. 'I'm thinking about which part of you I'd like to fuck first, if we got the chance.'

'Oh.' I couldn't find it in me to be shocked; we'd crossed a threshold of understanding some minutes back.

'I'm sorry.' He cast me an amused, sideways look. 'Would you prefer "make love" to "fuck"?'

'I prefer "fuck".'

'I thought you would.'

'It's not going to happen, though.'

'If you say so.'

'I'm married. You know that.'

'I sure do.'

There was a silence. 'Which part would you pick?' I asked.

He looked at me properly then, obviously pleased, and said, 'You won't find out by asking.' He straightened up. 'Shall we go get something to eat?'

There was a café out at the main entrance. By now it was the full blaze of noon and we were desperate for shade, so we went inside instead of taking an exterior table. There were a few other customers but it was so dark after the daylight glare that I could hardly see. Marcus led me right to the back of the room where the tables were unoccupied and we sat on a cushioned bench against the wall. There was an open window to my side, covered by a rattan blind, so we had a bit of a breeze without having to suffer the sunlight. A waiter came over as we were looking at the menu, and Marcus ordered a cup of coffee and a tea.

'Excuse me!' I protested. 'You didn't actually ask me!'

'Did you want a coffee?' he said, clearly not believing that I did. He was right too; I couldn't cope with the thick black stuff they served in tiny cups.

'I wanted a cold drink!'

He called out to the retreating waiter, ordering a couple of *limons*.

'Hoi! You did it again!' I didn't know whether to laugh or be annoyed by his overweening confidence.

'You'll like it. They just liquidise a whole lemon with icing sugar and water – very refreshing. And I asked him to make sure it was bottled water.'

'That's not the point, Marcus,' I hissed. 'You should have asked. Female choice, remember?'

He crooked an eyebrow. 'You're right; choice is powerful. But surrendering the power to choose ... that's powerful too.'

'What?'

'It's another order of power altogether.'

'What are you talking about?'

'I'll show you.' His teeth gleamed in the dimness. When he spoke again his voice was lowered. 'Lift your skirt up.'

I stared at him, my heart beginning to thump.

'Lift your skirt,' he repeated, leaning in ever so slightly. 'I want to see your thighs.'

I looked down at my legs. Sunlight shining through the little hexagonal holes in the blind lay in bright specks all over my white skirt.

'Show me.'

The table shielded me partially from the rest of the restaurant. I put my hands on the fabric and began to gather it slowly, revealing my knees. Why not? I asked myself. They were knees, that was all.

'Good. Now, all the way.'

Very slowly I pulled the skirt right up, almost to my crotch. I wasn't showing him anything he couldn't see on a poolside, I reasoned, but it wasn't the reasoning part of my mind that was in charge. The light-spots on my pale thighs were blinding white.

'Very good. Well done.' His voice sounded thicker. 'Now, do you feel that?'

I felt something all right: my knickers were full of heat and wetness, my clit was pulsing, and my entire lower body felt heavy and swollen. Marcus put out a hand very carefully and stroked his fingertips up my thigh. I bit my lip.

'You don't believe this is powerful? See what you've done to me.'

Very tentatively, not looking at him and trying not to move my upper arm in an incriminating manner, I stretched my fingers out to touch the fabric of his trousers. I found it tented. A foray discovered the thick ridge of his erection, as hard as bone, straining up against the cloth. Staring across the room with my mouth dry and my panties awash, I felt dizzy and dissociated, helpless under the tide of my arousal.

Then the waiter reappeared from behind the bar, bearing a tray of drinks. With one smooth movement Marcus tugged my skirt into place and I withdrew my hand. I let him order lunch without demurral. My sex was so wet I was certain I'd be leaving a damp patch on the cushions.

During the meal, and the ride back to town afterwards, we spoke very little. What was there to say, after all? It wasn't as if anything could happen. I wasn't going to let him fuck me out here in public and I wasn't going to conduct an affair under my husband's nose back at the hotel. The whole thing was an impossible fantasy. Marcus seemed quietly content anyway. I wasn't feeling calm at all, because it was the first time since my wedding that a casual interest in a man other than Rhys had hardened to serious temptation. I was glad there would be no opportunity to really mess things up. Well, a part of me was glad. The other part spent the whole journey back watching him furtively and imagining what might happen if he pulled up my skirt right there in the back of the taxi and ran his hand up the inside of my thigh to my sopping gusset and then pulled me into his embrace, while our driver watched us in the rear-view mirror with horror and delight.

Back at the hotel, Marcus walked me to my apartment. I think he was talking about visiting the Wadi Rum at this point, but I wasn't really listening to him, just to the thump of my heart and the surge of my blood. I wasn't going to ask him in, I told myself. I was going to let him go on the doorstep.

But the door was locked and no one answered my knock. I nearly swore then; I was so unsettled by my inner struggle. 'He's still out on the boat,' I groaned. 'Oh God.'

'You can come over to my room while you're waiting.'

I rolled my eyes, trying to hide how rattled I was by the suggestion. 'No. I need a shower. Oh, it's so damn hot ... And my swimming costume is inside so I can't use the pool ...'

He shrugged. 'Use my shower.'

'That's ... a really bad idea,' I said with feeling.

He laughed. 'I promise I won't join you unless you ask me. You trust me, don't you?'

I lifted my eyebrows without answering. It wasn't him I mistrusted: oddly, I felt as if I knew him well enough, as if I'd known him for years. In fact it had been less than twenty-four hours.

'Aha.' He looked both abashed and slyly flattered. 'Well, you could always lock the door, you know. And if you don't want a shower I've still got air-con and room service.'

In the end I went with him to his apartment, which was the same style as ours, with a double bed and kitchen area and a sitting room. I did use his shower, and one of his pristine fluffy towels. I did bolt the bathroom door in fact, but very quietly, so as not to be insulting. And as I stood under the wonderful tepid downpour I kept an eye on the handle, wondering if he'd try it. The thing never twitched, and though I did think I heard his voice at one point, it was so faint it couldn't have been meant for me.

Towelling myself down, I felt considerably better for my wash but no less precarious in my virtue. I could just open the bathroom door, I told myself. I could walk out there naked and he'd take one look and throw me onto the bed and fuck my wet hole. I wondered what his cock would look like. He'd be circumcised, I assumed, being American. I wondered how big it would be. I wondered whether he liked to go on top or beneath, and pictured him gripping my ankles and pushing them back and wide as his big stiff cock pounded into my cunt. He'd go for the difficult, gymnastic positions, I thought.

My freshly washed sex got a little less clean from the mental picture. I stood facing the door and just stared at it for a long, long time. To be honest, I think it was cowardice more than loyalty to Rhys that stopped me walking out there naked. I couldn't bring myself to take such a huge decision, so I pulled my dress back on, wishing I had a clean change of clothes. I couldn't bear to wear my sweaty bra and damp panties, though, so I stuffed them in the bottom of my bag.

The air-conditioner had made a difference to the main room during my sojourn in the bathroom; it was pleasantly cool now. Marcus was sitting on the low divan couch, faced in traditional fabric, that dominated the sitting area of the apartment. He wasn't reading or watching the TV or anything, just cradling a whisky glass and waiting for me. He'd changed into a fresh shirt, though. He smiled warmly. 'Drink?'

'Gin and tonic,' I suggested. 'Or – no, just some cold water. I've got a bit of a headache.'

'Oh? Not too bad I hope?' he asked, hunting in the mini-bar.

'No, just from squinting in the sun. It was so bright out there.'

'I could give you a head-rub if you like,' he offered. 'I learned Indian massage a while back.'

'In an ashram?'

He handed me my drink. 'In Canberra. There wasn't a lot else to do.'

He wasn't to know it, but he'd hit on my weakness. I love having my head massaged; it's the next best thing to sex. So at his suggestion I sat down on the couch and he knelt up behind me to take my newly washed head in his hands and rub it. And he was very good indeed – patient, firm and skilled. He eased all the tightness from the back of my neck and pressed smooth my forehead and scalp. He tucked his arms under mine, ordered me to relax and shut my eyes, then scrunched my shoulders until they unknotted. I lost all sense of time or thought under his kneading hands, dissolving into pleasure, as if he'd opened my skull and taken my brains out. More and more of my weight relaxed against him. His hands broke little murmurs of pleasure from my lips, and when he stroked my throat softly I groaned. His arms were around me gently, his firm body supporting me.

'That dress you wore last night,' he murmured in my ear, tracing my cheekbones with his fingertips.

'Mm?'

'Did you know it went see-through against the floodlight? Did you know I could see all your body beneath it?'

I was almost too relaxed to speak. 'That's not true.'

'No?'

'I think Rhys would have noticed.' I was faintly aware that I was using my husband's name as a talisman, to ward him off. It didn't work.

'What makes you think he didn't want to show off the beautiful body of his wife, for me to see?'

I smiled.

'You were wearing very sexy red lace lingerie last night. Right now, though,' Marcus whispered, 'you're not wearing either a bra or panties. I can feel your skin through this dress.' He brushed his hand across my hip to make his point. I forced my heavy lids open, trying to focus. 'No,' he breathed, his voice tender and heavy. 'Keep them shut.'

His fingers stroked my lids and my lips and I obeyed with a sigh. Cradling me in one arm, he kissed my lips softly, seducing them open with his gentleness. I tasted the smokiness of the whisky on his tongue. His free hand caressed the tips of my breasts and I realised that the air-con had brought them to obvious points under the cotton. I moaned into his mouth.

'Now I'm going to touch your pussy, Astrid,' he said. 'And you're going to let me.' He put his hand on me through my skirt and he was right; I not only let him, I parted my thighs a little. 'That's right,' he sighed, stroking me. 'Now. You lifted your skirt for me at the restaurant, didn't you. You're going to do that again. Slowly.'

Mesmerised by sensation I drew my skirt up my thighs, finger by finger. Cool air lapped at my damp skin. When I got to the hem he laid his hand on my bare mound, parting the swollen lips with a couple of fingers, delving between to find the syrupy slickness of my juices. When he traced the contours of my clit I writhed against him.

'Oh, honey, you're ready for this, aren't you?' His touch was like fire to my tinder: I felt flames rushing through my body. 'All day you've wanted me to do this, haven't you? And you've no idea how long I've been waiting to do it. Look how sweet and wet and open this is for me.' His lips brushed away any objections that might have risen to mine. 'Now unbutton your dress. I want to see that beautiful body, Astrid.'

I fumbled with the little buttons, unable to look because he was kissing me, and bared my breasts. He sighed with satisfaction.

'Now play with them, Astrid. Play with your breasts while I make you come.'

I cupped them, squeezing them together, fingering my nipples, but I couldn't do it for long. 'Oh – I'm coming now,' I gasped.

Marcus plunged his fingers into my slippery entrance, using his thumb on my clit. 'Yes. You are: right now.'

'Make her come,' moaned the echo.

I opened my eyes as my orgasm flooded through me. I saw Rhys standing against the kitchen bench, but it was too late and I couldn't stop; I just stared and moaned and spasmed in pleasure.

'Oh God,' whispered Rhys, wide-eyed.

'Rhys?' I whimpered, when I could speak again. For a brief moment I tried to sit up straight but Marcus's arms tightened around me in a hug.

'It's all right, honey.' His voice was warm and sure.

'Rhys? What're you doing here?' My voice came out husky.

'God, you're beautiful,' said Rhys. 'So fucking hot and beautiful.'

'He's not angry,' Marcus said.

I gaped. This felt wildly unreal. 'What's going on?'

'Astrid, I . . .' My husband looked shifty. I jumped to the worst possible conclusion.

'Did he *pay* you for this?'

'Far from it,' said Marcus smoothly. 'Astrid, there is something you don't know. Rhys and I met on the Net about six months back. On a cuckolding site.'

'What the hell does that mean?'

'It means that we both have certain specialist interests. My thing is married women –'

'Your *thing*?'

'My passion. My obsession: women who are faithfully, happily married, and just longing to be seduced all over again. And Rhys's single greatest turn-on,' he added, his voice hardening, 'the thing he fantasises about constantly, is the thought of his beautiful wife being fucked by another man. Of her being so aroused by this stranger that she'll do anything for his cock. Of him watching helplessly while she gets the shafting of her life, better than any he could ever give her, and she screams that other man's name and begs like a slut for him to fuck her more.'

I was stunned. It all made sense now: the way Marcus knew exactly the right things to say, the way he knew what I liked and what I wanted. He'd certainly done his homework: he'd been perfect for me. I'd been played by both men, but it was impossible to take the high ground when I'd just been discovered by my husband with someone else's fingers up my cunt. I couldn't even feel indignant. I cleared my throat to ask, 'Rhys told you everything, didn't he?'

'Everything. He gave me copious notes ... and photos. I've been looking forward to this for a long time.' Marcus stroked my damp hair from my face and kissed my cheek. 'Now I'm going to fuck you, Astrid, in front of him. Just like he wants me to. Just like you want.'

'Rhys?' I whispered.

'Please, Astrid.' He looked like he was in torment. 'I want you to fuck him.'

It took balls to admit that, I guess.

Quietly, Marcus slipped the button of his fly and unzipped his trousers. He adjusted himself on the couch so he was sitting next to me and hefted his cock out, stroking it reverently. It was a strong dark prick with clean lines, standing hard to attention. His pubes were shaved down to a neat shadow.

'Touch his cock, Astrid.'

I did, laying my hand on its quivering length. Marcus stroked my back.

'Is it bigger than mine?'

'Yes.'

'Longer – or thicker?'

I wasn't inclined to be tactful. 'Both, Rhys. He's much bigger than you.'

Rhys made a little noise of agony and delight. 'Suck his cock, Astrid.'

Marcus helpfully stood and dropped his pants. He had long hard legs; the body of a travelling man. As I bent forward and took him in my mouth he gave his balls a little squeeze and laid his other hand on my head. He hadn't showered yet of course, and I was delighted by the hot musk of his crotch. I explored his swollen glans with my tongue, eagerly.

'Take him down your throat as far as you can.' Rhys had moved round for a better view.

'That'll do, Rhys.' Marcus used my hair to draw me off his cock. 'I'm the one who's fucking your wife, not you. So you're going to shut up now and just watch.'

Rhys nodded.

'But,' Marcus added indulgently, 'if you look in that top drawer there you'll find a video camera.'

By the time our cameraman had sorted himself out Marcus had stripped us both. He lifted me onto hands and knees on the sofa and got up behind me, pushing his clean-cut all-American cock into my ready cunt. My pussy; that was what he called it. As in 'Give me that pussy, Astrid.' Or, 'God, that's a good tight pussy. Your husband hasn't stretched you enough for my cock, has he, honey?' I groaned in agreement, trying to accommodate his length. He obliged by reaching to finger my clit, taking his time, shafting me with long firm strokes. 'Look at Rhys,' he instructed, his voice warm. 'Your husband wants to know everything you're feeling. Let him know. Show him how you like having another man's cock up your pussy, fucking you good and hard.'

I let him know. I looked full into his face as Marcus fucked me from behind, so that Rhys saw every nuance of expression, every jolt of pleasure or shock that lit my eyes. My cheeks were flushed, my lips parted. I held nothing back, mewing my delight as my seducer's cock spread me wide and plunged into me. Sinking my hands in the cushion to brace myself against his penetration, I gasped half-coherent words of delight about how big he was and how strong, revelling in the way those words made Rhys quiver and his engorged erection heave against his trousers. I had never before felt how I did then, knowing myself the focus of lust for two men at once: the stranger who had crossed continents and rewritten his life for me; and the husband in whose deepest, filthiest fantasy, in the most vulnerable centre of his soul, I was the shining star. It wasn't just Marcus's thick cock thrusting into me that made me come, or the slap of his balls against my pussy; it was seeing Rhys's humiliation and ecstasy as, impaled on another man's cock, I got at last what I needed, I wanted, I deserved.

Marcus screwed me in half a dozen different positions that afternoon. I came noisily in every one of them, and twice when I was on top, staring straight into the camera, my bouncing tits cupped in my hands. Rhys practically had to hold me upright when we returned to our own room that evening, and then he took his own turn at fucking me, wallowing in Marcus's slippery wake, licking the taste of his spunk from my swollen lips.

The camerawork turned out pretty wobbly in places, especially where Rhys was working one-handed while wanking his boner with the other. But no one we've shown it to since seems to mind the shaking lens.

Rhys puts a lot of care into finding me the right sort of man these days. They've got to be good-looking and well-endowed and pleasant to hang out with. And they've got to work to get what they want.

Because I insist on being seduced, every time.

Janine Ashbless is the author of the Black Lace novels *Divine Torment*, *Burning Bright* and *Wildwood*. She has one single-author collection – *Cruel Enchantment* – and her second collection, *Dark Enchantment*, is published by Black Lace in early 2009. Her paranormal erotic novellas are included in the Black Lace collections *Magic and Desire* and *Enchanted*.

Rush

Gwen Masters

When Katie asked David how many women he had been with, he didn't know what to say. He was shocked that she would ask such a question. She was much too reasonable a woman, much too realistic to *really* want that answer. And he wanted to think about anything but an answer.

David didn't know how many women he had been with. He was thirty-nine years old and had never been married. Most of that time he had been a very single man without any ties to hold him down, but the truth was, even when he had ties, he wasn't the sort of man who was held down. David had cheated on more women than he could count, so how could he possibly count how many he had been with altogether?

Katie didn't need to know that. If she knew, what would happen to them?

David had known her for a few months before she took him to her bed. During that time he was fucking a stripper named Becky who loved nothing more than threesomes – or mo- resomes – with her best friend, so it's safe to say he was on the verge of wild even up to the moment he kissed Katie for the first time.

But he did kiss her and the feeling in his gut when he did it – well, there are some things a man can't explain, but let's just say that in one moment he understood where romance novels came from. The question of why she had been on his mind for weeks was suddenly answered.

She was the one. He could fucking *feel* it.

David had lived in his own personal heaven of Katie for over a year and he had started to see things in terms of diamond rings and decades. So there was no way in hell he was going to tell her about that stripper and her best friend and the way they liked to compete to see who could make him come first.

He wasn't about to tell her about the time he fucked four women either, one after the other, and then went to work and fucked another one. Five women? There might have been six. He would never remember their names, except for one because she was named Crystal Gayle, just like that country singer, but this Crystal was more into punk rock and had pink hair.

David hadn't exactly been picky. He wasn't looking at hundreds of women, he was looking at thousands, and he had probably stopped counting at triple digits anyway.

Katie did not need to know this.

She wasn't exactly an innocent but she certainly wasn't a slut. She could count her past lovers on two hands. And David didn't want her to count them, thank you very much. She had sparked a possessive streak he hadn't known he had. Many nights he had tossed and turned while he tried to get images of those other men out of his head. When he gave it enough thought, he rolled his eyes at his double standards.

'Well?' she asked. She was going to press the issue.

David was lying on their bed, her head on his chest, one of his arms around her and the other across his eyes. Her body was warm against his. Her breasts were so soft, obviously very real and very large to boot. He loved the way it felt when she snuggled up against him.

'Baby, we don't need to talk about that,' David said, stalling.

'I want to talk about it. I know you've been with a lot so I won't be surprised. How many?'

23

He was quiet for a long while. 'More than I should have had.'

Her breath was light across his chest. He hoped she would drift off to sleep but, of course, that would be too easy. 'You aren't going to tell me.' It wasn't a question, just a statement of fact tinged with a bit of sadness.

'I don't want to hurt you.'

She nodded against his chest. Her eyelashes flickered against his skin. Her breathing had changed, become more careful. She was guarded. Her body might be just as supple against his as it had been five minutes before, but in every other way she was drawing away from him.

'I will tell you,' David finally said. 'But please be sure you want to know, Katie. You're going to see me differently. I don't want to mess up what we have.'

She didn't move. 'Have you been faithful to me?'

'Of course I have,' he said, and wondered why she would ask such a thing.

'I trust you,' she said, reading his mind. 'I know you have. I was trying to make a point. What happened before me doesn't have much to do with us now, does it? Except maybe that thing you do with your hand. I like that thing you do and I'm glad you learned it.'

She buried her face in his neck, suddenly shy. He could feel the heat from her blush. David smiled, despite the fact that he was scared half to death.

'Asking a person how many people they have been with is always a bad idea,' he said. 'Someone always gets shocked. Or hurt. Or furious.'

Katie sat up in the bed. She looked at him with those big blue eyes. Were they wet? Was she on the verge of tears? He studied her mouth. No pouting downturn, no indication that she was going to turn on the waterworks.

David sighed. He was paranoid already.

'You're scared to tell me,' she said.

'Damn straight, I'm scared,' he admitted.

Katie ran her fingertips over his chest. She pulled at his nipples. David moved in the bed and one of her hands went down his belly, to where his cock was starting to show its appreciation. She stroked slowly and within seconds he was at full attention.

'You're going to fuck me into it, aren't you?' he asked.

'Probably.'

That was the thing about Katie. She had no hidden agendas, because she had no problem telling him exactly what those agendas were. Half the time it showed on her face anyway. She couldn't play poker if her life depended on it.

'You won't like me when I tell you,' he murmured. She wasn't paying much attention. Her mouth was descending on his cock.

She took her time, licking every inch and every ridge. She swirled her tongue around his head. She probed that sensitive spot underneath. He tried to think about baseball but all that came to mind was that one self-proclaimed slut who loved to have things pushed inside her, who loved to be stretched, and the time she looked at his aluminium baseball bat and asked him to fuck her with it.

'You're thinking about those other women, aren't you?'

It wasn't an accusation. Rather, it sounded hot as hell. Katie was breathless. She looked up at him with bright eyes and a wicked smile. Her tongue snaked out to lick the head of his cock. Any lie right now could get him into even more trouble than the truth surely would, and he knew it. Being honest was the lesser of two evils.

'Yes.'

'One in particular?'

This was getting rather uncomfortable. His heart was pounding, whether from arousal or from fear he wasn't sure. 'Why?'

'You have that look.'

'What look?'

She sank her mouth down on his cock. All the way. She did that thing with her throat and then his cock was all the way in, her nose pressing right against his pubic bone. She could make him do anything when she did that. She was the only woman who had ever had that kind of power over him, and suddenly he wasn't sure he liked it. Soon he would be confessing like a good Catholic boy to a goddamn priest.

'One in particular?' she asked again.

'Yes.'

'Which one?'

'Jesus Christ, Katie! What difference does it make? I'm not with her!'

'You're with me, and I want to know.'

David lay back and yanked a pillow over his head. He breathed deep into the cotton. Katie was working magic on his cock again, gliding up and every so often going all the way down, enclosing him in that slick, tight throat. She made deep-throating seem like a fine art. It hadn't come easily, though. She had practised on him again and again and again until she got it right.

Oh, did she ever get it right.

'Tell me,' she murmured around his cock.

David pushed the pillow away from his face. If she really wanted to know, he would tell her. Maybe just one little thing. Maybe that would be enough to make her stop asking. He felt as though he were giving her an intentional knife wound as his mouth opened and the words came out.

'I was thinking about the woman who liked it when I put things inside her.'

Katie paused in the midst of sucking him. This would be it. Surely she would stop and lie down and be mad at him for a few days and then this would all blow over.

'What kind of things?'

David stared at the ceiling. 'Bottles. My hand.' He paused. 'Baseball bats.'

Katie sucked him hard. It was a surprise, and he arched up into her mouth. She deep-throated him, then went back to bobbing up and down, sucking exquisitely on the head of his cock. What the fuck was going on?

'I want you to fist me,' she said.

David's cock went hard enough to make furniture.

'What did you say?'

'You heard me,' she purred, then started licking on his balls like a mischievous cat.

'No, I didn't.'

'How many women?'

She shook her head from side to side and slid her mouth down his cock like a corkscrew. He groaned aloud and reached down to touch her hair, but she batted his hand away. She looked up at him, her eyes demanding an answer.

'I don't know.'

'You don't know?' she asked, but she didn't seem surprised at all.

'No.'

She growled in the back of her throat right before she swallowed him into it. He tried to think of anything else but coming, but thought was becoming impossible. Her mouth bounced up and down, her tongue working back and forth like a whip, and he was on the verge within seconds.

She knew it. She stopped.

'Fuck,' David moaned in dismay.

'You've dipped this cock into more pussy than you can count, haven't you?' she asked, holding his cock in her hand like it was a throttle. Her thumb was on his cockhead, swirling in circles. 'I'll bet you've had more ass than you can count, too. And more blowjobs.'

He looked at her and said nothing.

'You've had so many fucks, they all blend together into a blurred chain of pussy. Don't they?'

This was it. She was going to crucify him for his sexual past. He knew it was coming. How could he have been so stupid?

'And I've hardly been with anybody. I don't think that's fair, do you?'

He opened his mouth to speak and nothing came out. He felt almost two inches tall.

'I think I should have some pussy, too.'

David blinked in surprise. His cock surged harder in her hand. She giggled like a schoolgirl and sank her mouth down on his dick. Her tongue sucked and her lips drew back hard and when she pumped him into her throat, he went to redline. She stopped sucking right before he could get off.

'What do you think?'

Never, ever ask a man what he thinks right as he's about to come. You just might get exactly what he's thinking, and it might not be tempered with common sense.

'I would love to see you fuck other people,' David said.

Her eyes widened.

'Holy shit,' she said with an air of wonder.

She sucked him deep, one last time, finally giving him a bit of mercy. He came hard. He shot everything into her mouth. He saw stars. She licked and sucked until there was nothing left.

'Other people,' she murmured, and giggled.

David knew he was in big trouble.

Of course, he reneged on everything as soon as he was coherent enough to do so. Sure, he would love to see it, but he would never actually be able to do it, he told her. It was a good fantasy. Sometimes he thought about it. Not often, though. Hardly ever, actually. And why would he want to share? He didn't *like* to share. He wasn't good at it. He didn't want to share her. Would *she* want to share *him*?

She looked at him the whole time with knowing eyes and that wise little smile.

'Do you have anybody in mind?' she asked simply.

David sighed in exasperation. 'Did you hear a single word I said?'

'Every bit.'

'Good. I think I made myself clear.'

'Sure. I've been thinking about a stranger. I don't want to run the risk of ruining a friendship, so any of your friends are out. My friends, too. Friends are better kept as friends and not made into fuck buddies, don't you think?'

He stared at her.

'Well?'

'You're insane. You're not fucking anybody else. That's final.'

She winked at him and giggled again.

'OK, big man. Whatever you say.'

David woke up the next morning hard as a rock. Which was convenient, because Katie was already on top of him, her legs spread wide, fucking him. Only her pussy touched his cock. She was braced on her feet and her hands, bobbing up and down. He had been dreaming about sex when he woke up, and apparently this was the reason why.

She looked down at him. Her hair fell loosely on either side of her face.

'Good morning, big boy. Guess what's for breakfast?'

'You,' David said, and flipped her neatly underneath him. She closed her eyes and purred like a cat while his cock stroked inside her. He'd had his turn last night and it was hers this morning. He angled his cock so that the thrusts went right against her clit. He ground into her at the height of each one of them. Soon she was writhing underneath him and moaning half-words that made no sense. He felt it when she came, a throbbing and clenching around his cock. He pushed as deep as he could go until her whole body relaxed under him.

David lay there with her for a moment to let his breath get back to normal. By the time he pushed himself out of bed to take care of morning business, she was sound asleep. He smiled at the way she looked, like an innocent young woman with an unusual blush to her cheeks. He brushed her hair out of her face.

Could he really let her fuck someone else?

The thought came out of nowhere and slammed him right where it counted. He tried to imagine her pussy spread open for someone else. He tried to picture another man's dick sliding into her. Would it be slow? Or would she want him to impale her with it? Would she taunt David while he watched? Or would she be loving and caring and give him reassuring looks while someone else made her moan?

His hand circled around his cock and began to stroke lazily, all thoughts of the call of nature forgotten. He was too busy thinking about Katie's light-pink pussy lips opening up around a cock while he watched it happen. He hadn't thought about watching her give him a blowjob, and he hadn't thought about another man's tongue on that hard little clit. He had started thinking about the fucking right away. That was the part that got him hornier than hell – the thought of her pussy being taken. The pussy that belonged to him.

David watched her sleep, sprawled out in the middle of the bed. Would she like him on top of her, so she could watch him? Or would she ride him like she rode David this morning? What about doggie-style, so David could get a good look at how hard he was fucking her?

His legs were trembling. He sat down on the bed, still stroking. Katie woke up when the mattress moved with the weight. She watched him with sleepy and satisfied eyes.

'You never come first thing in the morning,' she said. 'What got you all riled up?'

'You.' He was stroking harder. Pre-come was oozing out of

him, making his hand slick. He closed his eyes and imagined Katie lying under someone else.

'What about me?'

'Seeing you with someone else,' he admitted. She practically purred as she rolled to her side and wrapped herself around him. Her hand came around and touched his. Together they rode each stroke up and down.

'I'm going to make you watch,' she murmured.

That did it. Semen shot out of his cock and coated his hand. It dripped onto the floor. A splotch landed on his thigh. Katie giggled in approval. He lay back on the bed, almost on top of her, light-headed from the unusual early-morning pleasure.

'I'm impressed,' she said.

'What have you done to me?'

'Opened up the door to your fantasy world? You can't tell me you've never watched a woman with another man.'

David blushed. 'Guilty. But I can tell you this for sure: it was never a woman I was in love with.'

'And that makes things different.'

'You bet it does.'

Katie smiled down at him. 'More exciting?'

'It makes me jealous. And that's exciting. I have no clue why. It seems like the very opposite would be true.'

Katie kissed his forehead. 'We're going to have so much fun.'

Over the next few weeks, their sex life was revved up to redline. David walked around semi-hard all day. At work the guys teased him about the new bounce in his step. At night, he was fucking Katie with utter abandon. Muscles he had forgotten he had were sore now, and his cock was almost rubbed raw. Katie actually had to make him stop a few times, because pleasure had turned to pain. They were having too much sex, if there could possibly be such a thing.

But they couldn't stop.

The thought of watching her with someone else was an aphrodisiac beyond anything David had done in his past. And he had done everything. But in the past there hadn't been love thrown into the naughty sexual mix, and he found that it made for a curious difference. Every sexual act took on a new slant. Jealousy and possessiveness were new words to his vocabulary, but David loved the jealous feeling that sluiced through him every time he thought about another man's cock taking the pussy that had been only his for well over a year. It made no sense to the logical part of him, but it damn sure made sense to his dick.

No friends, she'd said, and David agreed with that. He was not the kind of man to make friends easily, God only knew why, and he didn't want any awkwardness with the friends he did have. Katie's friends were out, too. They might have been mature enough about it all but, frankly, David knew he wouldn't be. He didn't want to worry about someone she would see on a regular basis replaying the sexual romp every time he saw her.

So they placed personal ads on those websites that assure you that you can get laid, and tonight, if only you buy the gold membership. They opted for three months. They figured it might take that long to find someone who suited exactly what they were looking for: no strings attached, one-night stand, the man with her and David watching, nothing kinky, just many possible variations of a straight fuck. They described what they wanted, put up a picture of Katie wearing nothing but a thong, and waited.

The responses poured in. By the end of the week they were staring at a screen filled with over fifty messages that actually seemed legitimate. They narrowed them down to men in a town about an hour away. No way would they invite anyone to their house, and no way were they going to find anyone in their town. By the time they were done picking through what was left, they had three candidates. Katie sent those three emails. And again they waited.

She was particularly interested in one who called himself Rich. He was very fluent and well-spoken, seemed to be extremely mature about the no-strings deal and, better yet, he was in a very established marriage and simply looking for something on the side. In David's mind, that meant Rich wouldn't be a problem when the evening was over. Besides that, Rich worked in the health care field, and assured them he had to go through routine blood-testing. He was disease-free and he could prove it. That made David very happy.

What caught Katie's interest more than anything else, however, was the picture of his cock. He sent it to their email address, and when she opened the attachment, a life-size member filled the screen. Katie's mouth practically started watering.

'I want that,' she announced, and David knew that was it. They had found their man.

Rich was more than happy to oblige. No strings attached, no commitments beyond one night in a hotel room during which he would give Katie whatever she wanted.

That night David and Katie fucked so hard, the headboard slammed the wall and knocked a picture to the floor.

The week before they were to meet Rich was an exercise in torture. What if he changed his mind? What if his wife got wind of what he was doing? What if Katie backed out? David thought about backing out himself more than a few times during those long days at work when he stared at the computer screen and saw nothing but Katie spread-eagled on the bed with Rich on top of her, his cock ramming her in one hole after another. Could he really handle that? Was he really ready for this?

Then at night Katie would ride him and whisper in his ear about how much he was going to love watching her take on someone else, and David knew she was right. He wanted it as much as she did.

The night they were to head out of town, Katie showed up at David's office in a rental car. They were taking no chances. He climbed into the car and the first thing he noticed was the outfit Katie wore: short and flared skirt, black stockings, high heels and a blouse that seemed demure but somehow made her breasts look even larger than they really were. She was a knockout.

'I'm not wearing panties,' she announced, and he was instantly hard.

'And you're wet already, aren't you?'

The blush that flooded her cheeks was very becoming. She looked sexier than ever. David watched her drive and realised he hadn't ever seen her in high heels before.

'Are those new?' he asked, gesturing to them.

'The whole outfit is new.'

'You're gorgeous.'

She smiled a Mona Lisa smile and kept on driving. Her hand was trembling as she reached down to adjust the air-conditioning. She kept biting her lip, rubbing the lipstick off. She drove carefully, as if any wrong move might jeopardise the little outing. He slid his hand up her thigh, underneath her skirt. She really wasn't wearing any panties. He tried to delve into the space between her thighs and she quickly squeezed her legs together.

'That's not yours tonight,' she purred.

David withdrew his hand. She gave him a sidelong glance. David wasn't sure which one of them was more nervous. He leaned over to whisper in her ear, naughty things that made her squirm in her seat. He waited until the hotel sign was in sight before he handed her the coup de grâce.

'I'm going to let him come inside you,' David told her. She was so surprised, she let up on the gas pedal. The car lurched as the engine whined. Within seconds she was back up to speed, but her blush was fire-red and she was breathless.

'Really?'

'Really. I know you love it. It's the one thing you were so careful to sidestep this whole time, but I saw the package of condoms you bought the other day. You don't need them.'

'Did you already discuss this with him?'

'Yes.'

Her eyes narrowed. David had broken the rule about never sending Rich an email without letting her read it first. But it had been to plan this little surprise she really wanted, and he knew he was forgiven as soon as the admission came out of his mouth. She was too excited about all of this to care.

They pulled into the parking lot of the hotel. Katie slowed down to a crawl.

'My heart is beating so hard it hurts,' she confided.

'Mine, too.'

'Any second thoughts?'

'Of course.'

Katie whipped her head around and looked at him. Her eyes were wide and bright with anticipation. Her lips were swollen from the way she had been biting on them. Her face was flushed and her breasts heaved with every breath. She had never been more stunning.

'Have you changed your mind?' she asked.

'No. I'm jealous about what we're about to do. But I want this too.'

Just then Katie spotted his car. A silver Cadillac parked in front of room 108. That was what they had all agreed upon, and there he was. This was real. It was happening.

They cruised to a stop in the parking space beside it. The door was closed, but they knew he was in there.

'Honey –' Katie began, but David cut her off with a kiss. His hand was tight in her hair. She let out a little moan when he let go of her.

'Get out of the car,' he said.

She nodded slowly and opened her door. David and Katie met at the front of the car. Katie took his hand and shyly stepped onto the sidewalk. He was the one who knocked, and when he heard the rustling from behind the door, his knees almost went weak.

Rich was tall, about six feet, and solidly built. David gauged him at a good two hundred pounds. He had thick salt-and-pepper hair and a very good tan. His eyes were dark, but filled with unmistakable desire when he laid eyes on Katie. He hardly glanced at David.

'Come in,' he said in quiet invitation.

Rich looked right at David when he stepped into the room, as if noticing his presence for the first time. They didn't speak. Neither one of them knew what to say. Now that they were there, David wasn't sure what to do. What was the protocol? He was acting as though he had never done this before. With other women it had been smooth and easy, but Katie was the woman he loved. Everything seemed to take on a completely different dimension.

Rich reached out his hand. He took Katie's wrist and slowly pulled her hand out of David's grasp. David was instantly angry, but when he opened his mouth to speak, nothing came out. The door closed behind them and Rich used both the locks.

'Sit down over there,' Rich said, motioning to a chair next to the bed. 'Then you can decide what you want to do for the rest of the night. Where you want to be. What you want to see. Right now, I'm going to get acquainted with this pretty little woman here.'

Just like that, Rich had taken control of everything. David tried to hold on to the flash of anger, but instead he was excited. And curious. He wanted to see what Rich was going to do to her. He wanted to see everything. He wanted Rich to do everything.

David looked at Katie as he stepped to the chair. She was biting her lip and her eyes were wide. Rich ran his hand into her hair and tilted her head back so that she had no choice but to look at him. He took one of her hands and pressed it hard against his chest, then slid it all the way down to his crotch. The outline of his erection was clear behind his slacks, and he pressed her palm against it, then cupped her fingers around it.

'Is that what you want, sweetie?'

Katie slowly nodded. David's own cock was so hard it hurt. He swept his hand across the front of his pants as he watched them. That was his girlfriend with this stranger, and she was already rubbing his cock. He watched her hand move up and down while Rich examined her face with an air of dispassion, as if she were something he might like to buy, or might put back on the shelf.

'You're going to be a good fuck,' he finally breathed, and the shadow of a smile passed over Katie's face. 'Unzip me.'

The sound was louder than it should have been. David watched with interest as Katie opened his slacks and pushed them down. His shoes had already been discarded somewhere, and so there was nothing blocking him from stepping out of the slacks. He wasn't wearing any underwear. His cock was hard and jutted straight out from his body, pointing directly at Katie's belly. He pulled the polo shirt over his head and then he was standing naked in front of David's girlfriend.

She was staring at Rich's cock.

'You want to suck that, don't you?'

She nodded. She didn't once glance in David's direction.

'Strip for me first.'

Katie hesitated. She hated the stripping thing. She had told David once that she didn't know why she hated it so much, she just did. That was enough for him, and he hadn't asked her to do it again. Now a complete stranger was asking her, and though David knew she didn't want to do it, he also knew she certainly would.

She closed her eyes and started to unbutton her blouse. The fabric disappeared, layer after layer, leaving her creamy skin bare for their eyes. Her nipples were hard as little pebbles. She sat down gracefully on the bed and rolled the stockings off one at a time. The skirt came next, and David bit back a moan when the dim light from the bedside lamp caught the sheen on her inner thighs. She was so wet; Rich would slide right in without any resistance at all.

They were naked, and David wasn't. Neither one of them noticed his presence at all. David quietly slid his zipper down, freeing his cock, but he didn't dare touch himself. Not yet.

Katie stood in front of Rich and looked up at him. He nodded.

Without a word, she sank to her knees.

David gasped when she opened her mouth and took the first lick of Rich's cock. Her pink tongue swirled around the swollen head and licked its way down the shaft, all the way to the base. He was clean-shaven. Her tongue didn't stop there; she licked his balls too, everywhere she could reach, before coming back up and pressing her lips against the head of his dick. She slowly took him in, one inch after another. She hesitated when he got a little too deep. Rich slipped his hand into her hair.

'Suck all of it. I know you can. Show me.'

Katie struggled for a moment, trying to find the right angle. Then with a whimper that sounded more animal than human, she took him in all the way. Her nose pressed hard against his pubic bone. David's cock jerked and he had to circle his fingers around it. He stroked slowly while he watched Katie deep-throat another man's cock.

'Good girl,' Rich murmured.

Katie coughed when he pulled out of her mouth. She turned her head away and when she did, she caught sight of David, sitting in the chair. Her eyes were unfocused. Her face was filled with desire. She had probably forgotten he was in the room.

The jealousy that had been brewing in the back of David's mind all this time finally burst to the forefront. He gripped his cock hard to remind him of why they were here. He needed something to bring him back down to earth and keep him from bolting out of the chair.

'Are you enjoying this?'

The question was directed at David, but he hardly heard Rich through the pounding of the blood in his ears. Rich had to ask a second time before David could answer. When he did, his voice was reed-thin.

'Yes.'

Rich granted him a knowing smile as he hauled Katie to her feet. He did it by grabbing a handful of her hair. She scrambled up to face him.

'How do you want me to fuck her?'

David snapped out of the haze at that question. How did he want Rich to fuck her? How did he want another man to put a dick into his girlfriend? Was he insane?

'I don't want you to,' David blurted out, and Katie looked at him with something very much like amusement.

'Do you mean that?' Rich asked.

'No.'

'Are you sure?'

'Yes.'

'Yes, you are sure, or no, you are not?'

David shook his head and stared at Katie. He hadn't stopped stroking his cock, and he was right on the verge of an orgasm. Coherent thought was impossible. They watched David as he watched them, and finally Katie crawled onto the bed. She slithered across it like a cat, coming straight for him. She stopped on the edge of it and looked at David for a long moment.

Then she winked.

'Fuck her with her legs over your shoulders,' David said suddenly. 'She likes it deep.'

Katie's eyes widened. In seconds Rich was there behind her, his hand on her hip. He rolled her over onto the centre of the bed. They were close enough for David to see Rich's cock throbbing with his heartbeat, jerking slightly upwards with every pump. Rich caressed her legs for a moment before lifting them over his shoulders.

'No foreplay, huh? Just a good fuck? That's why you're here, isn't it?'

Rich settled between her legs. His cock pressed against her pussy. Katie wiggled underneath him; she was trying to get him into her, deep and hard. David watched her from the chair, knowing how that felt, knowing what every little cue meant. He knew her body like the back of his hand. He knew how it felt when he sank his cock into her, every little ridge and every little smooth spot, and the way she gripped his cock hard when she was really excited.

Rich sank the first inch of his cock in. David moaned out loud, right along with Katie.

'What do you want?' Rich asked, breathless already.

'Fuck her,' David said.

Rich impaled Katie with his cock. She arched up against him and shrieked like a fireball. David knew that sound, knew she was coming already, coming from the mere act of another man's cock pushing into her cunt.

She wasn't the only one who came. David's cock burst as soon as Rich sank into her. White jets of semen shot out of him and landed on the edge of the bed. He shook with the power of it, with the thrill of what he was watching. He kept coming until he felt absolutely drained, but his cock didn't go soft in the least.

He was still hard. He hadn't done that in years.

Rich was sawing in and out of Katie's pussy. Her legs were over his shoulders and she thrust up to meet him for all she was worth. The wet slapping sounds were obscene and delicious. She played with her nipples while Rich braced himself over her, thrusting downwards. It was hard and it was deep, and Katie was in pure ecstasy. From this angle David could see Rich sliding in and out. His cock glistened with her juices. His balls were already coated.

David kept stroking his cock.

'I was right,' Rich gasped. 'She is a good fuck.'

Katie looked over at David. Her eyes were hazy. She had already ridden out of the world on a pleasure train, and damned if she didn't look sexier than she ever had before.

'Her cunt is so tight,' Rich said to David. He looked over at him. Sweat was running down his face and he had a wicked smile. 'She's gonna make me come real soon, sport. I'm gonna fill her up with it. You both want me to come in her, don't you?'

Katie threw her head from side to side and let out a sound David had rarely heard. It was the sound of one of those really good orgasms; the ones that wiped her out, the ones that came only when the stars aligned and she was so hot her blood could boil. Rich groaned and thrust hard when she did that. David knew he was feeling the contractions of her pussy, squeezing and pulsing and smothering him in a silken glove.

Rich threw his head back and let out a grunt. He held his hips tight against her, his hands on her ass, pulling her into him and pushing as deep as he could go. Katie cried out loud. Rich's face took on a mask of pleasure. David stared at the place where his cock disappeared into her. He knew Rich was shooting his come into her, just the way she wanted it, and when David looked at her face, she was looking back right at him.

'How does that feel?' David asked, seething with jealousy and a fine edge of anger.

Katie didn't answer. She couldn't. She was completely taken by the pleasure. David might as well have not been in the room, but regardless, he was still stroking his cock. He was still watching.

Rich pulled out slowly. He spread her legs wider and looked between them.

'Show him,' he demanded.

Katie lay there for a moment, trying to catch her breath. Then she turned slightly towards David and lifted one of her legs with her hands, giving him a clear shot of her pussy. Her lips were red and swollen, and slightly open. A thin trickle of white slid out of her and down between her rounded cheeks. David watched Rich's come slip out of her until it started to stain the blanket underneath her.

'My God,' David breathed.

'She liked it,' Rich taunted. 'She came so hard on my dick. Did you see her? And now my come is deep inside that warm, wet cunt I just fucked. You want to fuck her too, don't you?'

David hadn't intended to get involved in the sex between them. He had intended to sit down in the chair and let Katie live out the fantasy and stroke his cock like a good boy. But seeing Rich's come slide out of her was more than David could take. He rose from the chair and walked towards them, pushing his pants down along the way, stripping the shirt over his head.

Rich had one of her legs over his shoulder. David climbed onto the bed and slipped her other leg over his shoulder. She was spread wide open.

And her cunt was oozing with another man's come.

David slammed into her with one thrust.

Katie's eyes opened wide in surprise. She seemed to want to speak, but nothing came out. She was too dazed with pleasure to do anything but lie there and take the fuck. David watched as Rich leaned over and sucked first one nipple, then the other. Then he bit on them.

Katie ran her hands into Rich's hair and looked up at David. The expression on her face was filled with such sexual thrill, such discovery, that the anger in him began to dull.

But the jealousy was still there.

David fucked her for all he was worth. He was determined to fuck Rich's come right out of her. He slammed in again and again, focusing on how she wasn't as tight as she usually was. She was slicker than normal and that was thanks to Rich. She was moaning and bucking and David was fucking into her hard enough to leave bruises.

The orgasm left him stunned and weak. He collapsed on top of her.

Rich moved away to sit on the edge of the bed. David vaguely heard the snicker and flare of a lighter, and then cigarette smoke drifted his way. Rich lay back in the bed, propping a pillow up behind him. David felt his eyes on him, and when he looked up Rich had a wry smile on his face.

'Rest, sport. Then we'll have round two.'

David buried his face in Katie's chest. She smelled like sweat and perfume and himself and a little bit of something he hadn't smelled before. That had to be Rich. The jealousy rose up in him like a tidal wave and he bit down hard on her neck, marking her with his teeth. Rich chuckled.

'The night is still young, kids.'

Minutes later Rich went to the bathroom. Katie sat up in bed and winced a little, then looked at David.

'You've never fucked me that hard,' she said.

'Yes.'

'Are you OK?'

David contemplated that and came up with no sincere answer. He shrugged. She wrapped her arms around him and asked if he wanted to keep going, or if he wanted to go home.

'Keep going,' he said.

'Me too. But only this one time, honey. Tonight is all. Then I'm done.'

David raised his eyebrows in surprise. 'Done?'

'We need time to think about all this. Don't we?'

They definitely needed that. He was already thinking about the other things they might be able to do, and especially about the comment Katie had made that first night they discussed all this, when she said she should have a chance to eat pussy too ...

No, David thought this might be the tip of the proverbial iceberg.

In fact, his body was already responding. He hadn't recovered that quickly in years, and he knew he might have only one more go in him. But surely between the two men, they could keep Katie satisfied all night long.

'Suck me,' David said.

Katie smiled and made her way down his body. She enveloped his cock with her warm, talented mouth.

Rich came out of the bathroom. He watched for a long while. By the time he settled on the bed behind her, he was hard again. Her whole body rocked when he thrust into her. He looked over her shoulder at David.

'Time for round two,' Rich said.

Malicious Intent
Sommer Marsden

I had absolutely no intention of seducing him. I just want that on the record. It was business. It was supposed to be food and drinks and schmoozing. A semi-hard sell, sure. I mean why would he want me to redesign his restaurant when his lovely wife was a budding designer? Why? Because I am good. I am beyond good. I am outstanding. And I was going to prove that to Samuel Radcliff.

I really am a bitch. I have to admit it. I heard his wife. Sitting at my table for one, picking at my hot and sour soup of the day, I heard her gushing over her project for her design class. And I heard her go on to say that one day she would totally redo The Tarnished Spoon. The name is why I eat here. Really. How can you resist a name like that?

Anyway, Deborah was going on and on about colours and swags and all of that as Samuel half-listened and nodded. He smiled but busied himself with lists and a calculator. 'Mmm-hmm,' was what he said.

Deborah was completely ignorant. She grinned and chattered and looked around with a great wide-eyed gaze as if she had never seen her husband's restaurant before. I watched her and she didn't see me at all. I eat lunch early. I eat alone. I usually sketch in my book or read as I eat. And she was too excited to see me, the lone woman in the corner.

'I have to go!' she gasped, glancing at her watch. She shot out of her chair. She was all thin legs and clumsy nature in her too-tight pencil skirt. She had a spectacular ass and I would have laid money on that being part of why Samuel had married her.

'Go on, Chicklet,' he muttered, punching more buttons.

'Kiss me!' she demanded and leaned forwards. She puckered her too-thin lips and teetered on her too-high heels. I thought for a moment she would fold up like a paper crane and fall into his lap.

He kissed her dutifully but his eyes never left his stack of paperwork. Interesting. I popped a button on my black dress and freed a little more cleavage. I had a job to win.

'Ah, the lovely Jillian! How is your soup? Can I get you more iced tea?' The hours I keep, I usually get Samuel or his second-in-command Robert. Robert is tall, lean and gay. He calls me Miss J. Samuel is taller and stockier and has brawn behind his walk that fills in the lines of his suits when he wears them. He reminds me of Dean Martin and that always makes me smile.

'No thanks. But I did want to talk to you about the restaurant.' I trailed a nail along my cleavage absently. The kind of gesture that looks completely innocent. The kind of thing that would make a man think, *Oh she didn't even know she was doing that. Surely seduction was not her intent.* And it wasn't. Not yet. I just wanted to redo the restaurant and put a pinhole in his little wife's plans.

Have I mentioned that I am a bitch?

His eyes found my fingers and followed the motion. It was like watching a man being hypnotised. And seriously, if it had been any easier I think I might have laughed out loud. 'What's that?'

'The restaurant. Can we talk about it for a moment?' I pushed the chair opposite me out with the toe of my black boot. 'Could you sit? Before the lunch crowd shows?'

He sat, still staring at my cleavage and my hand. The hand that had stilled at the swell of my breasts. Breasts that were more bared now than before he had joined me. What wonders one small button can hide.

'What can I do for you, Jillian?'

Maybe it was me but the word 'do' had a slightly wistful quality to it. He could do me, period, I thought and smiled a little. Still, I was only trying to steal the job at that point. Not the man. That urge came later. 'I want to redo your restaurant.'

He looked surprised. Maybe because of his recent conversation with Mrs Radcliff. And by conversation I mean her monologue. 'Why is that?'

I traced the seam of my cleavage with my fingernails. I had just had them done a lovely shade called Dame Red. 'I am trying to build my portfolio and your restaurant is one of the most popular in the city. I figure, I can give you deep discounts and you can give me a great reputation.' When I said 'deep', I leaned in towards him as if to tell him a secret. Samuel is a stern man. Friendly but strait-laced. Serious almost. But for a moment, I swear, if he could have dived head first in between my breasts he would have.

'That sounds interesting,' he said to my left nipple. Both nipples peaked against the soft black material. I was *sans* bra so visibility was roughly one hundred per cent. 'Do you have a colour scheme?'

'Actually, I have two. I can't quite decide,' I confessed.

'Can you sketch them up for me?' He shook his head softly like a man coming out of a trance.

'Absolutely. And since I will be back tomorrow for lunch as usual, I'll bring them with me.'

'Then lunch can be on me. A business expense,' he said.

I noticed for the first time how very imposing Samuel Radcliff was. How very blue his eyes were, like well-washed denims. And how very broad his shoulders were. My mouth went a little dry but my pussy grew wet. When he stared at me that way, I didn't give two shits about getting his business or foiling the young Mrs Radcliff's plans. 'Oh. Well, thank you.'

I stood a little too quickly and my heel turned. Samuel steadied me with a strong hand on my arm. Heat flooded me and my face flushed. His lips were very red and his stubble, just beginning to appear, was very dark. I suppressed the urge to run my fingers over his jaw to hear that coarse, somehow sexy sound. 'Easy there, Jillian. Be careful.'

'Sorry,' I mumbled. Somehow the tables had been turned and now I wriggled like the worm on the hook. 'I'm so clumsy. Free lunch wasn't my intent,' I said just for the record.

'I know that. But you eat like a bird! Even I can feed a bird. And the bird will bring me beautiful artistic sketches of a revamped restaurant. But I know it wasn't your intent.' He leaned in as if to give me the standard business peck on the cheek. Instead, he pressed his full lips to my ear and said, 'I think you have malicious intent, Jillian. But that's OK. I like it.'

Then he kissed my ear so softly I shivered. Then he turned on his heels. I left a ten on the table and walked outside to catch my breath. My heart was like a jackrabbit, my belly full of butterflies, and the crotch of my purple silk panties was soaked.

'Malicious intent. Yes, sir. I believe you are right', I said aloud. But the only one to hear was me.

I really did have two colour schemes in mind and I sketched them both out that night. It was truly one of those few times that I would joyfully let the boss decide because I loved them both. Thinking of Samuel as my boss gave me a delicious little shiver. It brought to mind having bound wrists and red bottoms freshly spanked and maybe a nipple clamp or two.

'Get a hold of yourself, woman,' I said to myself, sketching furiously to keep myself focused. I tried to ignore the vivid memory of his lips on my ear and the racing nerves along my neck and shoulders from his hot breath. I failed.

I dropped the sketch pad on the floor and hiked up my nightgown. The night was warm but not hot. The shades were up but I was below my neighbours' line of sight, I was almost sure. At that point, I didn't much care. My fingers played over my clit and my body hummed with a heat and desire that can only come from pure lust. Tight little circles pushed me so far so fast I hovered right there, Samuel's big broad shoulders and dark-blue eyes firmly in my mind's eye. The imagined picture of his hands gripping my hips as he moved into me. The fantastical fantasy of his cock ramming into me higher and higher until I felt like I would fly away.

I pushed my fingers into my cunt, stroking that spot deep inside of myself that always makes my breath catch. My hips shot up on their own as I let my mind take those lips of his from the shell of my ear down the back of my neck, trailing his tongue down the long, slender dip of my back to the swell of my ass. My brain played out light kisses over each buttock and big masculine fingers spreading me. And then him sliding into my cunt, yanking me back, fucking me hard. Slow for a moment and then frenzied.

I came on my cream-coloured sofa with a soft cry that sounded half-winded, half-confused. 'Jesus.' I was panting and splayed out like a tart in my living room. All the lights burned, my sketches littered the floor, and a soft rain had started to beat at the window glass.

I poured a glass of wine to steady myself and tried to finish my pages. Knowing that I would be expected to present them to my new boss the next day did little to still my hand. The steady beating pulse in my pussy that seemed to be insisting on just one more orgasm did even less. But I didn't give in, I worked. And I went to bed still thrumming with the energy of a live wire.

I knew without a doubt that if Samuel Radcliff so much as kissed me the next day, I would probably spontaneously and shamelessly come. I was that tightly wound. And that horny. That hot for him. I was in deep trouble.

I wanted to fuck him. I knew it for a fact as I got dressed. A calf-length diaphanous black skirt that somehow managed to be flowy but hugged me in the most perfect way. Underneath it, I wore fishnets. The diamonds were tiny, professional, but still ... fishnets. My tall black boots and a colourful, soft and, let's not forget, form-fitting cashmere sweater with a plunging neckline. Not so plunging that people wanted to ask what I charged for a blowjob; not so demure that I was mistaken for the kindergarten teacher.

I let my long honey-brown hair hang loose and in soft natural waves. A little perfume, a bare minimum of makeup. Under it all, black lace tango pants, and a black demi-cut bra that didn't quite match. I have issues with matching sets of anything but shoes and earrings. If you tell me it's a set, you have just lost a sale.

With my sketches under one arm, I grabbed my purse and my coffee mug and let myself out. My heels beat an anxious tattoo on the marble floor in the hallway. Honestly, I had hours before I could arrive at The Tarnished Spoon for lunch, so why was I in such a hurry? I knew the answer, though. I always walk too fast when I am nervous and excited. I was both.

I dropped off the drawings, booked some appointments, visited a site and schmoozed a client who was on the fence, all while keeping an eye on my watch. Lunchtime had finally arrived. Eleven o'clock and I was ready for some soup and bread and veggies. And Samuel. Maybe a bottle of wine to calm my nerves.

'No, no liquor,' I chided myself, walking briskly to my destination. 'You do that hyena laugh when you drink. No hyena laugh, Jillian. Water or tea with lemon, just like every other day.'

A man passing me on the street squinted as I chattered to myself. Then he smiled. Then he stared at my boobs and I didn't care.

'Sorry. Nervous! Talking to myself!' I said half to him and half to me. Then I laughed like a hyena and scurried down the alley that was a short cut between Bradley Avenue and Disher Street, where the restaurant was.

I rushed in and my eyes went crazy. Out of the bright sunlight into the low, romantic light of the dining room. He was waiting there. At his little booth in the corner, Samuel sat, with his mound of papers and his ever-present mug of coffee. He looked up, denim-blue eyes smiling along with the rest of his face when he saw me. 'You OK?'

I laughed, high and definitely hyena-like, and then I cringed. 'I forgot my sunglasses. I'm practically blind in here. I can't see.' More laughing. More cringing.

I felt more than saw him rise from his seat and come for me. My breath stalled when his big hand wrapped around my wrist. His warmth seemed to brand my skin and I pressed my thighs together, which was stupid because it made me wet and a little crazy from want. 'Come on then, Jillian. You should be able to find your table in the dark by now, but here, I'll help you.'

I let him guide me but he was right. I sat at the table almost every time I came here to eat. And I ate here three or four of my five work days. I should have been able to go in totally blind and find my chair. But Samuel had scrambled my brain and the arousal that rushed through me, feeling very much like heavy beating wings, was making me want to stand on tiptoe and kiss him until he fucked me on one of his tiny little tables. Right on the white tablecloth, with broken dishes and crumpled napkins scattered around us.

'Thank you,' I said in a breathy little voice, and touched his hand. But just for a moment. It was all I could stand. The electrical current that shot across my skin was borderline uncomfortable. I sighed.

'You sure you're OK?'

'You're electrocuting me,' I said before I could stop myself.

He stopped and faced me. His shoulders were incredibly broad. How had I never noticed that before? I had seen how manly he was, how athletically he was built, but never before had I really seen the sheer magnitude of his shoulders. 'I don't think so,' he said, cupping the sides of my head with his big hands. His fingers pressed into my hair and my heart fluttered wildly in my breast.

I nodded. I didn't really know what to say. So I nodded until he leaned in further. His lips were a hair's-breadth from mine, I could feel his hot breath on my lips. He smelled of coffee and warm cotton and tobacco. 'I think it's all in your head, Jillian,' he said and my pussy thumped in an ever-increasing pulse.

God. Wouldn't he just kiss me? Didn't he want to kiss me? Didn't he want to press his full mouth to my mouth and kiss me until I just came right then and there?

I waited and he chuckled softly. 'I'll bring you your lunch,' he said, pulling back and leading me the rest of the way.

When he pulled out my chair and seated me, it was all I could stand not to masturbate under the table. My body had gone haywire and my mind had too. Was I crazy? Was I the only one who felt that insane attraction? And the need to touch him, well, that was staggering. Was I the only one?

He set my water glass in front of me. Then came the bread basket, the butter, and my cup of the soup of the day. 'Cream of Crab,' he said.

'That's my favourite!' And it was. Plus, his place beat all other restaurants hands down when it came to cream of crab soup.

His eyes darkened just a bit as he looked me over. 'I know. And as I said, lunch is on the house since this is work.' Instead of sitting across from me, he pulled out the chair directly to my left and sat. Under the table, his navy-blue-clad thigh pressed against mine. My pulse ratcheted up and heat flooded my face. I clenched my thighs tight which only served to trigger a tentative flutter of pleasure inside my cunt. I bit my tongue.

'Aren't you going to eat?' He leaned in and I smelled his shampoo. Something woody and subtle.

'I don't think I could swallow,' I said and then blushed at the double entendre.

Samuel grinned. 'Oh, I bet you could. Show them to me,' he growled.

For a dizzying beat I thought he meant my breasts, and God help me, I was ready to hook my fingers in my sweater and bra and tug them down to bare it all. 'What?' Who was seducing who now?

'Your sketches, Jillian. Show them to me.'

I swallowed what felt like a stone but was only air. 'Which first?' I took a teeny tiny spoonful of soup and it went down easily. My favourite soup barely had any flavour, I was so worked up.

'You choose. You're in charge.' His voice was whisky and smoke and dark nights with glowing fires. I shivered because we both knew that was a lie.

'Let's start with the brown and blue scheme. Now what sets this off from what has become the norm of browns and blues is that the blue is really bright and the brown is so dark it's nearly black, actually. And the blue has such a turquoise undertone that it really pops. There are some cream accents and orange –' I threw my hand up to cut him off and he gave a sexy half-smile that nearly made me choke. 'Now I know you think I'm crazy suggesting orange, but just see the sketches before you balk. Orange is really quite versatile if you know how to use it.' I was loosening up with my designer chatter.

When Samuel took the sheets from me his finger brushed over the top of my knuckle. How could such a tiny touch hold so much sensuality? And how could I possibly keep my ass in my seat and eat? That was the true stumper.

'I like the orange,' he rumbled, really looking at the sketch. He was all business at that moment and I could catch my breath. 'And I like this idea of built-in extended benches that look like one continuous line but still offer private dining. Excellent. Your brain is gorgeous. But I'm not surprised.'

He handed the sketches back and this time all of his fingers took a gentle tour along the back of my hand. My nipples spiked like little slutty nubs eager for his touch or his tongue or even his hot breath blowing across them. I squeaked. Just a little. But still, it was a squeak.

'You hanging in there?'

I nodded and shifted in my seat. This rubbed my panties against my clit and I really did expect to simply burst into flames right there in my seat. 'Let's do the red, shall we?' I practically shouted and brandished the other sheaf of papers. 'I like this one, too. Very much. The barn red is not as offensive as a true red. A true red would seriously give the place the appearance of a rather brutal crime scene.'

Oh God. I was babbling. Honest babbling, but it was still a nervous running monologue. What had happened to the self-assured, cocky woman who had started this wooing venture? Well, that was easy. She had wanted a decorating job. Now she wanted cock. To be specific, Samuel's cock. In my mouth, in my cunt, I wasn't really picky. It had been ages since a man had made me feel half-insane with want.

'Crime scene wasn't the look I was going for.' He kept a straight face when he said it. He pointed to the ceiling fixtures I had drawn. 'Don't you think the ceiling is too low in here?'

'No, no, no!' My voice was hitting a pitch I was almost sure only dogs could hear. I took a great deep breath and blew it out, steadying my nerves. 'Look,' I said, grabbing my chair and hauling it to a current fixture. Samuel offered his hand and I took it, stepping up onto the wooden seat in my boots. 'This fixture hangs down about twenty-eight inches, thirty max. These are only thirty-two. Two inches is really no big deal.'

He grinned and I snorted. After the snort the ridiculous hyena laugh followed and the next thing I knew, I was teetering on my heels and losing my balance.

'Whoa, Jillian.' He grabbed my hips in his hands and steadied me until I stopped swaying. 'OK?'

I nodded, looking down into his face as it dawned on me that his beautiful full mouth was right about crotch level. Then the room was moving again but only in my head. Samuel bowed his head forwards, his brow hitting just above my mound. With the pressure, I could feel my pulse beating fast and crazy in my pussy. 'Samu–'

'Shh,' he said. He looked up at me and smiled. Inch by inch, I watched him lean in and place his mouth over my pussy. His breath seeped through the flimsy fabric of my skirt, snaking through the grid of my fishnets, the crotch of my panties, to invade my swollen sex. My head lolled back on its own and my heart beat so hard it hurt. I put my hands on his shoulders, feeling him breathe against my cunt.

His lips moved in a barely perceptible motion over my mound, effectively sealed over my pussy lips. I could feel the heat of his mouth through what felt like mountains of fabric and I was giddy with it. 'I . . .'

'Shh.' The vibration of his shushing worked through me and my cunt flexed, so very ready to come and then come again. But it wasn't going to happen like that today. I could tell already. Something like intuition told me that he was toying with me. And I liked it. His fingers fanned over my ass and he pressed himself more firmly to my pussy, the ridge of his teeth

55

lending a sharp pressure that was painful and pleasant all at once. 'I need fabric samples. Can you bring them?'

I was nodding, nodding like a lunatic and running my hands over the wide shoulders of his suit jacket. I had thought they were padded. They were not. That was all him.

'Can you bring them for lunch tomorrow? On me. We'll write it off.' He nudged my clit with his thin, sharp nose and my knees did a flimsy little curtsy that threatened to spill me onto the floor.

'Yes.' My voice was little more than a whisper.

He held out his hand to help me down. I took it, still feeling the moist warm spot between my legs left by his humid breath. 'And Jillian?'

'Yes?'

'Don't bring me those little one-inch squares. No one can tell a damn thing by a one-inch square. Big pieces of fabric so I can really see. OK? I'll pay if I need to.'

'Big pieces,' I repeated. I was slightly dazed and doing a piss-poor job at hiding it.

'Good girl.' He leaned in so his lips touched my ear like the first time and he reiterated, 'Good, good girl. Now I'll heat up your soup. You need to eat.'

While he heated the soup, I went into the ladies' room and hiked up my skirt. I braced my heel on the wall of the stall and shoved my hands down into my panties. One shaking hand stroked hot, eager circles over my clit. With the other, I finger-fucked myself until I sagged against the cold wall and had to bite my tongue to stifle my cries. I relished each honey-sweet contraction that worked through my cunt, the memory of his hot mouth over me there. So close and yet so very, very far.

This man was driving me crazy and I was loving every minute of it.

* * *

I had handkerchief-sized swatches of the brown, crème and blue fabric and another of the barn red with off white. They were stashed in my purse with my lipsticks and my BlackBerry and perfume. Six outfits! Six wardrobe changes before I settled on my taupe and black wrap dress with yet another pair of tall boots. No fishnets today, nothing but back-seamed black stockings attached to my garters. Something about old-school garters and hose made me feel undeniably sexy. Like a sinner with no hope of redemption.

'There's no way. He's married. I mean, she is like twenty and her boobs are clearly fake and she probably gives a killer blowjob. He's just fucking with you. He just wants to turn the tables. You started this and he's going to teach you a lesson. Like one of Aesop's fables or a morality play. Don't fuck with the married man or you'll get burned.' I muttered all of this to myself as I walked briskly to The Tarnished Spoon from my mid-day appointment.

I should have been super-excited about having landed the design job for Blow Out. The salon was going to be fantastic in chrome and black and red. But instead of excitement, I was gushing between my thighs at the memory of Samuel pressing his mouth over my sex and the heat that came from between his lips. It wasn't hard for my mind to take it one step further and imagine his tongue sneaking out to taste me there. Or the pressure he would put into the swirls on my swollen clit. Or how the rigid tip of his tongue would feel pressing past my entrance and dipping into the sweet cream of my cunt and . . .

I almost walked into the front door. A small sign had been taped to the door.

CLOSED FOR REPAIRS.

WILL REOPEN AT THREE.

I stalled out, confused. I stared at the sign and it seemed to stare back. Until the door cracked and Samuel peeked out. He smiled. 'It doesn't mean you. I closed *for* you. Come on in.'

My stomach did that roller-coaster dip and I swallowed a high nervous laugh. I was jittery and my body was reacting with Pavlovian ease. See Samuel. Want Samuel. Pussy gets wet. As easy as one, two, three. 'Thanks.' I stepped inside the dim dining room and found myself blinking again. We were alone. 'I brought you the fabric –'

'That's great, Jillian. But before we go any further, let's visit the kitchen. I can't have you redoing the Spoon without adding a few touches to the kitchen.' His eyes were dark and he had a nearly lupine look. Like he was the Big Bad Wolf and I was Little Red Riding Hood. My body was all chaos and urgency.

'I . . .' I felt a little dizzy and reached out to touch him to steady myself. The tingling of arousal that coursed through my fingers didn't help, so I let go. 'I don't do . . .'

I didn't do kitchens! Kitchens were a whole other animal. You had to know about floor drains and ovens and sinks. Pot racks and venting systems and walk-in freezers. A swell of panic that felt like a tidal wave rose in my chest and spots bloomed before my eyes.

'It's OK. I'm just asking you to look. You need to breathe. Breathe, Jillian.'

I did as instructed and nodded. 'Kitchen,' I said dumbly.

'Come on, it will be fine. I promise.' He took my hand and I felt that surge of predatory glee I had felt when I started this whole thing. I had only been trying to steal the job from Mrs Radcliff. And, if I were to be completely honest, to get a little male attention and an ego boost. And now he had shaken it all up and got me all crazy and . . . I followed dumbly, unable to even follow my own train of thought.

We pushed through the swinging double doors and stainless steel glowed all over the place. Walking from the dim dining room into the brightly lit kitchen was like walking out into the blazing sun. Nothing looked familiar to me. I saw sinks with an overhead rinse hose, and a huge griddle. Gigantic stoves, one with eight burners and one with four. Overhead racks held really big pots and swinging utensils. It was spick and span and shiny and might as well have been an alien planet for all I knew about the kitchen. 'Um . . .' I wanted to say something intelligent at least. 'Nice,' I said.

Brilliant.

Samuel chuckled and turned me to face him. I looked up into his face, holding my breath. He was big. Bigger than I had ever really realised. I was tall for a woman. I was wearing kick-ass boots and I was still looking up at him. Feeling small added to the overwhelming feeling of urgency and desire. I was ready to throw myself on the stainless-steel table and hike up my skirt. Instead I smiled and tried to keep eye contact. He moved in closer so that his pelvis hit mine and I felt the hard ridge of his cock in his slacks. My eyes drifted closed for a moment and I pressed back against him. Liking the feel of the hard-on. Liking the fact that it was for me. I opened my eyes but only for an instant when his lips touched mine.

And then he was kissing me and walking me back, my purse still tucked under my arm. I held his shoulders and let his tongue deep into my mouth. When my hips and ass hit the steel table, I gave a startled little sound but didn't break the kiss.

'Fabric samples,' he said against my lips. His hands settled on my hips, heavy and imposing. I wondered if he would leave fingerprints on me from holding me so tight. I hoped so.

I pulled them from my purse and handed them over, then watched, my heart beating wildly, as he examined the two fabrics. What the hell? Big hard cock, big deep kiss and then . . . fabric swatches? Odd. I yelped when he found a weak spot and ripped a strip from the brown print fabric. 'Nice. I like this one,' Samuel growled and ripped another strip from the large piece I had supplied.

'But . . . but, I thought –'

'Hands up, Jillian,' he said with a wicked smile. 'Hands up in the air like a good little girl.'

I could smell his aftershave and his clean skin and a trickle of wetness seeped into my panties. My cheeks flooded with colour almost akin to shame and I raised my hands like I was under arrest. 'Oh, OK,' I said.

'You are a very naughty girl. But so very interesting too, you know.' He talked softly to me as he tied one of my wrists to the pot rack overhead. I nodded but remained silent, twisting this way and that to try to relieve the demanding thump of my cunt and the constant nervous flutter in my belly. 'You come in here and seduce me into redoing my restaurant. You flaunt your body and your brain. I don't know which is sexier, by the way. And then you go and get all shy and girlish, which makes you that much more desirable. Makes me want to fuck you that much more.'

My throat seemed to grow small when he said the word 'fuck', and as if they had a mind of their own my hips rose up to bump against his so that I could feel that hard line of his dick in his pants.

'And I intend to fuck you,' he went on, taking my other wrist and pressing his teeth to the intense beat of my pulse where my skin was thinnest. He licked over the spot with the flat of his tongue and then stretched my arm up and tied me. 'And might I say, your wardrobe choice for today was genius. It's as if you knew. I bet you did. Somewhere deep down.'

I shook my head no and then found myself nodding. Details, I'd had no idea of those. The intent to fuck, that I had felt pretty certain of. Deep down I had known, if I was honest. He pulled the tie on my wrap dress and unfolded the halves until I was standing there in my hose and garters and tiny panties and a bra. My skin pebbled with goosebumps and he stepped back to look at me. It was a slow lingering look that had me testing my bonds by the end.

'Spread your legs.'

I did. Wantonly, ignoring my shyness, I spread my legs and when he touched me I hissed air like I'd been burned. 'You're so wet. You little slut. Are you a slut for me?'

And there I was nodding again. It all felt so surreal but so very, very good too. I pushed against his hand to see if he would slide a finger into me. I was rewarded when he pushed my panties to the side and knelt on the red tile floor. His mouth was as hot as I imagined, his tongue as good as I had hoped. He flicked hard circles over my clit with the tip before dipping his tongue into the wet, wet centre of me. When he added a few fingers to the fray and stroked my G-spot with a gentle kind of dominance I came swiftly. I let go and gave into the warm waves of orgasm, biting my bottom lip to try not to be loud. But I was still loud. I shook so hard as I came I set the pots and pans into a merry little melody of shaking and swaying metal.

'You're sweet like something off the dessert cart,' he said, looking up at me from the floor. His tongue toured my pussy once more and I jumped around in my ties. I was so sensitive his tongue felt almost brutal. He unzipped his navy-blue slacks as he stood and his face was set in a way that made me nervous and excited all at once. He fisted his cock as he came at me and I automatically spread my legs wide. So fast, my ass was on the stainless-steel table and he was sliding into me, my black panties still pushed to the side, my stockings and garters intact. I wrapped my legs around him as he fucked me. My upper body stretched so taut I felt the pull in my ribs, the discomfort only adding to the bright white pleasure of his cock sliding in and out of my body.

'My God, you are wet. You little slut,' he said again and I felt my cunt flex at the word. I would come again, I knew that much. He bit me gently above my collar-bone and when my pussy tightened around him like a fist, he bit me harder. 'You like a bit of pain, don't you?'

I was nodding again even though I had never responded to any kind of pain before. But hanging there at his mercy, I loved the feel of his teeth on me. His hands pinned me to the cool metal and he fucked me faster, the immobile table legs squealing with what sounded like glee. I rose up to meet him as I felt another orgasm sliding towards me. 'Oh, God,' I said as I came.

Clichéd but true. I called out to God and came again as Samuel bucked again and growled. The orgasm distorted his face. He didn't look as hard or in control or scary when he came.

The bright room was filled with the sounds of us panting. 'Christ, we sound like a pack of dogs,' he said and I giggled. He kissed me on the lips and I sucked on his tongue for a moment, wondering what it would be like to suck on his cock.

Samuel pulled free and opened the walk-in fridge. He disappeared and then returned with a cold soda in his hand. He took a long swallow, his cock still poking from his slacks. Then he put the bottle to my lips and tilted it so I could drink too.

'Aren't you going to untie me?' I asked, licking the soda from my upper lip.

'Why? We have tons of time. We have the place to ourselves till three,' he said softly. There was that lupine look again. My nipples went hard and he yanked back the lace cups of my bra to see. Then he leaned in and kissed me again. His lips were cold and tasted like soda, his eyes full of malicious intent.

Garden of Eden
Primula Bond

'I'd be touring America if I wasn't stuck in here.' Beatrice tore at the limp green shoots around the foot of the delicate vines. 'Imagine it, Caterina. The open road. Booze, blow. Boys.'

Caterina folded her hands under her apron.

'Gently, B. Those aren't weeds. They won't grow if you're rough with them.'

'Rough is best, believe me.' Beatrice thumped the wet grass back in and pushed at her headdress. 'I could be in New Orleans or Vegas right now, having rough sex, backstage or in the bus, taking my pick of the dancers. They're the best.' She smiled, her wine-purple lips rolling back to show the sweet pink inside.

Once, when Caterina was new, the pair of them had been digging at the far end of the vineyard when Beatrice started singing an old blues song. Her deep voice had cracked from lack of use, but it made Caterina's heart beat faster.

Someone had heard, though, and after that they had been lashed, made to prostrate themselves in front of the others at Matins, then separated for weeks.

'Strong, silent, hung like donkeys and oh so eager to please the lead singer. I was the star, Cat. I paid their wages. Sometimes I made them fuck me two at a time. And the performance on stage afterwards! You could smell it. But you wouldn't know about any of that, would you?'

Caterina tried to close herself off. Think of the muffled, powerful words like so many angry bees batting against her tight white cap. She plucked a couple of swollen grapes out of their leafy bed, and allowed herself a glimmer of pride. A year's tending, and they were perfect. So ripe in the palm of her hand. Oh God, she was hungry. Breakfast was a dry roll before daybreak, and now it was noon. So delicious if she could just take one tiny bite before taking the harvest to the wine press. Her teeth piercing the translucent skin, biting the red fruity flesh. The juice spurting onto her tongue, the cool, naughty liquid trickling down her throat. No one would know . . .

'You're gorgeous when you smile. Like one of those teenagers the scouts pluck out of Top Shop and turn into virginal-waif supermodels.'

'I'm not a teenager. I'm twenty.'

'What a bloody waste! Smiling is God's gift we should all share, rather than forbid.' Beatrice tipped her face to the sun. 'You'd never know we were in the middle of Tuscany. These four walls could be anywhere. Tennessee. Yorkshire. Anyway, what's so funny?'

Caterina liked the way smiling lifted her cheekbones. Her French mother used to stroke her face and call them *pommettes*. Little apples. But she pulled her mouth straight, back into its calm mask. 'Just that we've another lead singer to please now.'

'Very good. Try telling that to Mother Mary and see how she likes the analogy.'

Beatrice's smile was twisted.

'That's all behind you. Why are you talking as if it's still happening?' Caterina glanced at the bell tower. Five minutes before the next silence. 'You were the one who took me under your wing and convinced me this was the life.' Caterina blushed and leaned closer to Beatrice. Even this, being physically close, actually touching sleeves, was wicked because it was forbidden. 'You said hearing the Voice was like the rush of a class-A drug!'

'And it was. I meant it. I was running away. But it's been three years. Something's changing in me.' Beatrice sighed. Her breath was warm and smelt of honey.' I have these dreams, Caterina. Being on stage, being fucked on stage, those dancers taking me right there in front of the crowd, except the crowd is all of you in the chapel. How kinky is that? But that's why it feels like it's all happening now. Every morning I wake up, and my fingers are shoved right up inside me, and I'm really wet, and I'm moving with them, so I push them right in and all I can think about is a big hard cock fucking me.'

She ran her finger over Caterina's top lip. 'Smell that?'

Caterina sniffed Beatrice's finger, knowing she shouldn't. The sharp, sweet tang on her skin was instantly familiar.

'That's my pussy juice. From this morning.'

'Stop it, I won't listen, I can't listen to this!' Caterina put her hands over her ears and started muttering her prayers.

But Beatrice grabbed her and slid her hand up under the thick white linen veil flapping round her shoulders to touch the soft skin on Caterina's neck. Caterina flinched, and Beatrice breathed into her ear. 'If you respond that quickly to one little touch, sister, how do you think you'd feel to have a cock ramming up you? Two gorgeous men fucking you, front and back, both at the same time?'

Caterina shook her head wildly, the bees buzzing right inside her ears now. Sensations shot through her, straight from where Beatrice was touching her neck down to the place under her apron, under her dress, under her serge petticoat, under the scratchy bloomers where her white thighs, her bottom, her dark private parting, were warm and naked and loosening . . .

'Shall I tell you what else you're missing, Kitty Cat? All those earthly delights you've never tasted? Might never taste? The kissing, the licking, the way his cock goes hard when you stroke it. Even when he sees you. The feel of it sliding in, opening you up, pushing inside you.'

Caterina looked into Beatrice's dark-brown eyes. It was like she was being tugged by a string, no, a great thick rope, towards all those dirty things Beatrice was saying, all those wild pictures she was drawing.

'You can't give up all that pleasure. I don't care what Mother Mary says. Or what I said three years ago. I have to get back there, Caterina.'

And then the bell started to ring from the tower. They both glanced up to watch it swinging heavily from its wooden frame.

Beatrice jumped up then looked down at Caterina shivering on her hands and knees in the wet grass.

'Anyone visiting you today?'

Caterina breathed deeply. Thank God, the subject, the temptation, the buzzing of those bees, those stinging dirty thoughts, was going. She bowed her head. 'They've all turned against me.'

'Well, I have a feeling someone's here for me. I'll leave you to your precious vines.'

'Yes. It's time to make the wine.'

Beatrice took a step towards the convent. Already there was something different in the way she moved. Not the ghostly glide that made them invisible, but an obstinate stride. Caterina couldn't keep her eyes off her. The way she moved showed her body, her hips, the secret curve of her breasts. Even the divide between her legs. It was as if she could see right through her clothes to those long dark legs.

She turned, caught Caterina looking at her. Caterina felt coiled, her heart juddering in the chest she kept mercilessly bound.

'You might not be a teenager, sister, but you're about the only one of us who is truly a virgin. You really want to stay that way forever?'

* * *

66

The bees were becoming a distant drone in the back of her head, but they buzzed with a vengeance at the dead of night. In her cell Caterina's fingers strayed under her nightgown as she thought about those big black dancers taking her roughly in front of a congregation. Wondered but could guess how it would feel as her nails scratched over the cool white flesh of her thighs, sensed the warmth pulsating from her opening sex, yearned to go further.

Down the hall Beatrice and the other sisters slept. Or perhaps they didn't? Perhaps they all dreamed of their past lives full of lovers, remembering naked limbs and bodies rubbing against each other and getting sweaty, men kissing and touching, maybe even other women kissing and touching them. Her sisters, putting fingers inside themselves while they writhed silently on their unforgiving horsehair pallets.

But Beatrice was leaving. She would soon be free of that wicked whispering.

The sun was blistering and Caterina was at the far end of the vineyard, where Beatrice had once sung to her and got them both into trouble. The last basket of grapes was heavy, but she kept silent, didn't even grunt as she lifted it towards the cool press ready to be turned into intoxicating wine.

The air hummed with heat. Sweat gathered in a hot wet tangle under her veil. Pooled in her armpits. Snaked down her neck and formed a jagged stain down her back. She got halfway across the parched lawn and stopped. A motorbike was roaring up the road from Siena and with a climactic revving of the throttle it stopped at the end of the private lane. All her senses were alert. A deer sensing danger rather than a prisoner sensing freedom.

Someone was rolling barrels about in the wine house while the augur fed the grapes into the crusher, but no one else was visible. They would all be inside, scrubbing the floors or preparing lunch. But Caterina had shamelessly used what was left of her feminine wiles to get and keep this job. Chore, task, whatever. The red, potent wine from the fertile vines was the convent's main source of income other than anonymous donations, but they'd been about to abandon the press when, after that lashing she'd received last year, Caterina begged them to let her tend the grapes, even if she didn't have the skills to make the wine. And somehow, with eyelashes and innocence, she kept getting her way.

Now there were footsteps on the dusty road. Caterina crawled under the jungle of vines and ivy and clambering roses. She couldn't resist it. She pushed aside the glossy leaves to reveal a slit in the crumbling stonework and pressed her eye against the hole in time to see stones and grit being kicked up in front of the approaching feet.

Beatrice came into view. She was wearing faded old jeans and a white T-shirt. Caterina couldn't see as high up as her face, but she could see the outline of Beatrice's big breasts, pushing against the low-cut cotton, and the gleaming skin on her arms, and a sliver of chocolate stomach as she suddenly bent to put her rucksack down on the ground, right in front of Caterina's spyhole.

'You there, Kitty Cat? Breaking the golden rule?'

She rested her hands on her knees and stooped to grin straight at the wall. Caterina swallowed. Beatrice had ringlets coiling off her head. Bracelets on her wrists. And big black breasts dangling down inside the T-shirt, threatening to fall out of it.

'You know the first thing I'm going to do? My mate on the motorbike? Christ, how did I bear it in there?' Beatrice ran her hands over her breasts. Her pink tongue slipped wetly across her red painted lips. 'I'm going to pull my knickers off and I'm going to sit on his face, right there outside the gate, and spread my pussy all over his mouth, and I'm going to make him lick my sweet wet hungry cunt, make him do it real slow till I come in his face.' She moaned and tilted her head back, gyrated there in front of Caterina. 'Then I'll make him fuck me.'

Caterina felt the moisture springing in the curly hairs round her – what had Beatrice called it? – her cunt. Her pussy. Her sex. She pressed her thighs together. There was a pulse going, just inside, close enough to touch, the same deep throbbing she felt at night when those buzzing thoughts tormented her, those dirty things Beatrice had done and was going to do again. Her breath rasped in her ears as Beatrice touched herself out there in the deserted lane.

What would be the harm, no one could see, just one touch, just put her hand under her skirt and stroke there on the soft twitching skin, push through the curly hairs and feel that slick of wetness. She was safe in her garden. It would be like picking out a tune on the piano in the parlour. She moved her hands over her thighs, over the thick material of her garments, rubbed them up and down, each time shifting her skirt a little higher, over her ankles, over her knees ...

'But you'd better be careful, girl. You'll get a lashing. But maybe you'd like that. You know, I creamed myself when Mother Mary lashed me last year. That's why I like getting into trouble. You know that? All wet smeared down my petticoat afterwards.' She turned her back, stuck her bottom out and slapped her rump, hard. 'Hmm, maybe it's not so bad in there after all.'

Then she picked up her rucksack and was gone. Caterina was shaking, her fingers clawing at her skirts. Beatrice found sex everywhere, even in the lashing of those whips across their bottoms when they'd sinned.

She let the branches bounce back over the hole and staggered backwards into the sunshine, panting and doubled over. One of her stockings had come loose, rolling down her leg and irritating her, the black wool scratching her skin to leave it raw and sensitive as if she'd been burned. She pointed her toe like a ballerina, lifted her skirt and reached under it to yank up the stocking.

A bird screeched up behind her and she jumped round, leg still cocked, dizzy with heat and blinded by the sun. In the glare a tall figure stood holding her heaped basket of grapes.

'Oh, Sister Agnes, I was just – I thought I heard a swarm of bees.'

The figure said nothing and started walking off towards the wine press. It was wearing trousers.

Caterina shielded her eyes and stared. It was a man. The only man she'd seen in over a year apart from Father Christophe. And not a wrinkled old man like the priest, but a tall man with wild black hair and wide shoulders and long legs in baggy blue stained trousers. Strong, suntanned arms, the muscles flexing as he lifted her heavy basket like it was a punnet of strawberries.

Her stomach knotted right behind her navel. Her mouth went dry. Beyond the gate the motorbike suddenly roared into life, making her squeal with shock at the unaccustomed din. The man kept walking. The bike screeched off towards the horizon. Still he took no notice. So. Had Beatrice done it? Had she pulled down her jeans and her knickers and sat on her friend's face like she had said?

The bell, goddamnit, started to toll.

'What are you doing with my grapes?' She let her skirt drop down her legs, the fabric brushing her skin and settling back around her ankles. But her habit didn't comfort her. It suffocated her. She wanted to kick her skirt off, rip off her veil, her blouse, feel the sun burning into her skin. She tried a harsh whisper. 'Are you the guy coming to make the liqueur?'

He didn't answer. She tapped him on the shoulder, bristling with impatience. 'Excuse me?'

He looked round slowly. The curly hair was streaked with grey, and the stubble on his chin was flecked with white. How would Beatrice describe him? Handsome? Rugged? Craggy? Old? Horny. The word bit at her from nowhere, and she shoved her hands under her apron to stop them flying up to her reddening face. The way he hoisted that basket. And the eyes. Green and deep-set under a ferocious frown.

He didn't catch her eye, or speak. He stared, hard, at her mouth.

Caterina's hands clenched under her apron, pressing right into her lap. Into that secret warm place which felt every night as if it were coming alive. Her lips felt hot and swollen as he looked at her mouth. She could hear the breath rushing through it, and see the pulse pounding in his powerful neck.

A phantom hovered into view, and when his eyes flicked sideways it was like a match blowing out.

'Sister Caterina!' Sister Agnes crooked one white finger. 'To Mother at once, please!'

'The fact that he is deaf and dumb does not excuse you communing with a man out in the garden, sister. And we know Sister Beatrice poured pestilence in your ear. The only way to prevent you falling into the hands of the devil is by nightly flagellation and prostration.'

'And my work?' Caterina stood to attention in the dusty parlour that smelt of mouldy lavender.

'We will let you return to the garden, but you will not speak to him. He's here by patriarchal licence. Our sister convent in Venice sent him.' Sister Agnes and Mother Mary exchanged looks. They were like salt cellar and pepper pot, silhouetted against the window.

'It's a shame he's not blind, devoid of all the other senses as well,' hissed Mother Mary, her voice as sharp as the little black whip with three tails she had just handed Caterina. 'Because we cannot allow you to stray off your path, sister. You have heard the Voice calling you to purity.'

'He's the only man for the job, despite what happened in Venice. Because if we don't get our liqueur out to the markets there will be no roof over our heads.' Sister Agnes pressed her palms down as if to suppress such worldly concerns. Thin, white, hairy legs, Caterina guessed, under that worn old habit. Legs that had never spread open above a man's face. Oh, she might have had pretty eyes once, but after years of denial they were hard, blue, and veined as marbles. 'Meanwhile you will continue your nightly penance.'

Across the garden Zorzi would be toiling in her wine house, processing her grapes. His arms, with the muscles flexing under the skin, and his hands, those eyes gleaming in the wine-drenched shadows. And away over the hills Beatrice would be singing and dancing and fucking all she pleased.

The setting sun spiked through the stained glass in a sudden single ray like a warning and Caterina suddenly saw what the other nuns saw. Herself, illuminated by a heavenly light. She dug her nails into her hand.

'This is my chance to prove my purity to you.'

Caterina stopped to prop up a vine that had been beaten down by the summer storm and started to weep at all the neglect. In the end they had betrayed her. Kept her in solitary, away from the others and away from the garden, for a whole month.

'What did Beatrice tell you?' she had asked faintly when she was released from her cell by Sister Agnes. A month of contemplation and flagellation had crushed her. 'What am I supposed to have done?'

But it seemed they were all deaf and dumb, too. Nobody had spoken to her as they paced the cloister, even though it was communication time.

She licked her dry lips. 'She tell you we kissed, or fondled, or worse? Or did she tell you what she used to do with those dancers when she was on the road, what she was going to do the minute she got out of here? I'll tell you what I've been contemplating in there, shall I?'

But the words had stayed in her head. The words, and the thoughts that had buzzed, louder than before, when she'd been alone, straining up at the little slit of a window to see sun or moon or Zorzi, or lying face-down on the cold stone floor of the chapel in front of all the others.

She'd slapped the little cat o'nine tails across her bare shoulders and flinched with pain, then pleasure, gasping at the sharp sting on her skin diffusing into intense, invigorating heat. And yes, before the dawn prostration she'd pleasured herself, and while she'd done it she'd seen Zorzi's fierce green eyes, how he stared at her mouth, his muddy fingers wrapped around the vines, and what they might do to her, how they might feel taking hold of her, pushing up her clothes, straying up her legs, further in, and further, it was a habit she had not been able to break, her fingers pushing open the soft damp lips every night, poking at the secret hole that seemed to nibble and close around her fingers.

And then last night she had taken the thick leather handle of the whip, still warm from her flagellating, and eased it inside, oh so gently, back and forth in a little rocking rhythm, careful not to hurt herself, opening her knees wider to feel its brutal length, a scream bunching up in her throat as it touched a tiny bud that sent flares of excitement through her, gripping at her so hard that she squealed and pulled it quickly back out and tossed it across the room as if it were a snake . . .

'Zorzi is not going fast enough. He needs help with the packaging. We'll have to entrust you to him, after all.' Sister Agnes gave Caterina a big crate of empty bottles, unlocked the garden gate and pushed her out into the rain. 'Then, thank God, his work is done.'

Caterina stumbled under the weight of the crate. 'What did

he do in Venice that was so awful, sister?' She cleared her dry throat. 'I mean, will I be safe in there with him?'

'He took another sister's chastity.' Sister Agnes puckered her lips in so tight they looked like a cat's arse. 'Nothing you need to know about in detail, except that he is the devil and she was a very weak soul. This is your Garden of Eden, sister.'

Caterina was drenched when she got to the wine house. The rain thundered down on the roof but inside it was baking from all those hot dry nights, and she stood in the doorway panting.

Zorzi was bent over a barrel, turning the tap and studying the dark-red liquid pouring into a big jug. The sweet potent aroma made Caterina dizzy. She put down the heavy crate with a loud rattle and arched her aching back. He'd been out in the rain. His black hair curled on his neck. His wet shirt stuck to his spine and ribs. She could see muscles flexing as he breathed. Oh God! She could imagine that big body rearing up over the prostrate form of the sister in Venice, hidden in their vineyard, the busy canal just the other side of the wall, the boat that brought him every day rocking on the dirty green water. Her imagination homed in on the image of those strong arms propping him up as he tilted his buttocks, clothed in those blue trousers – she couldn't allow herself to imagine them naked, how they would look, round, firm, tanned, taut, tensing between the nun's white open legs, her brown apron and skirt askew, her arms outstretched as she offered herself like a sacrifice . . .

Silently he turned the tap off and squatted there on the dusty floor, sniffing the liqueur expertly before taking a deep swig.

Caterina's legs trembled as she went to stand in front of him. He swilled the liquid round his mouth, staring calmly up as if he had been expecting her, then swallowed. She massaged her fingers, strained from carrying the crate. His hair was wet, and a drop was elongating at the end of one curl, ready to fall onto his forehead. The silence and the heat and the still-falling rain hummed in her ears. All those nights of deprivation in solitary and her good intentions shrivelled because of the way he was looking at her. He studied her knees, which were on a level with his face, the his gaze travelled up her legs, resting briefly on her lap, where she was kneading her fingers, before moving up over her bound chest to her blushing face.

'I'm here to help you,' she croaked, and coughed. He waited, staring, again, at her mouth. She touched her lips, and they felt as if they were burning. 'They've punished me by keeping me silent for a month. Like you, I suppose!' She felt laughter sliding dangerously inside her, and waved her hand around the shed. Her sleeve brushed his hair. He started to smile. She took the labels she'd designed, reluctantly approved by Mother Mary, out of her pocket. The outline of a nun from the back, curvaceous in a ridiculously tight-fitting habit, reaching up to pluck a grape. He glanced at the image. 'I'm renaming the wine La Religieuse. Means nun, in French.'

He nodded. He stood up and came very close to her, then paused for a moment, waiting, maybe, for her to move away. But she didn't. She couldn't. She could feel the wall of warmth between them. The way he stared at her mouth as if he wanted to eat it. Then he lifted his hands and she held her breath, waiting for him to touch her. But instead he sketched her hidden curves with his big hands, tracing the same shape as her design, and she gasped as her nipples tingled in response.

The rain drummed on the roof. The drop fell off his hair onto his nose. Her veil was weighted with water. Zorzi took the hem of it, squeezed water out of it. Heat radiated out of him, even at arm's length. Caterina's mouth was open as she tried to breathe, and as he looked again at her mouth he yanked her veil right off and held it up disdainfully. Caterina slapped her hand over her mouth to stifle the shriek. She tried to grab at the veil, but he tossed it behind the barrels. As she flailed frantically for it he blocked her way. She put her hands up to hide the roughly chopped, hideous remains of her blonde hair, but he took hold of both wrists in one hand, wound a rogue strand of her hair round the finger of the other and rubbed it under his nose as if it were a herb or a petal. She could see her reflection, two miniature Caterinas in each of his dark eyes.

'Oh, God,' she croaked, as he tugged at her hair and her scalp prickled. 'I used to love my hair being stroked. I haven't been touched since – I've never been touched –'

His hands started to slide down her neck, lifting her wet collar away from the clammy skin there, and stroking her with his fingertips where her own pulse was hammering. Sparks of electricity seemed to crackle off her. He stared at her neck, her throat, down at her apron and the rough blouse underneath it. She looked down as well. The march through the rain had made the rough linen cling to her torso. Zorzi smiled slowly and instinctively Caterina pushed her shoulders back to thrust her breasts out.

His fingers moved round to flick open her top button at the base of her throat.

'We need to do the bottling.' Caterina tilted her head away. 'They'll check.'

He shrugged, took his hands away and picked up the jug. Now her neck felt cold. He pushed the jug against her mouth, the same place where he'd drunk, and tilted it until she was forced to drink. The wine was strong, and delicious. Some of it spilt down her chin, trickling where he'd opened the button. She wiped her mouth, giggling quietly, and felt the alcoholic haze spreading through her. He smiled and took a great big swig. Now his lips were red, and wet with wine.

Shards of excitement jabbed at her again. Having felt him touch her once, all of her was clamouring to feel one flick of his fingertips again. He was so close she could count every bristle pushing through the dark skin on his chin. She focused on his mouth.

His hands came back to her shoulders, and they started to massage the bones so that she was forced to relax. Her neck went limp and he undid the next button. And the next. But when the buttons were nearly down to her waist, she tried to cover herself. How repulsive she looked, her breasts bound beneath bandages. And sure enough, he stopped and reached behind him for something.

'That's right, Zorzi. We must stop.' She turned to do up the buttons, but he pushed her hands away, pulled open her blouse and started to cut, with his shears, at the bandages underneath. Now she was shivering with excitement and fear. Her knees were buckling. A pulse was throbbing deep between her legs. Her sensitive breasts tightened and started to swell, rising up like dough as the bandages loosened, cut into shreds, and dropped to the floor. Now they were offered, pale and soft in the shadowy wine house. Her nipples hardened, dark and red. He pushed her shirt further down her shoulder and traced the ridge of her collar-bone, treading his fingertips across the exposed skin and under the shirt again, threatening, no, promising, to creep down towards her breasts. Caterina was helpless now, her breath coming in uneven gasps of longing.

His features became blurred and fused in front of her. She closed her eyes, letting her head droop backwards as the soft caresses lulled her. He came closer, their knees colliding. He bent towards her shoulder and she could feel his breath hot on her skin. She moved her head round to meet him so that his mouth bumped up against hers. They both waited, mouths just touching. Her breath stopped totally then. She couldn't move away. Her lips softened and parted. He rubbed his mouth against hers. She slid her hands round him and up his back and she felt a quiver run down between his shoulder blades. Her hands pressed harder onto him. She was as desperate to touch as to be touched. He flicked the tip of his tongue against her teeth, and then around the inside of her lips, and he tasted of wine and so masculine, salty, sweet, wet, warm. She pushed her tongue in and his lips closed around it, trapping it, sucking it in between his teeth, so that her face was moulded into his and her breasts and body were pressed against the length of him.

This would be enough, she thought. This kissing is heaven. Perhaps if this is all, I won't have sinned. But it was like setting a taper to a candle as they sucked on each other. She was smouldering from her feet upwards.

She thought he was murmuring something, but that was impossible. He was pulling off his shirt as they kissed. He took her hands and placed them on his back and she squealed with the warmth of his skin. She stroked it, and scratched it, and he responded by reaching down and lifting up her skirt.

What was left of her sanctity struggled up and she battered weakly at his chest. 'No, Zorzi. I can't. The bell will go soon and what work have we done?'

But he lifted her and dropped her onto a pile of old hessian sacks, some empty, others full of crackling leaves. He stood and looked down at her. He was massive against the rainy daylight. They were enclosed in the darkness. Everything was wicked, and dangerous. She realised, as she lay there, that she looked like the sacrificial nun she imagined he'd seduced in Venice. The thought made her wriggle despite all her efforts to remain still.

He reached behind him to grab the jug of wine, and took two bottles out of her crate. He grinned as he tipped the liquid into the slim bottles until they were full. Still staring at her, he ripped a label off her roll, swiped one across his wet tongue, and stuck it onto the elegant brown glass flank. Then he banged a cork into the mouth and dumped it back into the crate before spreading out his hands triumphantly.

'Job done! How hard can it be?' She couldn't help clapping her hands. 'Christ, you are a wicked man!'

He laughed then, a kind of husky breath, filled up the other bottle and tipped some more into her laughing mouth. This time it splashed all over her breasts, dripping onto her nipples, and they both stopped laughing. They looked down at the dark-red, pointed nipples, wet with wine. He remained kneeling. She reached up, and pulled him down on top of her. He hesitated, then let himself sink down. He took her arms and held them above her head. The rough sacking scratched where her blouse had ridden up her back. She raised her spine off the bale to escape the prickles. Her torso was arched towards him and so were her breasts. Straining desperately towards him, his hands, his mouth. The most natural position in the world.

'They told me never to speak to you,' she said. 'But they didn't tell me not to touch you.'

He smiled then, and nodded as if he'd heard her, and the warmth inside her turned to fire. His nostrils were flared with the effort of breathing calmly. He was heavy on her legs. Her breath was shallow, barely there. One hand held her arms down while the other started to move down to her breast, feeling its weight against the palm of his hand. Then he bent down, muscles bulging in his arm as he supported his weight, and sucked the wine off her nipple. She moaned and flung her head back. He put one knee between her legs, still sucking, opening her, then he lifted her skirt, her petticoat, to reveal the cumbersome bloomers. Caterina squirmed with confusion, trying to cover the horrible undergarments, but he pushed the skirt and petticoat up to her waist, unaccustomed air playing on her thighs, and took hold of the bloomers. The slight ripping sound as he yanked them down was electrifying in its quiet violence and she opened her legs for him as he touched her, right there, in her wet crack.

Through the thin material of his trousers she could feel the thick outline of his cock jutting right up against her thigh, nudging against the cleft between her legs. The rain rushed through the door like hushed voices.

She became frantic now. She wrenched her hands free from his and grabbed at him to unbuckle his belt. She tore at his jeans. She wanted him inside her, his cock pushing up her. He grabbed her wrists again, pinning them down with one hand while he drew his cock out. It was hard, jumping in his hand. She wound her legs round his hips. The hay scratched into the crack of her bare bum.

Zorzi paused for a moment as if asking her permission. His eyes were glazed with desire as he searched her mouth for an answer.

'Yes,' she gasped. 'Fuck me, Zorzi.'

An explosive rush of excitement spurted through her, crazy and hot. She was lost. Any more words were stopped by her moans of pleasure as he started to run his cock up the soft skin of her inner thighs, guiding it to her swollen wet lips. Like some kind of harlot she knew to wriggle until he was deeper inside her. No niceties, no teasing as it slid inside and she gripped him tight inside her. The pleasure darkened to a hot peak ready to shatter her, no waiting, no possibility of waiting.

He pulled back for a tantalising moment, just as she'd envisaged, running the head of his cock round the tender groove, then he thrust into her, scraping her against the sacking, lifting her with his violence, until she heard her own animal shrieks of pleasure. He crushed her as he fucked her then shuddered violently, lying on her to kiss her again, licking and biting her mouth and her face as the excitement burst inside her, too, splitting her willing virginal body wide open.

Caterina let her arms and legs flop sideways and took his weight as he rested on top of her for a moment.

'If this is the Garden of Eden, that makes me Eve,' she said lazily, kissing his fingers.

The bell started tolling. 'The way you watch my lips all the time,' she said. 'That's because you're reading my lips?'

'No. It's because I want them wrapped around my cock.' His voice was deep and sexy and so shocking that he lifted her easily to her feet. 'That's going to be lesson number two.'

Primula Bond is the author of the Black Lace novels *Club Crème* and *Country Pleasures*, and the Nexus novel *Behind the Curtain*.

The Cicadas
Carrie Williams

They snaked through the narrow gorge, on roads running alongside sheer drops that would take them plummeting into the lush valley below were he to make the slightest error of judgment. She glanced, every few minutes, surreptitiously, almost shamefully, at her husband. The word still seemed strange to her, sometimes, as if she were living a dream – a dream that had lasted fifteen years now. Long enough for them to be making this trip, this second honeymoon. Why then did saying 'husband' still leave such an odd taste in her mouth?

She wasn't afraid; her stolen glances assured her that all was well, that he was in control of the little red convertible. He had always been a confident driver. In fact, that was one of the things that had first attracted her to him: his calm assurance, his hands lax yet firm on the wheel. He'd driven her out to country pubs, in the early days, and his prowess at the wheel had impressed her then, excited her even. On the way home he'd pull up somewhere – on an ill-frequented lane or in the gateway to a field – and, leaning over her in the passenger seat, push her mini-skirt up over her hips, yank down her knickers with the same assurance that he showed at the wheel, and finger her in the darkness. When she was on the verge of climax, he'd climb over onto her, fumbling for the side lever, and, once she was prone beneath him on the lowered seat, push his proud cock inside her and fuck her until the car shook to their rhythm.

She looked out of the window at the clefts and creases of the Provençal valley in all its green splendour. She missed those days so hard it hurt; sometimes she felt she would do almost anything to recapture the flavour of them, if only for a few moments. But the barrier of years stood between them and the present, making it seem impossible to re-experience them by any means except this burning nostalgia, a fire in her belly. Years of recriminations and resentments, years of spats and petty injustices batted between them, years of point-scoring. Sex was no longer something uncomplicated and spontaneous, but instead just another tool, or weapon, in the armoury of married life.

A second honeymoon, then, with the kids safely installed at their grandmother's house, watching too much TV and eating food forbidden at home. Bad habits instilled that it would take her weeks to undo. She glanced at Nick again, raising her hand and letting down her hair so that it swung with the movements of the car on the increasingly tight bends. As it brushed her bare shoulders in her halter-neck top, she felt a little freer: forget the kids and what they might or might not be eating – this was about her and Nick. It was a long-overdue break from the domestic and from the strains of his over-taxing career; a respite from daily cares and chores and from the fatigue of being responsible for other lives. A chance to find themselves again.

He slowed down as they ascended a road into one of the scenic *villages perchés* that dotted the hillsides of this region, and as he did so he turned his head a little and caught her eye.

'What?' she said, flustered for a moment, and she wondered what it was in her own regard that made him look so questioning, ill at ease even.

She shook her head, and he looked back at the road, a frown tautening his brow as he saw the streets narrow ahead. She watched his hand on the polished leather of the gearstick as he shunted the car down a notch and eased it around a corner into the labyrinth of the town centre. As he did so, she heard him sigh. She looked down at the map, traced a tiny white line on it with one fingertip.

'Not far now,' she reassured him. 'About three kilometres beyond Tourettes – this town – we cross a main road and the village is about another five kilometres from there.'

'And the hotel?'

She bit her lip, rustled through the papers on her lap. 'Mmmm – don't seem to have a street name on the email I printed out. But it's pin-sized on the map, the town. Can't be that hard to find.'

She watched as he nodded, checking the rear-view mirror at the same time, and though her instinct was to reach over and place her hand on the top of his thigh, as she had so many times in the past, she couldn't bring herself to act on the impulse.

The car swept down the broad driveway of the *mas*, bordered by silvery olive trees and aromatic lavender bushes, and entered the small car park. Beside the sleek black Porsches and glittering pewter Mercedes, their modest sports car lacked lustre. Sweaty and rumpled in the clothes she had worn for the flight, she felt unglamorous, middle-aged, although she knew thirty-five was considered still young these days. She glanced appraisingly at Nick; with his five o'clock shadow and salt-and-pepper hair, he too looked worn, past his sell-by date. She swallowed, wondering if they should have saved their money, spent it on improving the house. God knows it needed it.

But it was too late; already a porter was making his way over to them from the entrance, offering in faultless English to help them with their luggage. As the man opened the passenger door, he smiled down at her, and she felt a rush of blood to her face. His bronzed perfection, his flashing white teeth, the pressed black linen of his designer suit made her feel even more dishevelled and flustered. Accepting the hand he proffered her along with his smile, she stepped up and out of the car, smoothed down her skirt, attempted to smile back. Her mouth felt small and pinched, measly.

In their room, five minutes later, she opened the bath taps, poured in some of the complimentary algae salts, and then opened the windows onto a heart-stopping view over Provence hills and the perfume city of Grasse, shimmering in the sunlight like a mirage. Absently unbuttoning her shirt and slipping off her skirt, she stood mesmerised in her bra and knickers, letting the soft fragrant air caress her skin, teasing out the weariness of travel.

A flutter of fingers at her elbow brought her back to herself. Involuntarily she flinched. She knew Nick would be eager to make love, without preamble. He never seemed to understand that she needed some time to herself, to soak up the unfamiliar surroundings, to bed down in a new place and make it, in some sense, her own. His haste, his insistence, turned her off now, where once it had thrilled.

He sensed her reticence but persisted, and after a few minutes she had to shrug him off, telling him she needed to check that her bath wasn't overflowing. But the words were barely out and already he was turning away, expecting this.

At the bathroom door, she looked back over her shoulder, felt a pinch around her heart as she saw the same old dejection on his face, like a stain. He tried to hide it but never could; she knew him, and it, too well by now. How little it would take, she told herself, and not for the first time, for her to open herself up to him. Yet again and again she turned away. She frowned as she bent forward to swoosh the bathwater with one hand.

Freshly bathed, skin warm, pink and glowing beneath her fluffy white bathrobe, she found him gone, and was ashamed to feel relief. He must have set out to explore the hotel's abundant hanging gardens that they had admired together on its website; perhaps he had stopped for a cool drink in one of the hammocks strung between the fig trees, or was investigating the three pools – a large and a small swimming pool and then a hydrotherapy pool in the Japanese gardens by the spa. Beside the latter was one of the *mas*'s two open-air Jacuzzis. She wondered if the place were busy at this time of year or quiet now, a few weeks ahead of the season. She'd seen no other guests as they checked in. She and Nick might be lucky and have the place to themselves, or almost – there were always the staff flitting about, attentive to all needs, immaculate in their sharp black linen.

From where she was now sitting on the end of the bed, she let herself flop back, her bathrobe falling open around her, the sunlight pouring in on her from the open window. Her head on a pillow, she gazed down at her breasts, at her belly, with their fine hairs glimmering in the light. She thought of herself by the poolside, beside honed bodies fresh from the beaches of Cannes or St-Tropez. How would she measure up? Dare she go out there in the bikini she had splashed out on at the plush little lingerie shop that had just opened up around the corner from her house? And the spa? Would the French masseuse sneer secretly at this less-than-perfect body, marked by time, childbirth and the accidents of life?

She took a breast in each hand, brushed her nipples with the pads of her thumbs. A shiver ran through her, making her arch her back. She closed her eyes and pushed the rear of her head further down into the pillow, so plump, pliant and luxurious it must have been filled with the finest goose-down. Her eyelids burned acid-yellow. She emitted an involuntary moan, and let one of her hands move down to burrow itself between her legs.

She was surprised to find herself wet, already. Was it thoughts of the tanned bodies from the Côte d'Azur, or was the bronzed Adonis of a porter still in her mind? She shook her head. No – despite, or perhaps because of, his perfection, the latter couldn't stir her. Looks like that intimidated her, rather than inflaming her. The same went for the beach-buff bodies. For the first time in years, it seemed, she was finding pure pleasure in herself, in the feel of the breeze and the sunlight on her bare, cleansed flesh.

Legs parted, she slipped her fingers between her lips, delving inside herself. Her back arched further, without her knowing, as she pushed down on herself, responding to the pressure from her own hand. Like a fish flipping on the end of a line, trying to free itself, she bucked up and down, hips rising to meet her hand as it moved in and out of her, faster and faster as her orgasm began to make itself felt, mounting somewhere deep inside of her, in the blackest part of her, so hidden and secret she couldn't locate or even describe it. It was the place in her that was beyond words, barely accessible. Was that why it had been closed off for so long?

She opened her eyes. Beyond the window a summer haze had swathed the hills, made them dreamier still. A sense of unreality took hold of her as she felt her climax hit and carry her away, and it was as if from far away that she heard herself cry out, mindless of the window being open and of the possibility of any of the cool staff or her fellow guests being privy to her rapture.

When Nick got back, she was still slumbering, enveloped in post-orgasmic numbness. The first she knew of him was the light kiss on her forehead, like a butterfly alighting on her skin. Although she was still naked beneath the spread folds of her robe, he didn't try to take advantage, didn't make a move on her, and she was surprised and grateful. A burn did start up between her legs, where the ripples of her recent orgasm had barely subsided, but there was an anger inside her too, more powerful, simmering away somewhere beyond reach or reason, that made her resist even her own impulses. Denying herself was an inevitable side-effect of denying him.

Standing over her, he smiled down, a little ruefully it seemed to her. 'I've booked us a table for eight,' he said. 'I know it's early but I thought you'd be tired after the journey. I know I am.'

She nodded up at him. 'That's fine,' she said. 'Did you look at the menu?'

'It's posted outside the dining room. Pricey, but that's what you get with a Michelin star. There's a tasting menu with lots of seafood. Seven courses, I think. We should go for it, whack it on the credit card. We have come all this way, after all. No sense in being stingy.'

She sat up, enfolding herself in the soft robe. 'And the pools? Did you take a look?'

'They're even more beautiful than they look on the website. The main one – with the nude sculpture at the end – has incredible views over the valley. I may go for a swim right now, in fact. Fancy it?'

She shook her head. She was tempted by the thought of cool water on her skin again, even after her recent bath. But she wanted to be alone once more. Not, this time, to masturbate, but to think about what she was doing here. What *they* were doing here, and what they had expected this long weekend to produce. She needed to understand why it was that she had travelled so far with him only to want to be so utterly alone.

Not long after Nick had left, she went up to the second, smaller pool – the one without the racy modern sculpture or the views. Surrounded by umbrella pines and olive trees, it had a small wooden pavilion with fresh towels and a choice of fashion and news magazines and daily newspapers both French and English. She leafed idly through a copy of *Newsweek* and then, a little guiltily, through French *Vogue*, before helping herself to a couple of towels and turning around to decide which lounger to occupy. They were all currently free, as was the pool – the larger, glitzier one was probably more popular. But that suited her just fine. Solitude had become disturbingly desirable.

It wasn't to last: within a few minutes of her settling on her lounger with her book, a linen-suited waiter had appeared beside her, an empty tray dangling from one hand, and was asking if she wanted a drink brought out from the bar. She looked up at him, shielding her eyes; the glare of the sun behind him, despite the lateness of the hour, made it difficult to see his face. But she could tell he was smiling, and this smile unnerved her. She felt naked – as naked as she had been in her hotel room half an hour or so before, pleasuring herself. She had the impression that he knew what she had been doing back there, and that his smile was ironic, knowing. It was as if he had seen her in action, although she knew that was impossible – their first-floor room wasn't overlooked from any angle and she hadn't made *that* much noise.

'*Madame?*' he repeated, and she decided that his slightly supercilious air was more to do with his sense of himself and his own delectability than with anything she had done, or that he suspected her to have done. Her eyes were now adjusted to the light, and she saw in his chiselled face a model's angular beauty. The cheekbones jutted, the jawbone strong and wide. The eyes were a piercing blue. Chestnut hair flopped insouciantly down over his brow. He seemed to have stepped from the pages of the *Vogue* she had just been flicking through.

'*Un vodka tonique,*' she managed at last. It was early still, but perhaps a stiff drink would help her to relax. She was on holiday after all. For so long, she realised – ever since booking this trip – she had been thinking of it as a kind of test, an exam that needed to be passed if her marriage were to continue. Her entire future, and that of her family, seemed to hinge on this weekend and its outcome. How could she not feel pressure?

The waiter bowed slightly; she watched as he retreated, circling the pool on his way down to the bar to fulfil her order. A restlessness overcame her as she followed him with her eyes; like the porter, this man – this *boy* – was too young and clean and perfect for her. They just didn't do it for her. Yet something inside her was stirring her, reawakening unexpectedly. Something that, sadly, didn't seem to have anything to do with her husband, and hence made this trip something of a joke. A very bad joke.

She swam directly after the waiter had gone, not wanting to risk a plunge after having a drink; when he returned, she barely accorded him a glance, continuing to notch up the lengths as he placed the tray with her iced glass and nibbles on the table beside her lounger. Only after he had gone did she climb out, shaking her head to rid it of water, and sit down to enjoy her drink, imagining Nick by the other pool. What did he do when she wasn't there? The question had never presented itself to her before, and she suddenly asked herself whether she knew her husband at all. He certainly didn't look at other women when they were together, but what about when they were apart? Would he feast his eyes on beautiful silky brown flesh around him if he knew she wouldn't find out, or was he faithful to her even in his fantasies?

The sudden thought of him gazing at semi-naked women by the pool brought a throb to her pussy; she was shocked by how much the prospect aroused her, and by how something that by rights should have aroused her jealousy and ire shed a fresh light on her husband. A Nick staring at other women was, she realised, much more attractive to her than a Nick sitting primly by the water, reading the latest Jeffrey Archer, averting his eyes on principle – because he was married, because he loved his wife, because he *shouldn't*. A Nick with appetite – appetite for something other than her.

Dried by the sun, unable to flee the whirl and tumble of her thoughts by escaping in her book, she finished her drink, slung her silk sarong around her hips, slipped her feet into her flip-flops and made her way back to the room, wondering if Nick had beaten her to it. Her question was answered by the sound of music as she swiped her card and pushed open the door: a Santana CD that she recognised as one of her husband's old favourites was emanating from the Bang & Olufsen on top of the mahogany writing bureau. The music was accompanied by a low, laid-back whistling from the bathroom, the door to which stood wide open.

She approached, silently, heart in her throat. Nick was soaping himself in the same mellow way as he was whistling, his muscles no doubt softened by a vigorous swim, the last vestiges of city stress dissipated by the water and the sun on his naked limbs. He was on holiday now: that was clear from the slow sweep of the loofah over his thighs and buttocks, by the way his hand hesitated on his prick while his eyes remained closed, his face turned up towards the oversized head of the raindance shower.

She envied him for his ability to relax, to relocate his physicality so quickly. It had been what she had been seeking to do by masturbating, by swimming, but the relentless buzz of her brain had sent her indoors again, out of the sun, away from the pool. Why did she have to think so damn much? Why couldn't she just lose herself?

A rap on the door interrupted her reverie. She turned back in to the room and strode over to the door, checking her watch as she did so. It said five o'clock, but consulting it reminded her that she hadn't brought it a hour forwards since arriving in France, and she turned the little side dial to reset it as with the other hand she reached to open the door.

She looked up to see a man in the doorway, smiling at her, and her belly flipped over. This wasn't one of the movie-idol waiting staff, smiling deferentially while all the time thinking they were better than you. This was a real man – tousled, a little weather-worn, with a network of fine lines that bunched up around his eyes as the smile went on.

'*Bonsoir*?' she managed, after a pause.

'*Service du soir, Madame*,' he countered, and between her legs she turned to liquid.

She must have raised her eyebrows questioningly at the same time, for with one of his hands he gestured to a stack of clean towels balanced on the other. 'Fresh towels?' he went on, and his strong accent when he spoke in English had her legs and knees quivering.

She held his gaze, knowing that she must look quite insane. Without consciously thinking about it, she gauged his age at about forty, forty-five tops. Like the waiting staff, he was tanned, but unlike them there was an outdoor feel to him, something rugged and real. They reeked of the beauty salon, of *eau de Cologne* and expensive face creams. He seemed to come from the landscape around them: he was raw, as redolent of the rich red earth as he was of lemons, almonds, cedar, eucalyptus. Though she couldn't see them, she imagined the palms of his hands were slightly gnarled, roughened by contact with nature, honest.

All this came to her in seconds, as a tumble of fleeting half-thoughts, like water passing through a narrow canyon. Finally, as if awaking from a dream, she looked back confusedly towards the bathroom door. Did they need clean towels or not, she thought, more panicky than she would have been about the issue had she been thinking rationally. Nick would have used two at the most. One had to think about the environment these days.

She realised that the sound of the shower had died away, and was thinking to call out to Nick to ask about the need for towels when the sound of the man shuffling in the doorway made her turn her face back to him. His green eyes were fast on her; in them she saw a trace of friendly bemusement, as if he knew the thoughts that were going through her mind. As if he knew how much she wanted him.

'*Service du soir*?' came a voice from behind her, in an English accent this time, and she started at Nick's hand on her shoulder. 'Why, of course,' he went on. 'It would be rude not to.'

She felt her husband's teeth on one shoulder, risking a nibble, and swooned. He knew exactly how to get her going, knew that this was her erogenous zone. So why didn't he do that more often?

The man was still in the doorway, eyes flashing, full of a kind of well-intentioned mischief.

'Well?' said Nick. 'Ask him in. That's what you want, isn't it?'

She nodded dumbly, backing into the room, into Nick, who guided her with his hands, now looser on her shoulders.

'Where do you want to go?' he said, and she gestured towards the bed, feeling that she would pass out if she had to stand up any longer.

He freed her then, like a bird from a cage, and she half-fell onto the bed, forwards, excited and yet fearful. For a moment she remained frozen, hair hanging down on either side of her face, forming curtains shielding her from what was happening, for whatever was going to happen, affording her a reprieve. Then she inhaled deeply, and, turning over, lay on the bed, ready to confront her desires.

Nick was right. She did want this man. She wanted him more than she had wanted anyone in such a long time, even Nick. And Nick was making a gift to her of this stranger who had appeared on their doorstep: was that out of love or indifference? Was this his way of telling her he no longer cared, that he had had it?

The man himself seemed unquestioning, and the thought flitted through her mind that this might happen to him often – guests inviting him into their room, seduced by his ease, his unforced charm. Yet rather than feel revolted by such promiscuity on his part, this notion, too, aroused her. The idea of instinct, both on his part and that of other hotel guests, was enormously exciting.

Nick turned away momentarily, and she realised from the sounds coming from the other side of the room that he was pouring them some drinks. She looked back at the man, and something in his sea-green eyes made her reach to her side to loosen the knot on her sarong. Peeling the still-damp fabric away from her flesh like an insect casting off a skin, she slipped her hand into her bikini bottoms and let out a moan when she felt the dampness there. Holding the man's stare, she slid two fingers between her sodden lips and into her juicy core.

He reacted by pulling his white short-sleeved shirt up over his head, revealing a tanned chest and midriff covered with hair. She reached up for him with her free hand, and he climbed onto the bed, inching forwards until he knelt astride her. She let her free hand trail down him, from his neck to his lower belly: the hair was as soft and springy as it looked, something familiar and comforting. A place, she thought, of refuge. Already she could imagine cuddling up with this man when all the sex was done, finding peace in the feel and smell of him.

A movement at the edge of her vision made her turn her head. She had forgotten, for a moment, Nick, who was beside the bed again now, placing two glasses on one of the side tables. His own he kept in his hand, bringing it to his lips every few moments as he watched her carry on playing with her pussy.

The other man was now hunched over her, unhooking with deft fingers the clasp of her bikini top in the small of her back and then, when he had pulled the garment away from her and thrown it to one side of the bed, taking her breasts in his hands and bringing his face to each of them in turn. With his tongue he lapped and slurped at them, and his moans were like echoes of hers: deep, almost animal. Both seemed, for a time, to forget that Nick was there at all, as if the coupling of their flesh had spirited them away, taken them elsewhere.

But Nick refused to be forgotten. Nick was there, beside them but closer now, his bathrobe hanging open. She turned her head and within its shadowy realms she made out his prick, stirring, seeking a way out, seeking *them*. The man, sensing her turning her head though his mouth was still clamped on one of her nipples, looked up too. His eyes met Nick's; there was no animosity. They were not rivals for her – she was reassured of that now. She raised one arm up towards her husband, ready to share and be shared.

Taking her hand, Nick placed his glass on the table and then clambered onto the bed, advancing towards the pair on his knees. When he was beside them, she reached into the folds of his gown and took his firm prick in her hand. Then, raising herself on her elbows, she brought her mouth towards him as he in turn lowered his hips towards her, and as they met she folded her lips around his cock and jabbed at the end of it with her tongue as he moved slowly in and out of her.

Backing down away from her, the other man was now at her groin, his face buried in her sex, teasing at the fronds of hair there to get at the sleek wet lips below, and at the pert pink bud of her clitoris nestling at the top. Her breath came hot and heavy on Nick's cock as the man pleasured her, her orgasm mounting steadily and inexorably in her like a rising tide. She wanted the man inside her, wanted to feel the contractions on his cock, this cock that she hadn't even seen yet. He was still wearing the navy shorts in which he had appeared at the door offering fresh towels.

Nick's hips began to buck a little, to tremble, and she knew that he too couldn't be far from climaxing. Anxious that they shouldn't both come and put an end to the delicious, and deliciously unexpected, proceedings, she pulled her head slowly away, replacing her mouth with her fist but not moving the latter at all, just maintaining a firm grip that would keep him erect.

The other man, perceiving a change in pace, looked up, hair mussed around his questioning face. Raising one knee, she conveyed to him without the need for words that she wanted him to roll over now, so that he was the one on his back. With the hand that wasn't on Nick's cock, she pulled at the man's shorts; when they reached his mid-thighs, he took over and pulled them the rest of the way down his legs and then over his ankles and off.

She sat up, looking at Nick for guidance, or perhaps just approval. He nodded, and she knew then that he was happy with whatever she wanted to do next. She knelt, turned around and brought one leg over the man, who took hold of her hips and guided her gently down to him. She gasped as she slid onto the smooth baton of his prick, letting her upper body fold down onto his. As they brushed the fuzz of his chest, her nipples tautened.

The man's hands remained on her hips, and as their sexes melted into each other, he began to move her in slow circles on him. She looked down at him, but his eyes were closed. She hadn't kissed him, it occurred to her, and she brought her lips to his and did so. He returned the kiss, less chastely, his tongue prising open her lips and seeking hers, but he didn't open his eyes. For the first time she felt herself wondering who waited for him at home, and she was surprised to feel a tang of sadness. This would only ever happen once. Was that why it felt so beautiful and poignant all at once?

On her raised rump she now felt a second pair of hands, and as if acting with some kind of foreknowledge she moved her knees so that she knelt a little bit wider apart. Nick's hands grew tighter on her flesh, his fingertips sinking in, and she gritted her teeth. She felt his lips and then his teeth on the ripe flesh of her buttocks, heard his moans. His tongue crept between her splayed cheeks and flitted at the rosebud of her sphincter. She moaned too. This was too good to go on. Something was about to give, to erupt.

Then she felt the bulb of Nick's cock snuffling at her entrance, and she cried out. Was this physically possible, what he was going to try to do? Would it harm her? It was so long since he had taken her that way, and that was when there was nobody else inside her. She was afraid, and yet she felt more thrillingly alive than ever before.

Nick pushed inside her; primed by the movement of the cock inside her pussy, she came immediately, scarcely knowing, in her delirium, where she was. Somehow the two men staved off their own climaxes, and as she regained feeling she could feel how their cocks thumped against each other as they drove into her, establishing a tempo of their own. A few minutes after orgasming and then recovering from her numbness, she was coming again, and then again, in thrall to the friction from their combined thrusting.

Approaching exhaustion, she was astonished that either man managed to hold off for as long as they did. But finally, as if of some common accord, each of them grasped her hips, bringing their movement to a halt, and, their hands overlapping, gave themselves over to what seemed to be one single almighty climax that ravaged through both of their bodies like an earthquake of which she formed the epicentre, the origin. Then each pulled out of her and relinquished hold, the man beneath her falling away, shuddering, eyes closed, as her husband fell back, panting and swearing, onto the bed.

She lay with her hand on her pussy, not thinking about anything, and after a few minutes she heard the man get up and rummage around on the floor for his clothes. Nick rose too, helped him find his clothes, and then walked him to the door of their room. She raised herself on one elbow, knowing it was unlikely that she would see the man again, since they were only staying here for two nights, and tomorrow they had planned to dine out in a neighbouring village. She wanted to thank him, but then she realised that there was no need.

'You don't need to go, mate,' Nick was saying, one hand clamped to the man's back. Nick was still naked, his skin in the falling light of the unlit room covered with a sheen of sweat. 'Stay for a drink, won't you?'

But the man was waving his hand airily. 'It's not possible. I'm running late. You know – *service du soir.*' And as if remembering, he turned to take up the pile of towels that he had left by the door when they invited him into their room, into their life.

'Thank you,' she mouthed after him, knowing, even as she did, that he would never know how grateful she was.

She dozed off, and when she awoke the cicadas were in full song beyond the window, out in the Provençal night. Nick was bending over her, his lips brushing her earlobe.

'. . . table in five minutes . . .' he was saying. '. . . didn't want to disturb you . . . going to be late . . .'

She groaned, rubbed her eyes. 'Do we have to?' she said, surprised at herself – she was a sucker for gourmet restaurants, always had been.

He smiled down at her, and she revelled, for the first time in years, in his eyes on her, in her nakedness. She felt sexy, open, free of some kind of burden. She knew she would never be young again, and she didn't care. She thought of her eighteen-year-old body, and for the first time she didn't regret it. She was proud of the marks that experience had left on her, that time had inscribed on her still-glorious flesh.

She lay motionless, gazing up at him, attentive to the white noise of the male cicadas. The clicking noise they made – which, she had read in her guidebook, was not created by their wings rubbing together as with crickets, but by the contraction and relaxation of internal muscles – was their mating song.

She half-sat, reaching out for her husband.

'But what about dinner?' he said.

She smiled. 'Cancel the table,' she told him. 'Let's have room service.'

Carrie Williams is the author of the Black Lace novels *The Blue Guide* and *Chilli Heat*. Her third novel, *The Apprentice*, is published in April 2009.

The Rancher's Wife
Kristina Wright

He was waiting for her. She knew he would be, but his presence in the doorway still caught her off guard. He was six-three, two hundred and twenty pounds – his presence would have caught anyone off guard. She got out of her car, a BMW sports car that looked the worse for wear because it wasn't suited for the rough-and-tumble back roads of Montana, and took her time smoothing her skirt. Picking an invisible piece of dust from the black of the fabric, she flicked it away on the warm, dry wind that whipped her blonde hair around her shoulders. She tucked a wayward strand behind her ear and carefully locked the car door, though there wasn't another human being for twenty miles. There was nothing out here but horses and cows ... and Edwin Dobbs, her husband. To him, it would look like she didn't give a damn about being here, but she was really just trying to buy some time. As if a few seconds more would make any difference.

She'd had plenty of time to prepare for this moment. It had been thirteen months, after all. Thirteen months and six days, to be exact, since she walked out the door and left all of this behind. It had been longer than that, maybe twice as long, since she had told him she couldn't be a rancher's wife any more. It had taken her awhile to figure out how she was going to do it, make the break and leave him. She sometimes thought she had waited longer than she should for him to decide he'd rather have her than his damn ranch. She'd gotten tired of waiting.

She walked up the sagging porch steps to stand in front of him. 'Hey, Win. You're looking good.'

He *was* looking good. Win hadn't changed much in a year. His perpetual golden tan emphasised the pale blue of his eyes and the straight, white line of his teeth when he smiled, which he wasn't likely to do. His shoulders were as broad as she remembered, tapering down to a narrow waist. She knew that beneath the cotton chambray shirt and worn denim jeans was a flat, rock-hard stomach and well-toned muscles any bodybuilder would envy. Win's formidable body came from hard work and real sweat, not time spent in a gym. Win's body was a powerful, efficient rancher's body, but it was also a lover's body, capable of picking her up and carrying her from the barn to their bedroom upstairs without breaking a sweat. She shivered at the memory of his callused hands on her body, rough but ever so gentle, even as she reminded herself it wasn't 'their' bedroom any longer.

Win gave her a slow, lingering appraisal. 'City life has been good to you, Lee,' he said. 'You've got a little more meat on your bones than you used to.'

Only Win could compliment a woman with an insult. She could explain to him why he shouldn't have said it, as she had a hundred times with other comments, but Leslie just shook her head. It wasn't her job to fix Win Dobbs any more.

'So, are you going to invite me in or are we going to dance?'

He took a step back and gestured into the house. 'You don't need an invitation into your own home.'

She looked around. Not one thing had changed. The furniture, simple, practical and all in shades of beige and brown, was just as she remembered it. She had tried brightening the place up with colourful pillows and curtains, but it didn't help against the unrelenting brown. Win had always preferred a rather Spartan lifestyle, so there weren't any knick-knacks or magazines or pictures to break the neat, monklike interior. All of those had gone with her, except for one thing: their wedding picture. It wasn't a professional photograph, just an enlarged snapshot Win's brother had taken outside the modest chapel where they had exchanged vows.

The brown-framed picture sat on the brown mantel, just as it had for four years. A memento she didn't want of a day that was ingrained in her memory, for better or worse. Leslie had taken everything else when she'd moved out, but she had left their wedding picture because she hadn't wanted to be reminded of her failure. *Her* failure, as if Win's role in their doomed marriage didn't count because he wasn't the one who left. Now the photo caught her eye and she couldn't look away. They looked happy. Had they been happy? She really couldn't remember any more, though she could remember every other detail of that long-ago day.

'Why are you here, Lee?'

Leave it to Win to cut to the chase. He wasn't much one for small talk, but she had hoped for at least a little civil conversation first. Not that it would change the end result.

'Can I get something to drink?'

He looked at her, long and slow, his eyes seeing beyond her clothes and into the heart of her. He knew she was stalling, she could see it in the slight turn of his lips and the narrowing of his eyes. She looked away rather than meet that all-knowing gaze and confirm his suspicions.

'Sure. What do you want?'

What did she want? That was the question. Instead of giving him a list of things he could never fulfil even if he was willing to try, she said simply, 'I'll have a beer. If you have any.'

She knew there would be cheap beer in the fridge just as she knew the bed would be made with two or three of his grandmother's worn quilts now that the weather was starting to turn cooler at night; just as she knew he'd only let her nurse her beer for so long before he got impatient and reminded her there were afternoon chores to be done; just as she knew there was little she could say that would make everything between them all right again. All right. She could never settle for 'all right'. It had to be everything or nothing.

Win went to the kitchen and came back with two beers. He handed her one and sat on the couch, propping his booted feet on the coffee table. 'So, what's this little visit about, Lee? I don't imagine, judging by your Chanel suit and expensive heels, that you've come back to stay. So why are you here?'

She perched on the edge of the chair, afraid to get too comfortable. Afraid to make herself at home, even if it was her home, as he had said.

'Donna Karan.'

He blinked. 'What?'

'The suit is Donna Karan. The heels are Prada. The purse is Kate Spade. The wallet is Gucci and I earned every dollar in it, Win.' She hadn't meant it to sound like an accusation, but it did.

'Are you happy?'

It was her turn to stare at him. 'How do you mean?'

His sharp bark of laughter startled her. 'Happy, Lee. I know that translates as easily for a city girl like yourself as it does a cowboy like me. Happy. Do all these things,' he said, with a dismissive gesture towards her, 'make you happy?'

'The work makes me happy,' she said. 'I was wasting my law degree here. I'm being fast-tracked to make partner and the hours are long and the work is challenging. I'm excited to go to work every day.'

'I'm glad you found something that excites you.'

She cringed at his bitter tone. 'You knew what you were getting into when you married me. I told you I'd try – and I tried, Win – and you said you'd be willing to move if I wasn't happy. I wasn't happy, but you weren't willing.'

'Willing to do what? Move to some hard-edged city where everything is plastic, including the people?' He made a face like he'd just tasted something foul. 'That's not who I am. Hell, it's not even who you are.'

'You don't know who I am. You never did.'

He sat up, slamming his boots on the hardwood floor. 'All right, now that you've summed up our disaster of a marriage, what do you want?'

She stared at him, as if seeing him for the first time. A rancher, a man, her husband. Her husband with a wounded male ego. Men were the same, whether they lived on a ranch or in a condo, but Win's ego was as big as the state of Montana and she had driven a stake through his heart and his ego when she'd walked out.

She tried to smile and shook her head. 'I missed you.'

That caught him off guard. His chin jerked up as if she'd punched him. He stared at her, looking for the trick. His eyes were flinty bits of stone in his hard-set face. He was so unyielding. It had been what first attracted her to him. Win was a man who wouldn't be moved or cowed by anything or anyone. He was strength incarnate, masculinity in denim and chambray. And, for a brief time, he had been hers. When she indulged her sexual fantasies in those few minutes before sleep claimed her after a fourteen-hour work day, Win was hers again. His body as hard as his resolve – for her. She couldn't tell him any of that for the simple reason that her ego wasn't much smaller than his.

She shook her head again. 'I don't know why, but I missed you.'

'You missed the dust and the horse shit and the bugs as big as the palm of your hand and the three television channels and the wind whipping through here in the winter like the walls are made of paper?'

'No, Win, I missed *you*. Missed you a lot. I thought about calling you a hundred times. Did call you once, on your birthday.' She didn't want to cry. If she cried, he might think she'd changed her mind about divorcing him. 'I thought you might be around.'

'The work still has to get done, no matter what day it is.'

It was the answer she expected. 'Yeah, I know. It's a tough life and I hated it. But I missed you.'

He stood up, crossed the room to stand in front of her. His scent was pure cowboy: sweat and leather, musk and Montana. She resisted the urge to touch him. It would be so easy to reach out and rest a hand on his stomach; tuck her fingers into his waistband and anchor him to her. Instead, she knotted her hands in her lap.

'You came back because you missed me?'

She wanted to deny it, add a disclaimer to it, but the words needed no embellishment because they were true. 'Yes.'

As if afraid she would pull away, he reached out slowly and touched her hair. The weight of his fingers was nearly imperceptible and, like a cat, she stretched to meet his gentle touch. How many nights had she touched herself, quickly, efficiently, yearning for Win's hands on her body? Too many nights with only his memory to seduce her into forgetting everything that had made her leave in the first place.

'Yes,' she whispered again.

His touch was firmer now, both hands running through her salon-styled hair, tumbling the strands through his fingers the way she remembered letting hay tumble through her hands. He massaged her scalp, rubbing her temples until she moaned at the pleasure of even that simple, non-sexual touch. She had closed her eyes as soon as he touched her, but now she opened them, staring at his denim-covered crotch. He was hard, his erection straining at the front of his jeans. Hard from just stroking her hair. It was an incredible feeling – power and longing all in one. She dug her nails into the palms of her hands to resist the temptation he presented. Just as she knew how firm and taut his body would be from another hard year's work on the ranch, she knew the way his erection would feel if she reached out and ran her hand over the bulge. She closed her eyes again, afraid to give in to temptation. Afraid that if she didn't give in to temptation, she'd regret it forever.

'Touch me, Lee,' he said hoarsely.

She looked up into his hazel eyes and saw pain, regret and anger. She also saw need. Pure, raw lust mixed with all the negative emotions she had rained down on him. Her voice caught in her throat as she reached up and ran a trembling hand over his crotch. He was hard, so damned hard. As if they had spent hours tangled up in foreplay instead of just moments with his hands on her hair. He still wanted her. The thought sent a thrill of desire coursing through her veins and though her practical mind cautioned against letting this go too far, her body throbbed with the unrequited need of too many nights of unfulfilled fantasies of Win's body, Win's cock.

With manicured fingertips, she traced the length of his erection with a familiarity she hadn't expected. She had thought she'd forgotten him, the feel of him, but she hadn't. Though she still masturbated to memories of things she'd done with Win, those memories had faded to fuzzy images about people she didn't really know, unlike the bad feelings that seemed so much sharper and ran so much deeper. Now, sitting on the chair in the living room of the house she had once shared with him, the memories came rushing back through her to pool in liquid heat between her thighs. Her body remembered everything, every ridge and vein and inch of Win. She felt flushed, sitting here like this with her hand on her husband's crotch. Her husband. He was still her husband, not her ex-husband just yet.

Win groaned and the sound was primal and startling. Leslie jerked her hand away as if she had been burned. He wrapped his long, callused fingers around her wrist and pulled her hand back to his crotch, pressing it firmly against his erection, staring into her eyes. Here was the power she missed and longed for, the raw, physical power that had nothing to do with money or prestige. Here was Win, in all his masculine glory, and heaven help her, she wanted him more than she had ever wanted anything in her life.

'You want this,' he said, and it wasn't a question.

He had always been able to read her and had used it to his advantage. Teasing her, taunting her until she was out of her mind with lust and desire, a woman in need and only one man to satisfy her need. He knew her, knew her better than anyone, and she hated it – and him – in that moment. Hated him almost enough to get up and walk out and not look back. Almost.

Almost.

She nodded, that small acknowledgment costing her more than he could possibly know. Or maybe he knew that, too, because he pulled her up then, into his strong arms. She settled against his chest as if she had never left. She tucked her head against his shoulder, revelling in the softness of his well-worn shirt and the hardness of his chest as she rubbed her head against him, as if marking him. It felt good and right to be enveloped by him, to have his erection bumping her belly like a calf seeking sustenance. She made a contented sound, halfway between a sigh and a cry as he tilted her head up and kissed her hard.

She whimpered into his mouth as he kissed her, hating herself for being so weak. She tried to remember why she was here, telling herself that she was in control, but none of it mattered as Win teased her with his tongue and promises of so much more. She bit his lower lip, pressing against him and feeling the full, unyielding breadth of him. She never felt more feminine than when Win was kissing her. Everything she believed she had forgotten – or had wanted to forget – came rushing back as he kissed her senseless.

He anchored her to him by her hips, his erection nudging insistently against her as they rocked against each other in unconscious need. She reached between them, palming the rigid length of his cloth-covered cock. She wanted him. Wanted him so bad she could feel the wetness between her thighs soaking the wispy black silk of her lace-trimmed Agent Provocateur panties. Win wouldn't appreciate the panties, wouldn't know designer panties from a three-for-five special at the discount store, but he would appreciate her wetness. He would enjoy what he had done to her, what he had made her feel.

'Take me to bed, Win,' she breathed into his mouth. 'Now.'

She hated herself for sounding so needy, so damned feminine. She wanted to be the seducer, the one who made the calls, but she knew that once she admitted her need Win would be in control. Smug with his power over her even as he gave her everything her aching body desired. She would save the self-loathing for when she was back in LA. She didn't have time for self-recrimination anyway, because Win was picking her up. That swift, familiar motion took her breath away, made her feel helpless and powerful all in one instant. Her expensive pumps clattered to the floor as he swung her around towards the staircase. He took the stairs two at a time, the second and eighth steps creaking just the way she remembered.

She clung to him, running her hands over his shoulders and stroking his hair, as if she couldn't get enough of his body now that she'd been given a taste. He carried her through the bedroom door and tumbled her down on the big feather bed like a pile of clean laundry. She lay there, breathless, staring up at the exposed beams of the ceiling until he climbed on the bed and his face obscured the view. Then he was kissing her again, deep and hard, as if that short walk up the stairs had been interminable. She wiggled under him, anxious to feel the press of his cock between her legs. It was an ache that would not be denied and she whimpered in frustration because the angle was wrong.

He reared back and hiked her skirt up with one hand before lodging his knee between her thighs. It wasn't as good as having him inside her, but she rubbed against him anyway. She craved him, needing to be filled and fucked the way only Win could fuck her. She moaned and arched against him, digging her nails into his broad back. She didn't care that her clothes were getting wrinkled or that she might break a nail – she would break all ten if it meant having Win inside her. *Control*, her brain reminded her, but her cunt had other ideas.

'Little bitch in heat, aren't you?'

She moaned again, her head whipping from side to side, though not in denial. She *was* a bitch in heat, so hot she could feel a trickle of sweat between her shoulder blades. She wanted to be naked underneath him.

'Yes,' she moaned, as he rubbed his hard thigh between her legs. 'So fucking hot.'

He fumbled awkwardly with the tiny pearl buttons on her blouse. She bit her lip in frustration as he smacked her hand away when she moved to help him. Finally, he got them undone and spread her blouse open, revealing the black lace-trimmed push-up bra that matched her panties. He didn't admire the bra or the way it accentuated her tits, just growled as if it were in his way and then yanked the cups up over her breasts without bothering with the clasp. It was an obscene move, one better suited to new lovers in the back seat of a car than a couple in their marriage bed, but it suited her just fine. She knew every inch of Win's body, but something about this felt new, different. Raw.

Win palmed her breasts, pushing them together and making a valley between them. 'My cock would look good there,' he rasped, as he pinched her nipples between his fingers.

He twisted the hard nubs of her dusky pink nipples until she whimpered low in her throat. There was a moment of pain before he released her tender flesh, but it was an exquisite feeling that bordered on orgasmic. She put her hands over his and moaned, 'More.' He obliged her by pinching her nipples again, twisting and pulling them away from her breasts until she was writhing with the pain and pleasure of the sensation. She gasped in disappointment as he released her and sat back on his knees. He didn't touch her; he only looked at her.

She imagined herself as he saw her: blouse open, bra twisted up over her breasts, the nipples dark and hard, her hair a tangled mess from his hands and rolling around on the bed, her expensive skirt bunched up at her hips, thighs spread, a wet spot spreading on the crotch of her panties. She closed her eyes, the image too raw. She felt vulnerable in her half-nakedness, vulnerable and needy. But the darkness behind her eyelids was worse – what if he found her lacking in some way? Decided he didn't want her? The thought was so painful, she opened her eyes and studied his face as he stared at her, looking for some sign that he still wanted her. He looked at her for what seemed like a long time, until his gaze finally lingered between her thighs. She spread her legs wider, offering herself to him like a prize, her need a bone-deep ache of unfulfilled passion.

'Fuck me, Win,' she said, finally. 'Please.'

She hadn't talked much in bed when they'd been together, hadn't been one to demand or suggest anything. She would let him do what he wanted, and was usually more than satisfied at the results, but back then she had known what he wanted and was content to wait. She couldn't afford to play coy now. She needed him, needed him now.

'Fuck me,' she said again. 'Fuck me hard. As hard as you want.'

His blue eyes narrowed, the set of his jaw hard. A vein throbbed in his temple – whether from anger or desire, she couldn't be sure. She ran her hands up the insides of her thighs, framing her crotch with her French-manicured fingertips. Enticing him. The way his breath caught in his throat, she thought it had worked. But he didn't move.

'Why, Lee? Why should I? Don't you have a dozen hotshot lawyers dying to get into your panties?' he said, his expression dark. 'Don't you take a different guy home every Friday night?'

He was jealous. The thought thrilled her. He still wanted her and he was jealous that anyone else had been where he wanted to be. Instead of tamping his desire, Leslie knew his possessiveness only fuelled it to animalistic heights. Like an old prospector, he needed to claim his territory – or reclaim it. He needed to conquer her. And, heaven help her, she wanted to be conquered. Feminism be damned, she wanted to be fucked.

'I don't want them. I want you,' she said, not denying his accusation. 'The only one I want right now is you.'

Right now. As if there had been so many others since she had left the first time and would be so many more once he had satiated her desire. She wouldn't tell Win she had only taken two men to her bed in the year they had been apart and that neither of them had made her come. She wouldn't tell Win that once her would-be lovers had left she had masturbated to memories of his hard body driving into her and driving her out of her mind. She would let him believe what he already believed because she knew it would make him fuck her senseless.

'I need you, Win.'

He moved away and for one heart-wrenching moment she thought he was rejecting her. But he only sat on the edge of the bed and tugged off his boots, the action as familiar as the room. Then he stood, watching her as he pulled his shirt over his head without bothering to unbutton it and ripped open the button fly of his jeans with a *pop-pop-pop*. He dragged his jeans and underwear down his hips and his erection sprang free, thick and hard and so heavy it lay against his thigh. She stared at his cock as he finished stripping, mesmerised by old memories that seemed closer somehow now that he was standing naked before her. When he climbed back on the bed and knelt between her legs, she moaned with the memory of his touch even before he palmed her crotch.

'You're so fucking wet. Wet straight through your panties.'

She raised her hips from the bed, pressing against his rough hand. 'I'm wet for you.'

He hooked his fingers into the front of her panties and tore them off with one swift, startling motion. The fabric resisted for an instant, digging into her flesh before giving way beneath his brute strength. She would gladly have taken them off had he asked – or even demanded – but the sound of ripping silk set her heart racing, touching off some primal need within her. She wanted him to be rough with her and now was bare to his gaze, to his touch. She moaned and the sound seemed to echo in the quiet room.

Win braced one hand on each of her legs and spread her open, pinning her knees to the bed. He stared between her thighs as if he'd never seen her before. She supposed he never *had* seen her quite like this, with a Brazilian bikini wax and her cunt smooth and shiny with her juices. He slowly ran one callused fingertip between her labia and she jumped at his touch, her hips bucking in a way that would have embarrassed her if she hadn't been so damned needy for him to fuck her. He held his finger up to show her the moisture he had collected.

'Damn,' Win said, shaking his head with something like awe. 'You're a wet little slut.'

The word – *slut* – should have offended her, would have offended her if he'd said it at any other time. Win didn't talk to her like that in bed. When he talked at all, it was *baby, darling, sweetheart*. The fact that he had called her a slut meant he was angry, angry and horny and out of his mind with wanting her. Just the way she wanted him. She smiled, feeling as if she had regained some control even while he pinned her to his bed like a butterfly under glass.

'I am a slut, Win,' she said, replacing his finger with her own and stroking her slick flesh as she stared into his eyes. 'Don't you want to fuck this wet little slut?'

He all but growled at her, a deep, snarling sound that came from deep inside him as he stared between her legs and watched as she played with herself. 'Slut,' he said again, wrapping his hand around his engorged cock as if he couldn't stand to watch her and not touch himself.

'Put it in me, Win,' she whispered. 'Fuck me.'

She expected him to push inside her with one forceful thrust, but he surprised her. Leaning over her, he stroked the broad head of his cock over the back of her hand, still touching her pussy. She felt the trail of pre-come he left behind, slick and warm. She raised her hand to her mouth and licked the sweet moisture away as he rubbed the head of his cock over her swollen clit. Again and again, he dragged the tip of his cock down between the lips of her pussy but would not enter her. He only rubbed against her, covering the head of his cock with her wetness as he stared between her thighs.

Watching his face, she was aroused by the look of sheer concentration – concentration she had seen before when he was breaking in a new pony. Sweat glistened on his tanned forehead as if it were taking everything he had to be patient, to wait, to take his time with her. When her need became so strong she could barely stand it, she stopped watching him and let her eyes flutter closed for a moment, giving herself up to the sensation of his slow, steady strokes. She could almost come like this; just this, his thick cock rubbing her swollen clit and wet, wet pussy. That wasn't what she wanted, though. It wouldn't be enough. It was just a nibble and she wanted the entire feast.

'Fuck me,' she whispered, watching him stare at the point where their bodies touched. 'Please, Win. Please, please fuck me now.'

He dragged his gaze from between her legs to stare into her eyes. 'I should send you packing.' His expression was cold and hard. This was the Win she knew all too well. 'You just came back here to get laid and I should throw you out on your ass.'

'Please, Win?'

He hesitated, as if he had more to say. His jaw was tight and she watched the vein in his pulse throb. One, two, three beats. Then he was in her with that long-delayed and anticipated thrust, driving himself into her wetness so hard she slid up the bed and bumped the headboard. He hooked an arm around her waist and pulled her back down, away from the headboard and onto his cock, until it bottomed out against her cervix. She was so wet, there wasn't much friction and she growled in frustration and wrapped her legs around his back. There it was, the sweet spot. She clutched at him as he drove into her again and again, thick and hard and finally filling her up the way she had dreamed about for so many months.

It felt as if Win were fucking her with a year's worth of pent-up frustration and anger, and she met him thrust for thrust, digging her nails into his back and not caring if they broke or she made him bleed. She clung to him as he thrust into her, gasping and moaning but not telling him to stop because she never wanted him to stop fucking her. He moved inside her in a way that let her know he was after his own pleasure and couldn't give a damn about hers. It didn't matter, though. His pleasure *was* her pleasure. It thrilled her that he was taking what he *needed* from her body. It wasn't romantic or gentle, but in some strange way it was loving.

'So fucking wet,' he groaned, his narrow hips leaving bruises on her thighs as he thrust into her. 'Damn, baby.'

Baby. There it was. The endearment she hadn't wanted. She was his baby. Still his baby. Hot tears pricked her closed eyelids as she sunk her teeth into his shoulder. She didn't want tenderness, she wanted all the raw passion Win had kept pent up for so long. For her. For a moment she let herself imagine that maybe he had been with other women; maybe he had carried another woman to this bed. She took her own jealousies and let them shut down the tender emotions. This wasn't a seduction, she reminded herself as she gripped Win's ass and pulled him deeper into her, as if that were possible. This was fucking. She needed a good, hard fucking from Win. That was all.

She tightened her cunt around him and thrilled to his moan as his balls brushed her ass. 'Fuck me harder,' she demanded.

'Harder?'

'Hard as you want. I'm your slut.'

'My slut,' he growled, jack-hammering into her, his hands curving under her body to squeeze her ass.

His slut, not his baby. This was what she wanted. His cock in her pussy. That's all. A good, hard fucking. She let her body take over, shutting out everything else but the sensations of Win inside her.

Her orgasm took her by surprise. She barely had time to acknowledge the first ripple with a gasp before it was rolling over her in a series of intense contractions that hit her like a tornado and sucked her up. Suddenly, it wasn't Win fucking her, it was her thrusting up against him and pulling him into her, fucking him. She screamed his name as she came, holding onto him like he was a lifeline – in a way, he was. Every nerve ending felt exposed, her body radiating heat that started where

Win's cock went into her and spiralled outwards. She held Win close, letting him feel every undulating stroke of her cunt as she climaxed.

'Come, baby. That's it, come hard.'

'Yes, yes, yes,' she gasped.

Win kept fucking her hard, driving into her as if determined to break her. He lifted her up to meet his cock, rocking into her in the rhythm she had set, coaxing every last ounce of sensation from her cunt. Then he groaned, a deep soul-wrenching sound as his cock pulsed inside her, and she knew he was coming even as her pussy still pulsed with her own post-orgasmic ripples. She tightened her fingers in his hair and pulled his head down, kissing him and swallowing his moans as he came inside her, her mouth and her pussy taking everything he had to offer.

His cock slowly went soft inside her, but it was several minutes before either of them moved, before they caught their breath and their heart rates returned to normal. The feather bed sagged under the weight of Win's body on top of hers and she finally shifted, feeling uncomfortably claustrophobic. Win pulled away, his cock slipping free from her body, and rolled onto his back beside her. They lay like that for a long time, side by side and staring at the ceiling, as if reluctant to shake free from the memory of their passion.

'Is that why you came here?' Win asked finally, not looking at her. 'One more time, for old times' sake?'

She turned his head to study his unyielding profile. His eyes were closed, the long lashes delicate and out of place on his rugged face.

'No,' she said softly, though she didn't want to admit the other reason for her visit. 'I brought the divorce papers for you to sign. The rest ... that just happened.'

He nodded, as if he'd decided something.

'I – I wish ...'

'I know what you wish,' he said, his voice as hard as his body. 'I'll sign the damn papers, Lee. You didn't have to go to bed with me to get me to sign them.'

Leslie watched him get out of bed and dress, his movements smooth and fluid, as if the routine of dressing soothed him. He glanced at her, the barest hint of a smile on his lips.

'Leave the papers on the kitchen table and I'll put 'em in the mail tomorrow.'

'That wasn't what I was going to say,' she whispered as he bent to brush her forehead with a goodbye kiss.

'No?' He studied her, his expression shrewd now that his desire had been satiated. 'What were you going to say?'

She took a breath. 'That I wish I had torn up those papers.'

'You aren't thinking straight,' he said, though there was a hint of hope in his eyes before he blinked it away. 'You'll come to your senses once the high wears off.'

She laughed. She didn't blame him for not believing her. 'That's an accurate description – I feel high. And I want more.'

He evaded her grabbing hands and lightly smacked her bare thigh as if she were a disobedient mare. 'I've got chores that need to get done. I imagine you won't be here when I get back, so I'll say goodbye now.'

'Win –'

'Goodbye, Lee.' His voice was hard, all business. 'Don't forget to leave the papers. Hate to see you waste a trip and ruin your clothes for nothing.'

He was at the door now, a man with a bruised ego and a broken heart. Her fault. 'Thanks for stopping by, though. That was –'

'It was incredible,' she finished for him. 'And I still want you.'

He swallowed hard. 'Take care of yourself, baby.'

Just like that, he was gone. She listened to his heavy footfalls on the stairs, heard the creak of the second step and the slam of the front door. She pulled the soft cotton sheet up over her naked body and closed her eyes. She didn't blame him for not believing her. She had come to seduce him and had fallen back in love with him. Or maybe she'd never fallen out of love at all and had only used the divorce papers as an excuse to convince herself to see him again. She shook her head, sleep claiming her before she could make sense of it all. She only knew one thing: she still wanted Win and she would be here when he came home.

He would see she was back for good, even though she hadn't known it was what she wanted until she'd touched him again. She would be here when he came home and then he would see.

She would be here.

Christmas Present
A.D.R. Forte

I blame Gail's Christmas party, even though I didn't want to go. I never really *want* to go and listen to Gail sniff and pointedly Not-Criticise, but on the other hand, she's still my sister and Christmas is the one chance to see the whole family – Maddy and Thomas and Ed, our kids and their kids and all the cousins; three generations all gloriously crammed under one roof to make merry. That kinda stuff is important to me. So my daughter Jennie and I loaded up the presents we'd stayed awake until 3 a.m. wrapping, the dishes of pie and stuffing, and a few choice bottles of wine I'd been saving for the holidays. And we headed over to Gail's.

'So ... Mom. You never answered my question last night,' Jennie said as we turned onto the highway.

'Which? You haven't stopped talking since you got here,' I retorted. She hadn't, but then neither had I. We'd spent years counting the days until she left for college. Now we counted the days until she came home on break. Me more than her, I suspected.

'My question about if you'd found a boyfriend.'

'I answered you. I rolled my eyes, didn't I?'

'Mother ...'

I shrugged and overtook a guy cruising along in a Mustang. 'Dumbass! If you buy it, drive it for chrissake!'

'Mother, stop avoiding.'

She was relentless. My child without a doubt.

'I told you, Jen, I've been dating. It comes, it goes.'

'Dating who? The fuddy-duddy with erectile dysfunction?'

I gave her a disapproving glance. 'Dave. He's a nice guy! He buys me dinner. But no, not just him.' Rain began spotting the windshield and I turned on the wipers. 'I had a blind date which wasn't bad. And I got hooked up with an artist and we went out a couple of times.'

'And they all sucked.'

'No they didn't ... much.'

Jennie made an exasperated noise and tapped her fingers on the armrest, looking at me from the corner of her eyes.

'You just don't seem real happy, Mom. When I talk to you all you do these days is work. That's not you.'

'I throw candle parties.'

I glanced around and saw her roll her eyes. 'Yeah. You're turning into Aunt Gail.'

'Good God, no!'

'Yes!'

'No!'

The conversation degenerated from there, until we'd forgotten the whole point of the disagreement and turned to other stuff. But at the back of my mind some small voice I'd ignored for a while now piped up, encouraged by Jennie's accusation. I *was* bored and, yes, a little bit lonely. I *was* getting more jollies from making salad trays than getting my salad tossed, but that was life, right? I'd had more than my fair share and two amazing husbands into the bargain, and now ... well, it wasn't just about a quick fuck any more.

I hadn't told Jennie – and I wouldn't – that the blind date had been maybe two, three years older than her. Very smart, very firm in all the right places, looked mouth-watering in tight jeans, but he'd been on a whole different wavelength. I'd found myself with my legs around his waist and his cock pumping furiously between my thighs, trying to decide if I wanted tuna salad or chicken for lunch the next day.

It wasn't that I felt any less horny, I just needed more than a dick and pretty face. But what that 'more' was I couldn't have said to save my life.

Stifling a sigh, I pulled into the driveway of my sister's house. The door flew open almost immediately with grand-nephews and nieces tumbling out and running over to be hugged and kissed and wished a Merry Christmas. For a while I forgot my own angst in the hubbub, even with Gail looking over my loose hair and jeans and sweater with a little cough. So what? I was more comfortable than she was in her cashmere pantsuit and pearls.

I gave her a perfunctory kiss on the cheek and went to the kitchen where Maddy was already hysterical over an argument with her eldest and slicing tomatoes at a dangerous pace. Everyone had an opinion and the noise level was deafening, but I loved it. It took me out of myself and kept me busy, although it was nearly six by the time I finally put the last pie in to warm and escaped with a glass of Merlot for the blessed peace of the living room. There I found Bill hiding out too, presumably keeping guard over the appetisers and the tree.

We talked portfolios for a while and how college was turning out to cost way more than we'd ever planned. Luckily Bill and Gail's first two were already through and I had only Jennie, but we were going to end up helping Maddy out. As usual. The wine, the steady, sensible drone of Bill's voice, the twinkle of Christmas lights and the big, quiet room decorated in Gail's impeccable ivory and pastels took effect. I relaxed. And my defences were down. That had to be why, when the doorbell rang and I went with Bill to greet the arriving guests, I didn't stand a chance.

That, or it could have been the fact that he was drop-dead gorgeous.

Bill introduced him as the new manager of their national data centres. Magazine model was more like it.

'And this is my sister-in-law, Robyn. Robyn, Trent.'

'Hi Robyn. It's a pleasure,' he said.

Yeah, no kidding. He was mid-thirties maybe, grey eyes, a beefier version of Paul Newman. And he was alone. He'd tagged along with Bill's senior manager and his wife. Had to be gay, I told myself, but I didn't quite buy it.

After the introductions, I found reasons to keep occupied. Answering the door, making sure glasses were filled, acting like I didn't notice him glancing my way every now and then, but I did. I noticed every time those grey eyes were turned on me, probably because nearly every time my gaze had strayed to his ass or the width of his shoulders under the dark-red sweater, and when he caught me I looked away, blushing like a silly girl. Wondering what the hell my problem was. Too little sleep and too much wine? That had to be it. Hadn't I sworn off younger men?

I could hear the little voice in my head that now sounded like my daughter yelling, 'Oh bullshit!' at me, but I stood my ground. I avoided him right up until he sat next to me at dinner, snagging the spot on my left because Thomas was already planted on my right and in deep discourse with Jennie about something on plate tectonics. Academic jargon that all went right over my head.

'Hi again,' he said with a smile that made me fumble my fork and forget what was I about to do.

'Hi. Trent, right?'

'Yep.' He grinned like he was surprised and flattered I'd remembered and I found myself grinning back. Damned if dimples weren't my weakness.

'I'm glad I caught you,' he said, leaning in to refill my wine glass and then his. 'You've been so busy all evening. But . . . Bill told me you do transformation consulting?'

I nodded. 'Consolidations, centre launches, offshoring. Fun stuff.'

'Yeah, really,' he laughed, as he ladled stuffing onto his plate and then offered to do the same for me. 'Well, I'm looking to do exactly that in the near future here.'

'Oh my, that's enough, thanks,' I said, stopping him after spoon two of stuffing. 'Are you really? I'd be glad to help in any way I can.'

Oh crap. Me and my big mouth.

He put the stuffing bowl down since Thomas and Jennie were paying no attention, and unleashed those dimples again.

'I was hoping you'd say that. Bill said you were the woman to talk to and you know he isn't exactly heavy-handed with the praise.'

I blushed and shook my head. 'No he isn't. And thank you. I umm . . .' Crap, now I was at a loss for words.

'Well, the last thing I want to do is spend Christmas dinner talking shop, but I'd love to give you a call sometime after the New Year? Maybe we can do lunch.'

Boy, there was plenty more than lunch I wanted to do. I refused to meet his gaze, reaching instead for the gravy boat and puddling a generous amount between my potatoes and turkey as I nodded assent.

'Of course. Anything to help Bill out.' And to see him again. Even if all he wanted to do with me was pick my brain.

'Wonderful,' he said. 'I'm looking forward to it.'

'So am I.'

I gave him a generous smile and then attacked my food so I wouldn't have to talk any more. I knew I was giving mixed signals, but reasoned that it didn't matter because we weren't flirting. Not one word he'd said could have been construed as anything more than polite networking, and he didn't press me to chitchat beyond a few comments about the stuffing being amazing. I was sure there was no way he knew I'd made it.

After dinner, Jennie cornered me in the kitchen.

'Mom! That guy who works with Uncle Bill totally has a thing for you!'

I knew there was no point in playing dumb. 'No he doesn't, Jen,' I said, sounding tired and patient as I loaded dirty plates into the dishwasher. 'He just wanted to talk about work stuff.'

'Yeah, sure. He's been looking at you like a Chihuahua staring down a T-bone all night!'

'Jen!' I snapped as the door opened and others came in. 'Drop it, girl. Ain't nothin' happening there. OK?' I added, lowering my voice.

Last thing I needed was Gail thinking I was hitting on Bill's employees at her party.

'Just go talk to him, please, Mom,' she insisted in a half-whisper, leaning down to put silverware one at a time into the silverware tray. 'He's cute and I can't stand to see him giving you puppy-dog eyes and you just giving him the cold shoulder.'

She put the last fork in and I shut the dishwasher door and turned it on.

'If he's so cute, why don't you go flirt with him?' I grumbled under the noise of the washer starting up.

She didn't miss a beat. 'Because he's old,' she replied, sticking her tongue out at me. 'And, oh hell, I just have a feeling, OK? Just go be sociable. It won't kill you.'

She was right. It wouldn't kill me. But by the time I found another glass of wine and the courage to head towards him as he lounged against the sofa talking, I discovered he was about to leave.

'I'm sorry we didn't get to chat more,' he said softly, holding my hand after he'd shaken it goodbye.

It took all my effort of will to pull it away and shake my head.

'Me too. But we'll catch up after the holidays. Email me.'

I didn't mean it to sound quite so encouraging, but the husky note crept into my voice and I saw his lips curve upwards. No dimples, but just as dazzling.

'See ya, Robyn,' he said and my knees went weak.

OK, so he probably wasn't interested, but I could make him be. If I wanted to, I could bring him to his knees at my feet and he'd be consulting me on a whole lot more than the cheapest way to set up servers. But the question I had to ask myself, that I had to figure out between now and the New Year, was did I want to?

It was the end of January and I'd almost forgotten about the party. Well, not quite. I remembered one of the guests sure enough, but I'd long since decided that if I did hear from him, I'd pass him off to another associate and plead a full workload. I'd gotten back into my routine of candle parties and charity luncheons and romantic, platonic dinners with E.D. Dave. It wasn't exactly exciting but it was comfortable.

Only one night, when Dave cancelled, I was more frustrated than usual. It was the kind of cold but clear night that made me want to open up the French windows in the bathroom and crawl into the hot tub with good company. Sadly, the only available company ran on batteries, but the jets of heated water against the bite of the night air felt delicious anyway. It made my nipples pucker and tingle and I pinched them slowly, wondering if . . . if he had called. What he looked like under that sweater. What his face looked like when he came. Was he a loud fuck? A screamer? Maybe a moaner?

My pussy clenched tight, sending spasms up through my ass and thighs, and I spread my legs. I bent my knees and propped my feet against the edges of the tub, imagining that my fantasy knelt between them, ready to enter my pussy laid out so readily for him. I wondered what he'd want me to do. Rub my clit like I was doing now? The pad of my index finger balanced delicately on the hood, pushing back and forth in counter time to my hips sliding through the water. He'd watch my face and neck get red, giving away my hidden arousal. Would his cock twinge and ache like my nipples, longing to be inside me? Envying my fingers sliding inside my wetness?

I was shivering from cold and from the feverish heat of being so close to orgasm. But damn, how I needed a fuck! I needed something thick and hard inside of me; this damned finger-fucking in the tub just wasn't going to cut it tonight. Ignoring the protest from my knees at the sudden motion, I levered myself up and out of the tub. Didn't care if I got water all over the floor. I was so close, but I wanted to come the way I would if Trent was fucking me. Hard and slutty.

I slipped and slid over to the shower, slammed the door closed and pulled down the detachable showerhead. I turned it on and slid the dial around to the fast pulse setting. Cold. I was really shivering now, my teeth chattering and my fingers almost freezing, but inside I was still molten. Heat that couldn't be chilled even when I bent over, legs straddling the drain, and angled the icy spray up directly against my clit and pussy. I screamed out. Oh yeah, hell yeah!

That was good! That was what I wanted: relentless, burning cold pounding my clit. Punishing my tits when I moved the showerhead upwards. Gasping, stifled, sobbing for air, coming so hard I hit my head on the wall and didn't think about the colourful stars of pain until I'd finally let my hand drop and the stream of water was harmlessly pointed at the drain.

I didn't think about why I'd done it at all until I'd shut the windows and drained the hot tub and dropped towels over the mess on the floor. Then, when I'd wrapped my shivering, goose-fleshed body in a robe and lay absorbing the warmth of my comforter, I let myself ponder why. And I think I knew the answer.

He'd given me a challenge, he'd dared me without daring me. He'd woken up the sleepy part of me that didn't really give a shit about garden parties and scented candles and had only grown dormant from not finding the chance to hunt what it craved. With that smile and those bedroom eyes he'd offered me the elusive something else, and I wanted to claim it.

The next morning I was at work bright and early, having slept like a baby. Had to be all the exertion from the night before. With a grin, I sat down at my desk, opened up my email and stared at the message sitting at the top of my box. Sent the night before at 1.14 a.m. from an address I didn't recognise, but with a name attached that I absolutely did.

'Robyn. I apologise that it's taken me so long to get back to you. I have been travelling for the last few weeks, but I will be back in town on Monday and I'd like to see if you are free for lunch anytime next week. I am entirely at your disposal . . .'

I breezed through the rest of the email, but I was already grinning. So he wanted to play after all. Well, we'd see. I hit reply.

'Trent, it's great to hear from you and I really would love to meet with you, however my schedule is booked solid at the moment. I'd like to put you in touch with Jerome Houston . . .'

I carbon-copied Jerome and hit send, then leaned back and looked out the window with a smile. How bad do you want it, Trent? Bad enough to come to me when I make you? Bad enough to beg?

Yeah. Life was fun again.

But whoever said patience was a virtue obviously never tried playing chess. When you've made your move and you sit waiting for your opponent to make his, trying not to fidget and betray your nerves, wondering if he'll take your bait or see a move you never did, going crazy with every second or day that ticks by when he still hasn't budged. Nope, it ain't a virtue by any stretch of the imagination, just a masochistic exercise in frustration.

Then, just when I was about to give up and ask Jerome how things were going, I walked into the elevator on the second floor and right into *him*. I stopped short, teetering in my heels, and felt his steadying hand on my elbow, sure it was no accident that I ended up just a little closer to him as he helped me regain my balance.

'Robyn!' The pleasure in his voice, at least, he couldn't disguise or tone down. It made the sound of my name sexy and I smiled as I looked into his eyes.

'Well hi there! I wanna say I'm glad I ran into you, but ...'

He laughed, dimples and all, and let go of my arm, but he didn't move away as the doors closed.

'Well *I'm* glad you did. I'm really sorry I didn't get in touch with you earlier, I've just been on plane after plane.' He sighed and rubbed the back of his neck while I enjoyed the sight. 'I was looking forward to working with you.'

I tried not to let my grin show too much glee. I tempered it, or tried to, by putting on a half-frown of concern. 'But everything's going well with Jerome? He's one of our best ...'

'Oh yeah. Yeah. I ...'

Damn elevator. It stopped, opened, and we had no choice but to step out onto the white granite floor of the lobby, our heels clacking as we walked towards the front doors, making intimate conversation impossible. We were losing our opportunity, I was losing my advantage. We'd go through those doors and separate and it would be a stalemate unless one or the other decided to give in. And given how we'd played the game so far, how stubborn we both were, I didn't cherish much hope that either of us would.

My heart sank as the doors slid apart and he gestured me through. I had a moment to think how hot he looked in that navy suit, how elegant and confident, just the kind of man I'd always thought about having but never pursued. Both hubbies and most of the boyfriends had tended to prefer manual labour, dirty fingers and power tools, and I liked the way they balanced me.

But Trent, he was my final frontier, the last fantasy of taking on my equal and my mirror. I didn't want to let it, to let him, go. I turned, opened my mouth, and he spoke first.

'Robyn . . .'

We stood in the pale sunlight, warm for late February, spring already well on its way after the sketchy winter.

'Yeah?'

He looked down and then out at the parking lot and I knew I was holding my breath. 'Umm . . . I completely understand if I'm way out of line here, but . . . well, given that Jerome is handling our account I'd . . .'

His gaze swung back to me and his lips curved together in a way that made me suddenly very conscious of the lace on my panties.

'I'd like to ask you to lunch. In a totally non-professional way. Whaddya think?' For a few heartbeats I let him hang, mostly because I couldn't think of how to talk, but then I smiled and reached out to let my fingers linger on the sleeve of his arm.

'I think there's nothing I'd love to do more,' I said.

It started with lunch. Then lunch and cocktails. Then a movie sometimes. Slap me silly and paint me pink, but he was playing hard to get. I wasn't surprised, and to be honest, I didn't mind. Ten years before, I'd have been pulling down his pants by the second date, maybe the third if I was feeling sensitive, but now I enjoyed the excruciating pretence that nothing sexual was going on. Chaste kisses goodnight and hugs so careful they made my dates with E.D. Dave look downright pornographic.

Fine with me if he wanted to make me pant and squirm because I knew he was inflicting it on himself too. I could tell when his gaze strayed to my cleavage, which I always made sure was amply visible. When he flushed under his tan and had to find somewhere safe for his gaze so he could calm down. When he kissed me and I could feel the impatient pressure in his lips that wanted to press harder, wanted to crush my mouth and invade it and leave me breathless.

Oh, he was doing good, real good, but I had the upper hand. Age doesn't always bring wisdom, but it sure as hell teaches endurance, and I could hold out – I had my showerhead and plenty of batteries. Just like he'd given in standing before my office building, he was giving in on this too. I wanted total, unconditional surrender.

I *wasn't* ready for his phone call that Friday at 11 a.m.

'Hey there, girl.'

'Hey yourself,' I said, swivelling my chair around to look out the window and grinning as my hand went to the single-strand choker of garnets he'd given me on my birthday, which I tried to wear almost every day. Every day I didn't wear the silver tennis bracelet, that is.

'I need you to do something.'

'What's that?' I asked, smiling happily up at a tree outside that was covered in the bright shiny leaves of new foliage.

'Cancel your afternoon and meet me downstairs in fifteen minutes. I'm on my way.'

I laughed. 'I can't do that.'

'Sure you can. If there was something earth-shattering going on, you'd be tense. I can tell you aren't.'

Damn, that was creepy. It had taken Drew nearly ten years of marriage to figure me out that well and Steve never had.

'So . . .' he was saying, 'I'll see you outside. And Robyn?'

'Yes?'

'Before you come down here, take your panties *and* your bra off and throw them in the trash.'

I missed a beat. In fact, I missed a few before I managed to get out, in a very giggly voice that I absolutely hated myself for, something about how much my underwear cost, but he only snorted.

'I'll buy you more. Now, do it OK? Love you, gorgeous. See you in a bit.'

And he hung up.

The bastard hung up and left me to steal guilty glances at the door while I cleared my calendar and set the out-of-office message on my email. I shut down the laptop, and while it powered off I sat with my eyes still fixed nervously on the door and chewed my thumbnail. My heart was thudding. I couldn't seriously be considering it, not really. But if I didn't do it, wasn't that just admitting I didn't have the nerve? Would I see disappointment flash in those grey eyes?

For a minute more I chewed away at my thumbnail, then I stood and closed the blinds. And locked the office door.

Was I ever happy I'd worn a skirt today. Simple to pull my panties down and step out of them, even though I almost lost my balance as one sandal heel snagged, but a few seconds later there they were, lying peach and silky and abandoned on the carpet. Halfway there. My bra was harder; I had to take my jacket off and then wriggle the straps down my arms and pull the whole thing out through one sleeve of my blouse. But that was easy compared to the niggling thought that without the help of underwires and D-cups, I wasn't the perky gal I'd once been.

That shouldn't matter, I told myself. Once you got down to business and all the clothes came off, it didn't make a lick of difference; but my female vanity put up a fight all the same. It cringed and blushed as I wriggled the straps over my elbows and threw the bra after the panties. It blushed some more as I put my jacket quickly back on, and sat staring at the evidence of my shamelessness on the floor, but time was ticking by and my computer was off.

Before I could think too much about what I was doing, I

stopped at the ladies' on the first floor and transferred panties and bra from the depths of my purse to the garbage with yet another furtive glance around. Never mind that the restroom was empty and no one had seen me come or go. My heart was still pitter-patter as I left the lobby, as guilty as if I'd just stolen half the company secrets and a couple of billion into the bargain. I felt the glances of the security guards and the few passers-by as if they knew and saw right through the lined wool of my suit, and my face burned as I walked to the lobby doors. Who knew a little exhibitionism could be such an event?

He knew. Of course he did, as he leaned across and flung open the door of the Jag for me.

'I take it you followed instructions,' he said, grinning.

I dumped my laptop case on the floor and got into the car, careful to keep my legs together as I sat, and shot him a dirty look once I'd closed the door.

'That was $60 I just dumped in the garbage, thanks.'

He rolled his eyes, checked his mirror and pulled out.

'Save the excuses, girl. You like it.'

He turned out of the parking lot and we accelerated along the tree-lined path leading out to the freeway.

'But,' he said, looking sideways at me, 'I'm not *certain* you followed instructions. Did you?'

'I said so, didn't I?'

'How do I know that?'

I folded my arms and crossed my legs and gave him a slow smile. 'Guess you'll just have to trust me.'

I wouldn't give him the satisfaction, no matter how much my nipples were pointed and aching and how badly I wanted to feel his fingers exploring them through the silk of my blouse as he steered the car. Just the thought was enough to get my clit throbbing between my crossed legs, but I held out.

'Guess I will,' he said. He put both hands on the wheel and

looked straight ahead as we joined the freeway, but I saw the smile playing around his lips and I knew it was far from over.

'I figured the weather was perfect for a picnic.'

I could only agree as we got out of the car. He'd driven out to Briar Park, and followed the winding roads down to a spot where springy, soft grass rolled down a gentle embankment to a small inlet of the lake. Trees clustered around and above the embankment, creating a green grove shielded from view of the roadway and the lake itself. But it wasn't hidden to anyone walking by, especially any game wardens or rangers.

I helped him lay the thick blanket out as if this were no more than a romantic picnic, as sweet and innocent as all our dates thus far, but when I sat and bent to take my sandals off he looked up from where he was fiddling with the picnic basket and shook his head.

'Leave them on.'

We looked at each other for a long moment. He'd left his jacket and tie in the car, but I still wore my jacket. Because once it came off there was no more pretending, no more playing modest.

So when at last he nodded at it, when he broke the silence of whispering trees and songbirds and distant water and told me to take it off, I knew we'd finally crossed the line. Although, now that we were here, I wasn't sure just which side the surrender was happening on.

I unbuttoned the single button and let the jacket fall from my shoulders. In the stillness, it felt like I was moving in slow motion. He forgot the picnic basket and leaned back, just as slowly, bracing himself on his elbows as he watched me take my shirt off too, unbidden. Bit his lip as I untied my hair from its twist and combed out the long, still-fiery curls with my fingers.

'God, I love your hair,' he said. 'I love how you keep it long.'

I smiled, but he wasn't done.

He sat up, eyes alight, and let his gaze travel over my bare torso to my legs, neatly crossed at the ankles, sandals still in place on my feet. Still bracing his weight on one hand, he hung the other over his knee and lifted his fingers like a symphony conductor, guiding my movements.

'I want to see you play with those beautiful tits. But first I want your skirt up over your hips. I want to watch you.' He paused and his gaze met mine. 'Will you let me?'

God, how do you say 'no' to something like that? For that matter, how do you say yes?

I couldn't find words at all. I just nodded and turned to recline on my side, facing him. I hiked my skirt up as I turned, so that my lower belly, my trimmed bush and the lips of my pussy were visible. I propped one hand under my head and with the other I caressed my nipples and the heavy weight of my breasts. He looked at me and his hand moved across his crotch, and I knew he didn't care about the stretch marks from carrying Jennie on my thighs and hips or the fact that my tits weren't perky.

I looked at him and knew he could have gorgeous young women but he'd chosen me, and my stomach went all butterflies and I think I fell a little bit in love all over again.

He took his clothes off piece by piece while he watched me pinch and stroke my nipples and rub one leg along the other so that my tormented clit could find some relief. He stripped down to nothing, and I in turn didn't care that he didn't have a six-pack. I cared more about the width of his shoulders and the dark curls sprinkled across his chest. I cared about the cock rising thick and erect from the darker bush between his legs.

I thought of how often, how much, how viciously I'd fantasised about his cock and the sight of it, so close, made me dizzy with wanting. He followed my gaze and smiled as he took his length in hand and stroked the skin up and down, rubbing

the head and watching my lips part and my fingers uncon-
sciously clamp harder on my nipples.

'Do you want this, Robyn?' he asked me and I gave him
another dirty look.

'If you don't bring it over here, I'm going to come and take
it,' I threatened.

He chuckled. 'Do it then. I dare you.'

Wrong words. I kicked the sandals off and then the skirt and
then I went after him. He didn't run far, just a few feet away
from the blanket before he let me catch up with him and
grabbed me and pressed my naked body to his. We kissed and
groped each other under the trees like some wild creatures out
of Greek mythology, with the springtime breeze caressing our
sweating skin and the music of the wilderness as background
to the rough beat of our blood.

Then he led me back to the blanket and knelt over me and I
spread my legs for him. Just like I'd planned, just like I'd
fantasised. Only with the scent of grass mingled with the scent
of sex and skin; with the heat of afternoon baking up from the
earth and the touch of wind all over my body; with him kissing
me more gently than I'd ever thought about even as one of his
fingers thrust hard into my pussy and the other into my ass
and I cried aloud from the sheer confusing pleasure of it all.

He wiped his fingers on the grass while I panted, and smiled
at me.

'*Now*,' he said. 'I want to fuck you.'

'You got protection?' I demanded.

'Of course.'

I let him retrieve it from his pants pocket, tear the wrapper
and pull the condom out before I snatched it from his grasp,
stretched it out and tossed it aside. He stared at me, and I smiled.

'Been years since I've needed those, love.'

He gave me the dimples, but he still had to get one last jab
in. 'And you're sure I'm safe otherwise?'

'No,' I told him. 'But I'll take the risk. I want you like this.'

And I had him. He couldn't say another word. He just filled me and fucked me like his life depended on it. Like it was all he'd ever been created for or meant to do. He fucked me until I hurt and the white blanket under us was spotted with red, and still I begged him for more. He lifted my legs and kissed the soles of my feet while he drove deep into me and I didn't think about tuna salad or anything else. I couldn't think at all; I could only lust and feel and come, and this – him – was what I'd needed all along.

I watched his face as he came and listened to him yell and I smiled. I wiped tears away from my eyes and his and played with his hair while he lay still on my breast and our breathing slowed, melded and at last found the same rhythm. He kissed my nipple and made me laugh and I thought that it had been worth the wait of half a lifetime: this silence, the satiation, the ache between my legs that told me I was alive. This feeling of being complete.

I closed my eyes and sniffed his hair.

'Know what?'

'What?' he replied, his voice drowsy and husky and delicious to my ears, muffled by his lips against the curve of my breast but vibrating through his chest and into my belly on the single word.

'I think you're the best damned Christmas present I ever met.'

He laughed.

Not Knowing It
Charlotte Stein

He's such a dark horse, that's the thing. Always with that peaked cap pulled down low over his eyes, and those eyes always pretending to be naked and vulnerable and like they're telling you everything.

But they don't really tell you anything.

He has none of the flat bland allure that the conventionally handsome usually have, and so none of that easy by-the-numbers readability, either. Back in college, when he read out that gross fat chick story, his face should have read: I hate you, gross fat chick.

But it didn't. It read like nothing, as it does now.

'Hey Hobbs,' he says, and kisses my cheek – awkwardly – and then we sit down – awkwardly – and wait for the rest of our former writing group. Also awkwardly.

I guess it's always been that way between us. I'm too aware of how handsome he is and he's too aware of how unfuckable I am and it's all because he's not like Ryan, all charming and able to banter with me, and I'm not like Kate, all cute and confident.

'So how've you been?' he asks, and I don't know. Good, I guess. Good enough that I don't care about what he thinks of fat chicks.

Though I still think about it when Kate and Ryan get here,

and everyone's talking all at once. I fade into the background and remember every inch of that story he read out, more sure than ever that he wrote it as an answer to some of mine.

Mine were celebratory, voluptuous, sunk deep in a sensual blur. Never focusing on an excess of hip or breast, but brushing over them, soft as gossamer.

His was morbid in its detail. The deep dimples that crowned her buttocks, the ripples of flesh undulating under his main character's hands, the creases and folds and slopes. And the sad-sack loser obsessed with it all, as though no normal man could ever be interested in anything like that.

But I do remember a line from his story – one line in particular – that was as lovely as his story was obviously not intended to be.

The soft crushed velvet of her skin that begs for my body.

Yes. I remember that.

He thinks I begged for his body. I'm sure he does. We're all sat around drinking too much, lounging on beanbags like harem denizens, sharing stupid fantasies just like the good ole days, and I'm sure he expects me to say: *you.*

You were my fantasy. You were right; I wrote those honeyed stories about a glittering honeyed land for you, Julian. The head of my queen's harem was modelled after you and your long liquid limbs and your limpid unreadable eyes and that sultry cast of your sultry mouth.

That's what he thinks I will say, but then I guess he doesn't know me half as well as I know handsome men. He wrote that gross story to ward me off – keep away from me, fat chick! We handsome men can't be touched by the likes of you!

So I tell some little thing about how I've always wanted to be a nineteenth-century proper lady, married to a proper husband, who then, on our wedding night, gives me the fucking of my life. Oh I never knew it could be this way, etc.

Ryan laughs and says exactly that, but Julian just stares at me with those storm-blue eyes. He looks sullen, I think, or angry. Because now he's wrong wrong wrong – he'll never be my nineteenth-century husband with his over-styled hair and his peaked cap and everything about him, Mr IT Whiz Kid.

'OK, OK – what's yours, Julian?' Kate says. 'Still the same? Or has it changed?'

'It never changes,' he replies, and I try to recall what it was before. All I can remember are a dozen boring stories about robots and the fat story, however.

'My favourite fantasy,' he begins, 'is the one with the girl who doesn't know I'm there.'

We all immediately sit up straighter. He's never told this one before.

'I guess it's kind of a voyeuristic fantasy. Though maybe not really. I don't know what it is. But it's my favourite anyway.'

'Are you sure?' Ryan asks. 'Because we can all still go back to believing you're dead inside at this point. I think I speak for everybody when I say we thought you only had robots in you.'

'I do,' he replies, in that slightly uncertain yet lazy way he has when he's about to say something possibly funny. 'They operate the cogs in my cock.'

I take too big a drink of wine, and almost go over the wrong way on my beanbag. He, on the other hand, looks like he was born to loll on beanbags. As though he's the sultan of our harem, only it's a harem of people who never, ever have sex with each other.

Unlike the people in my stories, who do nothing *but* have sex with each other. My harems are filthier than a garbage truck. Only not disgusting. Never disgusting.

OK. Maybe sometimes disgusting.

'So you were spying on someone,' Ryan says.

'It didn't happen like that,' Julian says, and I'm sure he now looks half as though he wishes he hadn't said anything at all.

No one ever honestly wants to share their perverted fantasies with friends they've barely seen for years.

'It was in our final year. Remember Tawny Housam?'

Boy, do I ever. She had legs longer than my entire body. Did he spy on her striding over the Eiffel Tower?

'After we'd split up, I guess I was feeling pretty weird. Wondering how I fitted in, wondering if I'd ever meet anybody right – the usual college stuff. Or maybe seventeen-year-old girl stuff. Whichever. Anyhow – that's when it happened.'

'You started your new life as a seventeen-year-old girl?' Ryan says.

Kate giggles. I drink.

'I went to the Hallsdale party.'

'The one where Curtis Blalock dislocated a testicle?'

'That's the one. I got bored trying to pretend I was charming after around twenty minutes, and fell asleep playing on someone's computer upstairs somewhere. Woke up covered in coats.'

I'm sure that's happened to him at a dozen parties. I've seen him trying to talk to women in the corner of kegfests, looking glorious but sounding like a computer manual. Though I can hardly knock him – I've woken up in my own fair share of coats.

'I think it was maybe morning, or close to it, and the house was deserted. Or at least I thought it was.'

'Dun dun duuuuhhh,' I say, but I think I'm drunk so it's understandable.

'I went downstairs, and saw the door to someone's bedroom ajar. And I could hear running water, too, which sort of made me want to pee. So I went into the bedroom thinking I'll talk to this left-behind person, and then use the bathroom, and then go home and kill myself.

'But I got into the room and it was all quiet and dim, with that soft morning feeling and someone's bed covers all ruffled,

and even before I saw what I did I felt real relaxed and kind of
... warm.'

If only he could talk like this at parties with women. But I
think he has to be comfortable. We're apparently comfortable,
like old shoes.

'And then I turned, and the bathroom door was ajar, too.'

I think I've heard this one before, but there's still something
about the way he's talking. He seems kind of breathless, and
even beneath the shadow of his cap his cheeks look flushed.
Like he can hardly bear to get it out, it's so scorching hot.

I can hardly bear for him to get it out, either. I'm on
tenterhooks, waiting to hear what he's going to say.

'I didn't mean to look. Or at least, I didn't mean to keep
looking. I can remember seeing a flash of pink and knowing
that I should walk away immediately, but I didn't. I wanted to
look – which makes it worse and better at the same time.

'I think the thing was – she was so unexpected. Everything
about it was unexpected. Her being there, the way she looked,
the effect it had on me. She didn't look like anything I was used
to – she had tiny little legs and broad square shoulders – but
those things only served to make me more interested. They
made me not want to look away.'

I can't picture this short boxy woman.

'She was completely naked, and wet from the shower.'

Which makes the doors being ajar completely implausible,
but do go on anyway, Julian. You're still making it sound as
though it's the truth, and that's the important thing. The
delicious thing.

'Her skin was like syrupy icing sugar, all glistening and pale
and edible, and I remember that *thud*, that kick of sex I felt,
thinking about eating her up.

'There were so many nooks and crannies to her body: that
dark secret crease between the top of the thigh and the edge
of her triangle of hair, a dip where her hips met her upper

body, the place at the underswell of her breasts. I wanted to map out her secrets, and give all of these places names. I wanted to write the names on her skin with my tongue so they'd always be on her like burns.

'All the other girls I'd ever had faded away as her hands glided over the blooming crescents of her breasts and the deep hollow of her belly button. They couldn't compete with that sudden desire to have my hands be her hands, and discover that body she obviously had no idea about. She had no idea it was capable of having this effect on anyone, I know.

'And that fact excited me more. She had no idea she was seducing me – wouldn't have even if I had done all of this legally and made small talk with her and got her back to her bedroom and laid in semi-darkness, waiting for her to take her clothes off in some clumsy hesitant way. I think that, more than anything, turned me on. She was doubly oblivious of her seduction of me, so oblivious that she could have read me erotic stories as lush as her body and thought only that I was stone.

'Of course I *was* stone. Just not in the way she might have imagined.'

His liquid voice is what makes a wet dream wet. I'm convinced of it. I hadn't realised it before right now, but it seems as though his voice can make even the words 'nook' and 'cranny' into fluid sinuous sex.

Unless it's all just the wine. Though I hardly think it is. I didn't think I'd ever hear Julian talk like this. I mean sure, sure – he told that fat story. But that was a pointed commentary on losers who like heifers. This . . . I don't even know what this is. His eyes are molten and hooded, and he seems to have sunk into some unholy wash of lust, and I swear if his lips part one more time to let out that little wicked pink tongue, I'm going to set this beanbag on fire.

And it gets worse! I don't know how he can go from robots

and computer manuals to this. How much has *he* had to drink? How much has he had to drink in the last ten years?

Too much. Even though he kind of looks like he's ripping off a plaster.

I bet the guilt over this is just burning up his staid robotic insides. I bet he just wants us to tell him how normal he is. Which he is, oh he is, oh if only he were always like this: near-readable and seductive and open.

Maybe I wouldn't be so afraid of his sultry handsomeness, then.

'She had lots of hair made into streamers by the water, and she lifted it all up and pinned it away, and when she did it her glorious tits lifted – so soft and ripe and plump. I'd never seen breasts like it outside a *Playboy*, and they made the pit of my stomach take on that hot low hum, that total need for sex. So did her mouth, as she inexplicably slicked it with lip gloss. Only it was explicable – she did it just for me.

'I know what you're thinking – that perverts make up any old bullshit to justify themselves – but so be it. I'm a perverted phantom-seduction lover. Even though I don't think it was entirely that. It wasn't that I had to pretend she was secretly doing it for me.

'It was just as exciting thinking about her doing it for herself. Seducing herself, maybe.

'Which she did. I watched her apply the gloss and then bite one of those gleaming lips, as though contemplating her own naughtiness. And then she glossed her tiny little pink nipples, too. Slowly, very slowly, until they were like the glistening insides of ripe cherries.

'I think she was watching herself in the mirror as she did all of this, but I can never really know for sure. I've checked that bathroom since, and there *was* a full-length mirror propped in between the sink and the wash basket, but maybe her eyes were half-closed. Maybe she was looking at a picture of Alan Alda on top of the wash basket – who knows?

'But I like to believe in the mirror. I like to, because then she lifted one leg and placed it on the edge of the bath, and the view she revealed to herself must have been glorious.

'Those black-as-anything curls, the split of her sex, and all wet, as wet as her skin. She must have been wet – by that point, I was stiff enough to put pressure on my zipper and that was just from watching her play with her spiky nipples and caress herself and pout.

'Watching her dip her hand between her legs was too much. I was ashamed of myself, then, but that only seemed to make it worse. Shame stroked right up and down my cock while she tried out that place between her legs as though she'd never heard of it before then. As though this – at what must have been twenty years of age – was her first time masturbating.

'She looked vulnerable and like a good girl, only not, just stirring something beneath her fingertips – enough to make faint juicy sounds, but not enough to really put her over the edge. Her movements were lazy, which made me think she'd done this many times before, but then her sighs of pleasure were so fragile.

'She didn't moan – just made these breathy little frustrated sounds while her cheeks grew pinker and pinker. One hand squeezed at her breasts hard, reflectively almost, as she rocked herself against her fingers, and then the languid pace gave way to something more obvious and frantic.

'I remember thinking: *How can she stand up like that?* At that point I could barely stand, but she kept it up through trembling and watching and fucking herself.

'She slid her fingers into her pussy only as she was about to come, and I would have given anything to have been in her place and touch that slick heat instead of her. I wanted to push her over that last little edge, push my cock into her while stroking her clit, but all my tricks – which are hardly any at all – were nothing next to her. My pretty face wouldn't work on her. Her own hand and her reflection were enough. I had nothing to seduce her with.

'So I walked away, with the sound of her coming pressing into my back.'

Immediately I want to ask: *How do you know your pretty face wouldn't be enough?* But that seems like a strange and shallow question, and I'm far too busy being turned on.

I feel as though I've been dipped in hot chocolate, and then poured into a volcano. I am molten and loose-limbed and angry at him for seducing me like this. Doesn't he know that I'm impervious to his charms? That a pretty face and a saucy story and a liquid voice aren't enough for me?

Why can't he just go back to being a charmless robot?

I actually say that to him, too. Later, when I'm in the kitchen substituting sex for ice cream. Ryan's freezer has *great* ice cream, like Bubbleyum Hopscotch and Toffee Dream Daze, because he's cool and sexy and he's the one who charms me. He's just as handsome as Julian, and he also buys great ice cream – probably because he knows I like it.

What have you done for me lately, Julian Walker?

'You've always thought that about me, right?' he says. He doesn't look exactly hurt, however. He looks somewhat amused in a way that makes me uncomfortable.

I spoon almost-melted Double Chocolate Sex into my mouth while I pretend to consider the question. While I keep him hanging by his balls. Only not, because when did I ever have such power over handsome Julian?

And then I say: 'Always.'

His eyes look dark, like before, when he was telling his story that should have embarrassed him but didn't.

'I realise it wasn't as good as one of yours.'

One of my what?

'But I'm glad it was better than usual.'

The story, my brain supplies. His story.

'I guess you have a sexier time in reality than you do on the page, Julian,' I say, but he skips right by that.

'So you thought it was sexy?'

'Sure. Why not.'

'Now it sounds like you're lying.'

'Why would I lie?'

'To make me feel less embarrassed?'

'Wouldn't me telling you that your story was hot make you *more* embarrassed?'

This conversation is going to a weird place that I don't like. Also, he's looking at me really weirdly, too. It's like his gaze is making me small, somehow, though not necessarily in a bad way. He's zeroing in on me. I'm a tiny little creature that he's caught in his headlights.

'It never embarrassed me to hear the things you used to come up with.'

'Because you're dead inside.'

'So you think they had no effect on me?'

'I think –'

I pause. It would be very easy here to tell him the score. Too easy. He's probably trapping me.

'I think you always felt I was trying to seduce you with those stories. That's what I think. Handsome boys always think every girl wants to screw them. Even mediocre boys think that every girl wants to screw them.'

His eyebrows meet his hairline.

'Isn't that what you thought, Julian? That I wanted to screw you?'

For some reason I don't want to examine too closely, I feel aroused again. Though I'm sure it's just a side-effect of lip gloss on tits.

'I . . .' he begins, and then he laughs. 'I always thought you were oblivious to me, if I'm honest. Seeing as I'm a charmless robot.'

'I was oblivious to you,' I say, though now that he's appeased my pride I'm not sure that's strictly true.

'That's what I figured,' he replies, and now he looks . . . rueful, I suppose.

'But if it's any consolation, your perverted fantasy was very *not* worthy of oblivion . . . wait. Is that the correct thing to turn oblivious into?'

He laughs.

'No idea. But thanks, anyway. I prefer being a pervert to a charmless robot.'

'It was a great perversion. Even though it's obvious that it never actually happened.'

He quirks just one eyebrow, this time.

'Oh, you don't think so?'

'Giving it an air of *actually happened* helped it, but you've got to cover up the holes.'

'Such as?'

'Such as – why would a woman shower and then wank with the door open, the morning after a huge party when there's bound to be people around?'

He glances away, squinching his mouth to the right in that *you got me* sort of way. I have to say, I never thought it would be Julian who would be so casual and friendly with me after all these years. I thought it would be Ryan and me that slipped back into each other. Maybe literally, this time.

But I guess charmless robots change.

'OK,' he says. 'OK. So what if . . . it wasn't the night after a party.'

'Like, just when everyone's gone to Hoboken?'

'Sure. Everyone's gone someplace. And it's not a house. It's a dorm.'

'So . . . someone's dorm room?'

He snaps his fingers.

'Ex-*actly*.'

'But then, why would she leave her dorm door unlocked?'

'Let's say I have a key.'

He looks full of laughter and knowing and it makes me feel even weirder than I did before. Sort of like I'm the butt of a joke, but not quite.

'Why would you have a key?'

'Because she's my friend. She's my best friend, even though she probably doesn't think of herself that way.'

'So you regularly spy on your best friends naked?'

'Is that worse than spying on a stranger?'

'Yes. No. I don't know.'

'Make up your mind, geez, Hobbs.'

'So you – you spied on your friend.'

'I did.'

'And you never told her you spied on her and then you blabbed about it to everyone.'

'But in my defence, I changed a few details. To protect the innocent.'

'Naturally.'

'Like: she wasn't out of the shower. I saw her through the glass door. And there wasn't a mirror, but I like to add that detail because it's sweeter that way.'

He's kind of leaning down towards me, and I can feel myself trying to lean away. Trying, but failing. When he puts one hand on the table next to me and gets real close, I feel offended and like a fool and turned on all at the same time. I can hardly look at him, but then I do and his eyes turn my hot chocolate insides to something even worse.

'And then what?' I whisper. 'And then what happened, in the story?'

His smile grows more teasing, and this time I can read his eyes perfectly: relief. Relief, and maybe a lick of triumph, too.

'I guess I realised how much I wanted her.'

'So you didn't before?'

Before you saw her naked. All of her, naked, utterly.

'On some level, maybe. I just didn't understand what she was doing to me. She wasn't like the girls I usually dated ... she was –'

'Different. She was really different. And special.'

He chuckles.

'It wasn't so clichéd.'

'Really?'

'I just didn't realise how much I fucking love a big ass until that moment. Does that sound different enough to you?'

This *all* sounds different to me.

'You had a kind of fat-ass awakening, then.'

But he doesn't laugh.

'Yes!' he cries. 'Yes!'

Like he's singing hallelujah.

'Before that moment, I was starting to think I was gay. Because the girls who I thought I should be dating got no reaction. But she did. She got a reaction.'

'Because she was so special.'

'Because she seduced me without knowing it. She'd just read her little stories as though reciting the phone book, and lather herself up in the shower and love herself and not even notice that anyone was there, and wear shirts too tight for her and play with her hair and it was all like this amazing secret that no one knew but me.'

'Because *you're* so special,' I say, intending sarcasm, but my voice comes out worse than a whisper. It comes out hoarse and weak and I think I'm actually tilting my face up to meet him even as he's definitely coming down to meet me. And I don't want to think what we're meeting in the middle to do but I'm sure it's going to happen nonetheless.

I can see his lips parting, and his eyes smouldering, and all the things that are supposed to happen when someone you really want to screw is about to kiss you.

'Just like you,' he replies, and I think: God. That was the *best* end to a story ever.

I attempt resistance. Really I do. But who am I fooling? A wet fish could probably seduce me. I have no chance against the Most Handsome Man in the Universe, who has possibly just admitted to spying on me naked in the shower. Which should make me disgusted, but only makes me brim with joy in some disgusting sort of way.

Still I try not to kiss him back. I try not to think about that dimple in his chin and his movie-star hair and his lean vulpine face like something out of all my fantasies about werewolves. I try not to think about how he knows about all my fantasies about werewolves and nineteenth-century husbands and harem slaves and so on.

Crap. Is he going to expect me to be that way? Maybe it's not my huge ass after all. Maybe it's my smutty mind. And what about –

Oh mother of God I don't care, he has his hands on my huge ass and I don't care. I don't care because I'm remembering now how he has a lot of tattoos – probably done in an effort to make himself less of a computer nerd – and I want to lick them all.

I never thought I'd get to touch those tattoos. What's more alarming, however, is that it seems he never thought he'd get to touch my gigantic ass. He's been longing for my gigantic ass, and that is not a worry to my libido in any way whatsoever. My libido is apparently twenty feet tall and devouring his face.

Not that his face minds. *Oh my God*, he keeps saying, while his eyes roll up in their sockets and his hands do a dance all over my back and butt. More than a dance, in fact. They're like Indiana Jones discovering the lost city of Atlantis. They're excited and extremely thorough. I don't think an inch of my back and butt goes unexplored and good Lord his fingers are dexterous.

Of course I've seen them be dexterous before. He's always clicker-clacking away on some keyboard with his wriggling extra-long fingers. But it's a whole different story when they're roaming your back, finding those dimples that rest just above your ass and unhooking your bra both through your shirt and without your knowledge. I'm only aware of my bra being open when skin meets air.

'Oh man, I've waited years to see these not through a shower door,' he says, and then shoves his head underneath my shirt. I thought he'd seduced me with all that spying and butt talk, but his head under there really does the trick. I giggle, and he giggles, and it suddenly seems OK to be about to fuck someone as glorious as he is.

Because we're definitely about to fuck. Even if I weren't half-sprawled across the table with him between my legs and my boobs almost out, I'd know that much.

Still, I'm not sure how to get from A to Z. Until he steps back, flushed as anything and grinning broadly, and words come out of my mouth I had no idea were in me.

'My turn, perverted spying boy,' I say, and then I seat myself properly on the table and lean back on my hands, and tell him what I've secretly always wanted to. Like the queen of the harem, ordering her best slave: 'Strip.'

The amount of eagerness on his face is alarming in such a good, good way.

'All right,' he says, breathless and boyish. And then he yanks his jersey over his head in one motion, and there are just acres of man flesh for me to feast my eyes on. One thing I always liked about Julian is his entirely non-weedy man body. It's not muscular, like Ryan's, and it's not skinny, like Kate's, and it's not thick, like mine. It's just solid.

I'm Goldilocks, and he's just right.

He shucks off his jeans, and there's nothing wrong there, either. Solid thighs like twines of heavy rope, and jockeys that show off the other heavy things he might have. Of course he has heavy things. He probably wouldn't be so eager to rip off his underwear right here in the kitchen if he weren't ready for his *Playgirl* close-up.

And then he stands there with his hands on his hips, looking better than ice cream.

'You want me to lather up now?' he asks, and I immediately imagine what I must have looked like to him. Like a soap-covered cake, I'd imagine, judging by the way he's looking at me now.

'Maybe with some ice cream,' I reply, and to my greatest joy he seems to have no problems with that whatsoever. He takes the Hot Lickable Fudge from me and with one finger paints a stripe over a perky little nipple.

Which I lick off with great enthusiasm. And then he paints another stripe down the centre of his mouth, and I lick that up too. And I can totally see where this is going only I can't, because he then says, 'Your turn now.'

And then I suppose I have to take all my clothes off and have him lick ice cream from my copious curves. Which sounds frightening, in one way, but in another is electrically exciting. He makes me feel exciting. I've never had someone write a story about me before, and God only knows what stories he's going to write about me from now on.

How about: The Time I Peeled Off Her Clothes on the Kitchen Table?

Which he does, one item at a time. So slow, so very slow that it's agony-riddled bliss, like being unravelled into sex. He eases my shirt up so that it ruffles and slides against my skin, and then as he removes my bra he slithers the silky cups against my nipples so that they ache and shiver pleasure on down between my legs. And all the while he follows every inch of my body with his eyes, as though he's never seen anything like it.

I want to ask him why he waited so long – his cock sure seems to think he shouldn't have waited so long – but then again, why did I? His excuse doesn't seem as good as mine, but then, I don't know what it's like to be so into something. I like all sorts of men: small, fat, skinny, thick, big and all the things in between.

Not like him, who only likes me.

He unbuttons my jeans until I squirm and tell him to go faster. But he just laughs and says, 'As though I'm going to rush this.'

And I suppose that I love him saying that more than I love going faster. Besides, slower means that I get to feel every tiny step towards utter all-consuming desire, that ache in my nipples spreading to liquid heat that blushes and swells my pussy until I'm concentrating on nothing but it, and even better than that I get to consider everything in his story as it relates to me. The ink-black curls he exposes when he tugs down my panties, all the soft hollows and curves of my body, and his hands stroking them as though he loves them all.

He licks the inside of my thigh on the way back up from the crouch he's in, and his tongue is just about the sexiest thing I've seen. It's even sexier when it flickers briefly but unerringly through that split of my sex he wanted to see so badly, and when I make a surprised sound he makes a little answering sound back.

He doesn't have to say it but he does anyway: *I'm so hungry for you.* And then he bites me, he bites the flesh at my hip, and the soft underswell of my breasts. And then my throat, deliciously that much harder than he bit the other places, and I realise with a jolt of heat through my clit and my nipples and everywhere that he got that from my stories. That I like to be bitten hard just at the beginning of my throat.

And I know what he likes, too. He likes to watch.

So I push him away, and lie right back on the table, and wrap my legs around his waist so that his erection can only press into the place I want it to go.

'Watch, then, in close-up,' I say, and put my hand between my legs.

It takes him around ten seconds to put the condom on – which he gets without moving from between my legs, from the pocket of his discarded jeans – and while he does it his eyes don't leave my hand. Of course I hardly do anything to myself but spread for his delectation – mainly because I'm so liquid anything else would be hard – but that's not really the point. The point is that now he's ready to go fast.

Still, he tries to be careful. He tries, but I'm so wet that he just keeps right on sliding until he's good and deep inside me. It feels amazing to have something fill me up in just the right sort of way, while my fingers slip over and around my swollen clit. So amazing that my hungry pussy clenches and pulls at him, and his hands grip my thighs sudden and tight.

'Oh honey, that's too much,' he says, and I love that flushed cast to his face and the way his lips part, and just thinking about how worked up he's been getting himself and then how worked up my body and my slick hot pussy is getting him makes my clit jump against my fingers and my cunt cream.

'Just fuck me,' I tell him. 'Fuck me however you want.'

At which point he grabs great handfuls of my ass and surges against me hard enough to make the table move. He actually pulls me onto his cock that way, over and over again until I know we must be making a racket and the table is almost up against the fridge, but it feels too good for me to care. Someone could be spying on *us* and I wouldn't care. I just hold on to the edge of the table with one hand and fuck myself with the other, and let him pound me until my tits jiggle.

When they do, he moans *Oh fuck, oh fuck, you're magnificent*, and not only do I believe him as every part of me undulates, I feel even better than that. I feel like the queen of my harem, making this gorgeous man flush and sweat and fuck me like he's possessed.

He grunts and groans and I know he's about to come, but he presses the heel of his hand down on my sliding fingers first and rubs, and the demand is just enough to make me twist and come around his cock in wracking shudders.

Oh, oh, oh, I tell him, and he answers me in similar style. *Oh yeah*, he stretches out, in between each one of my high tight moans.

And then we're done. Fucking in Ryan's kitchen, completely naked and somewhat covered in ice cream. The tub's over-turned, and I look as though I'm wearing an ice-cream sleeve. But as he gazes down at me, eyes still stormy and hooded, glazed in perspiration, I don't think he's going to have any problems with that.

'So how come that story worked, and the first one I tried went down like a lead balloon?' he says, much later, as we lie in the rubble we seem to have created. I can hardly speak, but I manage at least, 'First one?'

'The first one I tried. About the guy with his curvy girl.'

The gross fat chick story. Oh for the love of – the gross fat chick story!

Of course, I don't say that. Mainly because I feel like a massive fool. But also because what I really want to say is this: 'Stick to reality, honey.'

Just One Night
Terri Pray

Claire swirled the remains of her Matinee around the glass. 'I need a good long hard shag. It's been too long and I'm about ready to jump the nearest man and fuck him senseless. Or let him do me. God, this is insane.' It wasn't helping that nearly every man that walked past her set her body on fire. Maybe it was just the club, or the drink, but whatever was going on her sex drive had slammed into overdrive. 'This just sucks, big time, and I'm running out of batteries!'

'No luck on the boyfriend side of things?'

'None, dried up. Drake split. Besides, I don't need a boyfriend, I need a fuck buddy. Dates, relationships, they're a waste of time lately. A man in my life? For what? To complain when I stay late at the office?' That was the last thing she needed to deal with right now.

'So, do something about it instead of sitting here with me.' Sharon gave a half-shrug and glanced around the busy bar. Smoke curled upwards from a dozen tables as couples, small groups and single men and women mingled. Music thumped out from the nearby jukebox, adding to the background noise. 'Get proactive on this. Or don't you have the guts?'

Claire's shoulders tensed as she sucked in her bottom lip. 'What?'

'Come on, it's not like you. So what are you going to do about it? Sit back and sulk, or get out there and grab a man?'

'I hear a dare coming on.' She sipped the last of the drink and set the now-empty glass down. 'So spill. What are the terms?'

'Just like that?' Sharon drained the last of her drink. 'Give me a chance to think here, I wasn't expecting you to dive right in on this. Damn it, woman, you don't like to make things easy, do you?'

'Why not, you're the one who made it a challenge.' Claire smiled; if nothing else, she'd caught her old friend off guard. 'Or is it too much for you? We can always change the subject if that's the case. I can find something else to do. Or someone.'

'All right,' Sharon growled and closed her eyes, shutting out the distractions around her. Her long, French-manicured fingernails tapped against the table, her lips pressed into a tight, thin line. 'The dare. You're to find and seduce a man from this club, and bring back a trophy to prove it. His fly button. I want to see his fly button in the palm of my hand tomorrow morning at coffee.'

Heat flushed through her cheeks. 'Tonight? You sure about this?'

'Yes, that way you don't get a chance to change your mind, or have something come up. Now, choose your target!'

'You mean my prey?' Claire grinned and licked the tip of her tongue slowly over her lips.

'That works, as long as you get this done tonight. You need a good long screw with a guy that will leave you walking bow-legged for a week. All you've got to do is pick one out.'

Yes, it did work and in more ways than one. Hunting down a man for sex – well, she'd never done that one before but there was a first time for everything. Pick one. Sounded easy, but the reality was another matter. 'Hm, now which one to pick, perhaps the blue shirt over – no, there's a blonde hanging on his arm.'

'Ah, yes, that would be competition for you.'

'No, not that, trouble. I'm in no mood to end up in the middle of a cat fight and she looks like the type that would scratch the eyes out of any woman who went near her man. Look at the way she's glaring at the brunette.'

'Hm, good point.' Sharon pursed her lips and nodded towards the bar. 'What about the dark-haired hunk there?'

'Gay.' She barely glanced at the man in question.

'How do you know? Come on, you're dodging!'

'I know his boyfriend.' Pity about Gavin, he was one gorgeous piece of man flesh, but his interest in women as sexual partners ranked right up there with cleaning up dog shit from his shoes. 'Great guy, if you need a fake date for the night, but that's as far as he goes. He's great when it comes to choosing wine as well.'

'I'll remember that, always useful to have a back-up.'

This wasn't helping. Who was she going to target? It wasn't as if the bar was short of likely subjects. It was a pick-up joint, that's why she'd come here in the first place.

'Mike.'

'What? The bartender?' Was she kidding? Mike didn't date people from the bar, everyone knew that.

'Why not, you've had your eye on him for months now.' Sharon nudged the empty glasses across the table. 'And you've got the perfect excuse, or don't you think you've got what it takes to land him? Is he out of your league? Imagine that, a bartender out of your reach.'

Claire growled. 'Out of my reach? Bitch! Oh, now you've gone and done it.'

'That was the entire idea.' Sharon flashed a smug smile and leaned back in her chair. 'Go get him, if you can. Though I'm betting he says no, he always turns customers down.'

Oh, she could and would go and get him. Without another word she slipped out of her chair and snagged the two empty glasses from the table. Claire made her way through the semi-crowded bar, taking in the men and women who had descended upon it for an evening of alcohol, sex and entertainment.

Was she any better? She'd come here with Sharon for the same thing. All right, so she was taking a more direct route on the sex aspect and if it all worked out then she'd be going home with Mike.

Sure, if I can get him to break his record in turning women down.

Six foot with an inch or so to spare, with dark hair caught in a ponytail at the nape of his neck. The play of muscles beneath his clothing spoke of a man who took care of himself, or played sport. No beard, not even a hint of growth, which meant he had shaved before work. Good. Not that she minded a hint of whisker when she was in the mood for it. Just not tonight.

'What can I get you?'

'Two chocolate Martinis and you.'

Mike leaned on the bar, snagging the empty glasses with an easy swipe. 'Now, if I didn't know better then I'd assume that was a come-on. But out of all the women in here, you've been careful not to try and hit on me.'

'It *is* a come-on.'

Mike laughed and shook his head. A light danced within his eyes. 'Well, your common sense had to do a runner at some point. Look, do you know how often I get that line? You're the third one tonight, so what makes you so special? Why would I go home with you, or take you back to my flat?'

Third one? Great, that wasn't going to help her situation. 'The fact that all I want is one night, no strings attached, no calling you, stalking you, hell, I'll even change bars after tonight if that would help.' She leaned against the bar and pressed her arms in close, forcing her cleavage fully into view. How the hell was she supposed to trap him for the night if he was used to being hit on?

'Hm, now that's an offer I haven't had before. Not phrased that way at least. Still, I can't see why I'd take the risk with you. Oh, don't get me wrong, you're attractive enough, my type even, but this is my job and I'm not about to fuck myself over a quick shag.' Mike turned away and started work on the drinks.

Risk his job? Shit, didn't think about that one. The reason he'd turned down women in the past and planned on doing so tonight was clear now. 'And what if I could prove to you that I'm worth it?'

'How?' He turned back and set the two new drinks on the counter. 'How are you going to prove to me that you're worth the risk of my job, and with it my flat?'

If he was willing to risk his job, she had to be willing to do something equally dangerous for her reputation. But what? Music, the bar . . . oh, the answer was staring her in the face, if she had the guts to follow through with it. 'What if I get up on that bar and do a little Coyote Ugly for you?'

'And what does that prove?'

'That I'm willing to risk my reputation.' How much of a risk it really was, she couldn't be sure. 'So it's not my job, but I'd have to live with the comments from people who know me, and maybe a few people at work. There's a bonus – you'd get a good idea of just how our night would be.'

'What gives you that idea?'

'Because I'm going to use that dance to seduce you and by the time I'm done you won't be able to turn me down.'

'You're on.' He grinned and looked down the length of the bar before glancing back at Claire. 'So, go pick a song and get up there, unless you're having second thoughts?'

'Bring it on, I'm going to show you the dance of a lifetime, Mike. One you'll never forget.'

Mike didn't say a word. He stepped back from the bar, checked to see if anyone else needed to be served, and then turned his attention back to Claire.

If she was going to do something about it, then she had to do it now. Claire walked away from the bar and headed for the jukebox. When she'd first started frequenting the place she'd found the old-fashioned jukebox to be an odd addition, but now she was more than a little grateful for it. At least this way she could pick out the right music for her new challenge.

Claire traced her fingertip over the list of music. What would work best for this? Some of the songs were too slow, others too fast. She needed something that would stand out, something he wouldn't expect her to dance to in order to seduce him. One song caught her attention, but it didn't fit the bill and she continued to search through the titles. Then she found it. 'Lady Marmalade', by Pink.

She slipped the coins into the box and hit the number. The time it took to find the song gave her enough time to walk to the bar and climb onto it. Mike arched an eyebrow as the music started and Sharon waved from her chair, grinning like a Cheshire cat.

Don't think, just do it. Easier said than done.

The opening beats of the song rang out through the bar and she let her hips roll in time to the beat. She turned and fixed her gaze on Mike, mouthing the words of the song. It didn't matter that the men and women around her whistled, and cheered her on. Her focus was on Mike, nothing else mattered.

She strutted down the length of the bar, her hips swaying with each deep beat. Her body set the pace. The song played through her mind, urging her steps across the bar. She'd tease him. Torment him. Show him how her body could move. Claire teased her hands over her hips, then up along her waist until she cupped her breasts and turned back to face him.

Her tongue traced over her lips, wetting them, her gaze fixed on his face. His eyes widened. Lips parted. Sweat beaded across his brow. He groaned. She couldn't hear the sound, but the shape of his lips made it all too clear what he was doing.

What would those lips feel like against hers?

She didn't know, but planned on finding out in intimate detail.

Her hips rolled, thighs tensed, and her breasts bounced, nipples hard against her top as she strutted back towards him. No, that wasn't enough, she needed to up the ante. She waited for the right moment in the song and lowered herself down to her hands and knees on the bar, smiling as those who needed to snatched their drinks out of the way. With the beat firmly in the back of her mind she crawled, stalking him across the bar, her breasts pressing against her top, her cleavage clearly seen by anyone who cared to look.

What they saw didn't matter to her.

Mike, his view, his reactions, those were the only things that mattered to her now. He belonged to her. He didn't know it yet, but there was no way she was going to let him get away. Not tonight.

By the time the song was done, so was he.

Claire stepped down from the bar with the help of Mike's hand. His eyes glowed. Small beads of sweat coated his brow. She licked the tip of her tongue over her lips. 'So, did I manage to interest you?'

'Something like that.'

'Then what are you going to do about it?' She purred the words, resting one hand on her hip.

'Jim, cover the bar for me, I've got some business to attend to.'

'Yeah, bet you have!' Jim laughed, and winked. 'Have fun and don't do anything I wouldn't do!'

Claire shivered, heat claiming her being as she walked with him out of the bar. So, he was willing to take the risk. Good. So was she. She'd done it. Now all she had to do was complete the rest of the dare.

After what she'd already done that should be easy. She leaned into his touch as they walked around the back of the bar towards the stairs to his flat.

* * *

'So, will you really be fired for this?'

'No, I don't think so. Doing this once in four years working here isn't going to get me canned. Warned maybe, not sacked.'

'Good, I wouldn't want to get you in trouble. No matter how much I think it might be worth the risk.' He smelled of honest sweat and leather rolled into one. Where the leather smell had come from, she didn't know. Aftershave maybe? She'd find out later.

'You're trembling.' He leaned in, brushing his lips over her throat. 'Something wrong?'

'No, I'm fine, really.' *Sure, I just made a fool of myself on the bar, everyone knows what I'm about to do with Mike and ...* And she didn't care. This was what she wanted.

He opened the door and stepped to one side, letting her enter first. 'Welcome to my not so humble home.'

'Wow.' Whatever she'd been expecting it hadn't been this. The small flat wasn't a hovel, or a bachelor pad with all the markings of a man left to fend for himself. No dirty laundry. No dishes scattered across the floor, waiting to be stepped on. A computer sat in one corner, in a sectioned-off area set up as an office. The rest of the main living room of his flat was equally well cared for.

'Right, you were expecting a cross between hell and a dump?'

'Something like that.' She turned to look at him as the door closed behind them. The time for talking was over. Claire reached up and wrapped her arms about his neck, brushing her lips over his.

'Hm, is that all you have?'

'No, not by a long shot,' Claire whispered against his lips. Her nipples pebbled beneath her bra. Heat flared through her body. 'I've got a lot to show you, and that dance, this kiss, is only the beginning.'

'More like a hint of a beginning from this side of things.'

'Then let me show you the rest.' She licked, slowly, along the seam of his lips. 'It'll be worthwhile. Trust me. I'm going to make this a night you never forget.'

He grabbed her by the arms, his voice dropping to a low growl. 'If you're trying to make this one night into something more . . .'

'I'm not, and if I was do you think I'd tell you?'

'Fair point.' He smiled and eased up on her arms. 'So, what do you have in mind?'

'Let me show you.' Claire moved into the circle of his embrace. 'I've watched you for a long time.'

'I know.'

'Cocky, aren't you?'

'That was never in doubt.'

He was arrogant. Sure of himself. Powerful in his own way. Men like him were rare. Most would have used their job, regardless of the risks, to enjoy as many women as possible. Not Mike. He'd shown restraint. Yes, there was something powerful about him that she hadn't come across before. And he was hers. If only for the one night.

She reached up and pressed her lips, gently, against his throat. Her teeth scraped over his skin. He growled beneath her touch.

'Nice.'

She licked across his pulse, teasing the tender flesh as her fingers claimed the buttons on his shirt. She tugged the edges of his shirt apart and traced her nails over his taut abs. God, she'd waited a long time for this. His skin tasted so good, so tempting beneath her lips. Her nails scraped at his chest and she struggled to keep control of her body.

'Bedroom.' His voice was little more than a low moan.

'Where?'

'Behind and to the left.'

'Good.' She didn't want to move more than she had to. Not with the way his body felt beneath her touch. It felt right. He felt right.

He turned and took hold of her arm, leading her back towards the bedroom. His fingers found her buttons, opening them, pulling off her shirt, his already lost to the floor of the flat as they stumbled through it.

'You're hungry.'

'Tell me something I don't know,' she whispered and leaned up into his kiss. 'I'm starving and you're the cure.'

'Is that so? Well then, maybe we should try and cure that hunger.' He leaned down and nipped at her throat.

Claire opened his pants the moment she felt his legs touch the bed. She tugged at them and pulled them down, the outline of his cock beckoning her through his soft grey shorts. It throbbed beneath her first touch. 'What do you have here, hmm?'

'If that's a serious question, then I've got a few worries about this that I didn't have before,' he half-laughed. 'Or maybe I should show you exactly what I'm capable of doing?'

'Oh, I think I've got a few things I can show you myself.' She pushed him back onto the bed and tossed her skirt aside, leaving her in her bra and panties. 'I can dance in more ways than one.'

'Can you now? Well then, let's see what you can do.' He shifted a little more onto the bed, and looked up at her. 'But you're over-dressed.'

'So do something about it.'

'I plan to.' He reached up and cupped her breasts through the soft peach of her bra, thumbing her nipples until they hardened. 'Nice, very nice. Bigger than I thought.'

Claire growled, 'And if they hadn't been?' Just her luck, a man with a breast fetish. Not that she minded. Not fully. She ground down against his cock, teasing him with the damp heat that emanated from between her thighs. Her vulva was eager, hungry for his cock.

'Ah, I'm not complaining. Small breasts. Large breasts. I like

165

them all, as long as they're attached to a real woman.' He leaned up and latched his lips around one nipple, sucking hard.

Claire groaned. She arched her back, her hips pressed against his groin. His cock twitched and pressed against her. 'Yes!'

His teeth grazed her nipple, his free hand massaging her other breast. Her belly tightened. Her body was hungry for more, so much more than she had been shown so far. She needed this. Needed him.

No, I don't need him. He's just a quick fuck. Nothing more.

Her panties moistened, damp, eager, heat coating her inner walls. She groaned, surrendering herself to the sensation, for now at least.

Prey. The tease had been there from the challenge that Sharon had set. He was prey, fair game. She could do anything she wanted to him – well, she could try. If he didn't like it, he'd stop it. He was strong enough to stop it and take whatever he wanted from her.

The thought forced her to stop. If she pushed too far would he turn the tables on her? *So don't push things.* Easier said than done. Her thighs clenched on either side of his hips. Pulling off her panties and riding him would be so easy right now. No, he wasn't ready, she wasn't ready.

'Something wrong?' He pulled away from her breast and smiled. 'Second thoughts?'

'No, not at all, just thinking this through.' Claire leaned down and claimed his lips. He groaned beneath her kiss, his lips parting, welcoming her touch. Her breasts brushed against his chest. His tongue explored her mouth, tasting her. Without a word he took control of the kiss as he rolled them on the bed, pinning her down with a low, eager growl.

'You like this, don't you?'

'Yes.' She looked up into his eyes.

'Good, because I don't play meek and mild.' He leaned down and reclaimed her lips fully. His tongue conquered her mouth.

She struggled for dominance for a moment, only to surrender. His lips bruised hers. Her breath hitched in the back of her throat, her body tight, heated beneath his. Her nipples ached for his touch, his mouth, his fingers, anything that would tease her, torment her a little more.

She groaned, arching into his kiss. This was where she belonged. In his arms and in his bed.

'Sweet, so damn sweet,' he murmured against her lips. 'Take this off, take it all off.'

'Do it for me. I want to feel your hands. Your touch on my skin. Not just here, everywhere.'

Her hips rolled against him. The feeling of his thick erection teased her. Tormented her. She needed to feel it between her thighs. In her body. Within her fully.

'You only had to ask.' He reached up, opening her bra from the back and sliding it down from her breasts. 'Beautiful.'

You're not so bad yourself. No, she couldn't say that to him, too damn over the top. 'And you're just going to stare at them?'

'No, not just that.' He edged down between her thighs and grabbed the sides of her panties. 'Maybe I should just rip them off.'

'Not unless you want to replace them.'

'Or send you off without wearing any. Do you like that idea? The thought of being sent out there, nude beneath your skirt, the cold air caressing your sweet pussy. No one else knowing that you weren't wearing anything, no one but me that is.'

'You wouldn't.'

'Wouldn't I?'

Silly statement. Of course he would. He'd tear them off, use her and send her on her way. A part of her liked that. Wanted that. She pressed her lips together in a tight, thin line. Her hips trembled, a soft jolt working through them.

'Well?'

'Take them off.'

'Take, or rip?'

'Either, whichever works best for you.' A low shiver claimed her being as Claire looked up at him. 'Or are you just going to push them to one side?'

The lace snapped in his hands. She hissed. A moment of pain and shock hit her hips with the snap of the lace.

'Nothing left to stand in my way, is there?'

'One thing.'

'Oh?'

'Condom.'

'Covered.' He lifted up the small foil-covered package. 'I'm not leaving anything to chance.'

Claire smiled. 'Good.'

Mike eased down a little more between her thighs, pressing on them, parting them further. 'God, you smell so sweet.'

Her inner walls clenched. Heat claimed them, coated them, her clit throbbing beneath each touch of his breath. Would he touch? Lick? Kiss? Or just tease? It didn't matter, she'd enjoy whatever he did to her.

Mike leaned in closer, parting her lower lips with a touch of his fingers. Teasing them apart. Her thighs clenched, her body aching for his caress, for the soft brush of his lips, his tongue, his fingers, something, anything that would help ease the heat that tried to claim her being.

His lips closed about her clit, his tongue flickering over the small, ripe bud, and she grasped the edge of the bed, her hips half-lifting from the bedding. She groaned. The walls of her sex clenched. His tongue circled her clit. Her hips rolled, pleasure surging into life, her belly tight as she pressed her heels against the bed. God, that felt so good.

How long had it been since a man had touched her like this? Too long. Far too long. Her eyes closed, a soft shudder playing through her body as she writhed beneath him. He growled against her clit, the sound sending small vibrations through her tight nub.

'Yes!' She arched her back, her hips bucking from the bedding. 'God, yes!'

He eased away from her clit and smiled. 'You're hot, slick and ready.'

'It's been a while,' she gasped, reaching for him, trying to bring him back against her clit. 'Finish what you started.'

'I plan on it.' He moved back to her clit, sucking it into his mouth until she screamed in pleasure. One finger slid between her lower lips, pressing against her inner walls. She groaned. His finger tapped, then searched, finding that secret spot deep within. 'Right there.'

Each touch against the small spot within her core sent a jolt of sheer pleasure through her being. Liquid heat claimed her sex. She whimpered, her body no longer her own. Thought lost all meaning. She groaned, writhing beneath his touch, her core rippling on his finger, her hands clenched in his hair as she struggled to keep a grip on her sanity.

It didn't work.

Without warning it hit.

She arched up, her back tight, hips lifted from the bed. She sobbed as pleasure, pain, fear and hunger ripped through her body. Waves hit her, one on top of the other, as his finger caressed her inner walls. She couldn't stop it. She had no control over it – he set the pace, not her. Her body was no longer hers, but a plaything under his command.

No, I'm not like that. I'm not submissive. She tried to move, to regain control, but the grip on her hips prevented her from moving and that only added to the pressure in her body, the delight that played through her core.

'I can't do this.' She pressed her hands against his shoulders and pushed away from him. 'God. I don't know what's going on. I need this and I can't do it.'

'What?' He looked up at her and rested on one arm.

'I'm not – not submissive.'

'Aren't you? Funny, it looks like you are from here.' He shook his head and moved back up along the length of her body, grasping her wrists and pinning them to the bed.

'What?' Claire cried out, struggling beneath his grip.

'Your lips say one thing but your body says another, so let's put that to the test.'

'You're insane.'

'No, I'm determined.' He eased himself between her thighs, the head of his cock nudging against her lower lips. 'Your body likes this. The heat coming from this sweet pussy of yours tells me how much you enjoy being held down. You're not screaming for help. You know they'd be able to hear you, and you're not threatening to call the cops . . .'

'I – I don't know.'

'Too scared to test the limits?'

'No.'

'Then let it happen. I'm not going to hurt you, unless you like that sort of thing. And maybe you do. I can see the doubt, the hunger and the confusion in your eyes.'

Confusion didn't even begin to describe it. Was this why she'd been so drawn to him? *No, I'm not submissive! It's just not possible. I'm in control of my life!*

'Any words of protest? No, I didn't think so.'

I can't let this happen! 'Mike,' she murmured, unsure what she wanted him to do.

He moved her wrists to one hand, holding them against the bedding as he reached for something. She barely knew what was going on until he fastened a set of simple leather cuffs around her wrists. 'Better, much better.'

'How did they get there?'

'I've always kept cuffs on the bed.' He grinned. 'Just in case.'

'You – you've done this before?'

'Not with customers from the bar, but you could say I've had more than one woman bound and helpless on my bed.' He leaned down and claimed her lips, parting them beneath the play of his tongue. She struggled to control the kiss. It didn't work. No matter how she tried to take control of the kiss he conquered her, turning her sensual attack aside and reclaiming her.

Her breath hitched in the back of her throat. *Fight it*. Why? *Because I'm not submissive*. If that was true why was his kiss having such an effect on her? The cuffs? The feel of his body pressed against hers. *Just – it's nothing more than a new experience, that's all*.

He pulled away from the kiss, reached down to the left of the bed and brought up a scarf. 'Now, your sight.'

'What?'

'Trust me.'

Trust a stranger she'd picked up from the bar? *Like I have any choice right now?* No, she didn't. She was bound. About to be blindfolded. Helpless on his bed and – *and I love it*. Mike tied the scarf over her eyes, stealing her sight. She tensed, hissing through her teeth.

'Relax,' he murmured.

'I am relaxed.'

'Sure, that's why you hissed at me.'

'I just – sorry.' What did he expect? She hadn't done this before. Hell, she'd never even thought about doing this.

'Shhh.' He brushed a light kiss against her lips.

They tingled. His kiss, even after being bound, her sight stolen, still affected her. She whimpered into it, parting her lips fully. God, she wanted more. Needed more from him.

He shifted away now that she was bound and helpless, tracing his fingertips down over her breasts, circling her nipples before he left her alone on the bed.

'What are you doing?'

'You'll find out.' His voice was some distance from the bed, his steps barely audible.

Claire frowned and listened, wondering what he was up to. Something opened, a door, not in the room. Out in the kitchen? What the hell did he need from out there? Claire sucked on her bottom lip, chewing it slowly. How long was he going to be? God, she didn't like waiting like this. It didn't make sense. She had other things to do with her time.

Like what?

Find another man to sport with? One that wouldn't tie her to the bed?

And just what's wrong with being tied to the bed? Other than the fact that it went against everything she thought she was, nothing at all.

'You look uncomfortable there. Something wrong?' His voice was little more than a low purr.

'No, just – I'm – I was wondering where you'd gone.'

'Oh, I think you know where.'

She frowned and then tensed as she felt something cold and wet drip onto her breasts. Claire shivered, her nipples tight and hard. She hissed between her teeth. Hunger flared through her being as she tried to fight what he was doing to her. Ice. Cold, melting ice that dripped onto her breasts and left her shivering and waiting for the next touch.

'Yes, you like that, don't you?'

'No. Yes. God, I don't know,' she whimpered, her thighs tight, a deep roll claiming her hips as she tried to hold onto her reactions instead of letting him control her. Another drop hit and clung to her left nipple. 'Please don't.'

'Please don't what? Stop? Start? Tell me what you want, Claire. Or don't you even know right now?' He traced the edge of the ice cube over her breast, outlining it. Then he leaned down and closed his lips on a ripe nipple. She gasped and arched her back. Cold. Warmth. The two combined to tease her senses. Her belly rippled and tightened, only to ripple again.

'Yes, you like that, don't you? I can see it, smell it in the air, the way you need it, want it, crave it, and so much more.' His voice was little more than a low whisper as he traced the melting ice cube further down her body. 'You want to deny it. But I saw it in you even when you walked into the bar the first time. You're submissive. All you needed was a man to show you the way. Or perhaps a woman.'

'I'm not bisexual.'

'You said you weren't submissive either.' He chuckled and dipped the ice cube between her thighs, tracing it over her clit.

She arched up, crying out in pain and pleasure combined. 'God!'

'No, I'm not one of those, not yet at least.' His deep laugh filled the air. 'But I might be in time, at least in some small way. I'll make you cry out in delight before the end of this. You'll call out for me. You'll need me. Then you'll come. You'll come so hard and long that you'll lose track of who and what you are.

'No, what I have to do is show you how to deal with this. You're mine for the evening. For as long as you're bound to my bed. And I'm going to enjoy it. You will too, just as long as you let your walls down. It's time to see the real you.'

The real her? What the hell was he talking about?

Thought fled as he pushed the ice cube fully between her thighs. The cold ice melted over her body, over her clit, the pain of it merging with the pleasure of his touch as he slipped one finger between her lower lips. 'God, what are you doing to me?'

'I think you know.'

Yes! How could she not know with the way her body was reacting? She groaned as each new touch brought a wave of pleasure through her body. She sobbed, her hands clenching into hard fists. Her back arched tight. 'I – I can't go through this, I won't be able to go through this.'

'Yes, you will. You've got no choice but to go through it. Remember that.' He nibbled his way along one breast, then down over her belly towards her mound, not quite touching it with his lips. 'You're mine.'

'No, I'm – it's just one night.'

'And that's all I need.'

She swallowed hard and tried to force her thoughts into some semblance of order. His fingers danced between her thighs. Touching her clit. Teasing her. She sobbed, her hips pressing forwards. Lifting. Needing him. Needing something more than just his fingers and the cool remains of the sliver of ice.

'That's it. Move for me. Lift yourself into my touch. You need it.'

Pressure built between her thighs. Pleasure cascaded through her senses, threatening to spill her out of control. 'Don't. I can't!'

'Yes, you can and you will. I'm not going to give you a choice.' His fingers slid over her clit, teasing her, tormenting her until she lost the ability to do anything but sob, moan and lift into his touch. 'That's it, move for me. Move for me and let it happen.'

Her vision blurred, her breath hitching in the back of her throat. Pressure claimed her sex. Her lower lips throbbed, her clit burning. She couldn't stop what was happening. She didn't want to stop it.

Her heels pressed against the bedding.

'Please!'

'Come for me. Come for me now!'

'I can't!' She needed something more. Something she didn't want to admit to. Not here. Not now.

'Tell me why.'

'No!'

'Do it!'

'Fuck me. God, please, fuck me!' The words tore from her mouth before she could stop them.

He moved before she had the chance to regret her words. His thick cock slid easily into her clenching pussy, filling her, stretching her walls until she sobbed in delight. His balls slapped against her body. Slick, hungry sounds filled the air. Nothing else mattered beyond the feel of his cock within her tight, heated pussy.

He thrust into her, slamming her body against the bed. The springs creaked beneath them, her hips lifting to meet each demanding, sensual slam into her body until she no longer knew where he ended and she began.

'Come!' The order was clear as it cut through the fog of her arousal.

What other choice did she have? She screamed, her body tight, wracked by pleasure, pain, fear and need all rolled into one. Lights danced across her vision. She tried to hold back, but her body wouldn't let her. It hit in waves. Delicious, sensual, frightening waves of hunger and pleasure, pressure that ripped through her being until she collapsed on the bed in a sobbing, shaking heap, barely even aware of Mike's roar of delight.

Yes, just one night, that's all she'd wanted, but who said the night had to end now?

All for One
Rhiannon Leith

What was it about weddings and 'Dancing Queen'?

It had gotten to the stage where as soon as Megan heard those first *ahs* she fled for the door, with some *ahs* of a very different tone ringing through her head. In her midnight-blue taffeta gown she swept out onto the hotel veranda while the evening took off inside. She breathed a sigh of relief that another round of bridesmaid's duties could be struck off the list.

Always the bridesmaid, and all that. Maybe she should consider it as a professional option. It would be a break from the office.

The thought of work made that part of her mind pop back into life, like the genie from the bottle. Although work didn't grant many wishes. It paid the bills, bought her a comfortable life, apartment and car, and a wardrobe out of *Sex and the City*. But did that make up for a lot of very long, lonely hours? Megan let out a sigh. Perhaps she should be inside celebrating. But the thought of the Parker House project file sitting on her desk overshadowed the evening.

She couldn't really leave this early. Not as a bridesmaid. It wasn't fair on Sally.

A low chuckle rippled over the bare skin of her back, toying with the sensitive hairs which had come loose at the top of her neck.

'You're not going to do a Cinderella, are you, Meg?' asked Richard. He leaned against the wall, a drink in one hand, his collar unbuttoned.

'Richard?' She gave a squawk of surprise as she saw her old college friend. 'My God! How are you? Have you just got here?'

Richard laughed as he hugged her. His fingertips lingered against her shoulder blades before he released her. Megan's body jerked in response to his touch and she flushed. 'Just an evening invite for me. Then again, I haven't seen them since college so fair's fair.'

'I haven't seen *you* since college. Where have you been? Wait: are Blake and Daniel with you?'

She tried to look back into the room, seeking out the two other familiar faces from their college years. Richard, Blake and Daniel had always been together. The three musketeers, she used to call them. Damn, she had done everything with them, same courses, same social clubs. Everything except the obvious. But, to be honest, the three of them came as a unit. She had loved them all. How could she ever have picked just one?

'I don't think the blushing bride wanted to blush quite as much as she would if Blake turned up. He might give the groom some tips.'

Megan's disappointment was shot through with mirth. She had forgotten about Blake's fling with Sally. Then again, Blake had 'flung' just about every girl in their year, not to mention the years on either side. Some of the boys too, so rumour would have it. 'How is he?'

'The charm is still very much intact. Daniel is running a rare book shop.'

'And you?'

He had changed over the ten years. No surprise there. So had she, no longer the pushover she had been. She wouldn't have survived in business if she'd stayed that way.

Richard had filled out, grown into himself perhaps. The same good looks carried a different tone now, more masculine. His blue eyes exuded control and practicality, command, such a bright blue that she wanted to breathe a little faster. Travelling – his only long-term goal on leaving college – had obviously suited him. Somewhere inside her, something was unwinding, something unexpected.

'As you'd expect, I suppose. Dad died.'

'Oh, I'm sorry!' She hadn't expected that. Not at all. 'Recent-ly?'

'Five years ago. I've been running the estate since then. You should come and visit.'

Megan remembered the manor house which Richard called home and couldn't help but smile. The thought of a lazy weekend there was certainly tempting. But ... how could she afford the time away? She sighed again. 'I'd love to but –'

'Great,' he said, not allowing her to finish. 'What about the Bank Holiday weekend? If you want, I can see what Blake and Daniel are up to.'

She squirmed. 'I have a lot of work to ...' Her voice failed her as Richard reached out and tucked a lock of her hair behind her ear, his touch delicate as a butterfly. His eyes trapped hers, nothing like as harmless as they used to be. Heat warmed their depths and that same heat welled in the base of her stomach. To her surprise, Megan's core melted and a jab of desire left her breathless.

'Come,' he said. 'It would be so good to catch up. And they would love to see you again.'

The others ... the others would be there as well. Her breathing eased a little and she shifted, embarrassed. 'Well, why not? You're right. It would be like old times, a weekend with the three musketeers.'

Richard lifted his glass to her in a toast. 'All for one,' he murmured.

* * *

Megan was late leaving the office. It was almost eight when her phone rang. Her PA sounded flustered. Meg began to smile, because he was normally unflappable, but his words made her breath stop in her throat.

'There's a gentleman here to pick you up. Blake Regan.'

'I'll be out in a minute.' She hung up and stared at her reflection in the monitor, amazed at the schoolgirl reaction that had seized her. Her stomach flipped and she swallowed hard.

A cough brought her head up sharply. Blake stood in the doorway, glowering at her.

'Aren't you meant to be driving down to Richard's?' His voice sounded deeper than she remembered. He'd let his black hair grow long, and it curled thickly against his broad shoulders. The smile had never looked so wicked. 'I've come to carry you off, so shut down the laptop, there's a good girl.'

She laughed to hide her irritation. 'I'm really behind.'

But Blake didn't back down. 'You certainly are. Now are you coming with me, or am I going to have to tip you over my shoulder and carry you out?'

Only Blake could have said it to her. Uncertainly, she lifted her gaze to meet his. 'It's good to see you too.' She kept her tone stiff and formal, giving him the withering look that made office juniors shrink in on themselves and seek ways of escape.

Blake cocked his head to one side and the grin turned rakish. 'This is new. I like this. So am I kidnapping you, Madam CEO, or are you going to come quietly?'

Megan threw up her hands. 'All right. I surrender,' she laughed. 'Whatever you want?'

'That's the general idea, love.' Blake pulled her out of her chair into an embrace, kissing her cheek with surprisingly soft lips. She pulled back awkwardly, surprised. Blake had never shown any interest in her in college.

'My . . . my bag's in my car.' Her cheek burned where he had kissed her, and she fancied she could still feel phantom lips brushing against her there.

'Good,' he said. 'We'll pick it up on the way. I'm driving.'

Megan dozed off in the car. It had been so long since she had sat with nothing to do and Blake, for some reason, was none too talkative on the long drive through the dark countryside. They chatted idly at first, his old playfulness returning as soon as he got his own way. He made a good living as an alternative therapist, massage and aromatherapy, which made her smile. His answering grin turned wickeder than ever.

Megan woke when the car slowed, crunching across gravel. Opening her eyes, she found Blake watching her, a peculiar expression shadowing his face.

'We're here, Sleeping Beauty. Need a moment?'

Megan discovered her neatly pinned hair undone and the jacket of her business suit unbuttoned. She glanced suspiciously at Blake as she slipped the button back into place and tried to tidy herself up. Megan ran her fingers through her chestnut hair, smoothing it back from her face, and then checked her watch. It was after ten.

Her stomach rumbled. There had been a fairly insipid sandwich around lunchtime but that was hours ago. A lot of hours ago.

'Hungry?' Blake chuckled. 'Come on, Meg. Richard was expecting you for dinner. Some of it might not be ruined. You were never this difficult to distract in college. When did you lose your sense of adventure?'

'Me?'

When had she *had* a sense of adventure?

She sat in the bubble of light of the car's interior, while Blake crunched around the car to open her door. He took her hand, helping her out, holding on longer than strictly necessary. 'Yes. You.'

* * *

Daniel greeted Megan at the door and her heart leaped with delight just to see him. They'd kept in contact at first, but soon it was just emails at Christmas, and then nothing. He knew how she had struggled in the early years. She saw that in his eyes.

'It's been too long, Meg.' He whirled her around in strong arms. 'You look amazing. You've haven't changed a bit.' Behind her, Blake gave a snort of laughter. Nothing dimmed his cynicism. 'Ignore him.' Daniel drew her into the hall, studying her in the light. 'You look tired. Have you been burning the candle at both ends?'

His remonstration made her feel ashamed. She had thrown herself into her work, but then again what else could she do? A couple of disastrous relationships had persuaded her that no man could embody everything she was looking for. She was good at her job, damned good. It didn't seem fair that she'd had to work three times as hard as everyone else to be considered an equal.

She almost sagged right there where she stood. Daniel saw right through her, just as Blake had been unimpressed by her business persona. They knew her better than anyone in her life today. They weren't out to charm the boss, or make a profit. Or worse. She missed their company so much, her musketeers. Just being with them was like awakening from a bad dream. Shame she felt so tired.

Daniel's hands on her upper arms were both a comfort and a strength. Always the most perceptive of the three, his rich brown eyes soothed her heart.

'Food first, I think. Then a bath and a good night's sleep.' Blake growled something from behind them, but Daniel – gentle caring Daniel – cast him a sharp glare and to her amazement Blake retreated. 'We have the whole weekend together.' He slipped his arm around her shoulders and steered her further into the house.

* * *

The three men had not changed much, Megan decided, but their characters had become more deeply ingrained in the years since she had seen them last.

Richard poured her wine and pressed the glass into her hand. 'I'm so glad you decided to come.'

Megan rolled her eyes. 'You didn't give me a lot of choice, sending the muscle.' She glared at Blake. 'If you say as much as a word, Blake . . .'

A thousand corny retorts sparkled in his eyes, but he pressed his lips together. Megan fought back a laugh. It was hard not to forgive Blake anything when he looked at her like that.

Daniel placed an omelette in front of her, rich and fragrant, filled with melted cheese.

Megan sighed. 'Remember these on Sunday mornings?'

'I remember the hangovers,' said Blake.

Richard poured more wine. 'I remember *your* hangovers.'

They watched her eat, chatting about old times, and Megan felt the regret of the time she had missed with them fading to a memory as the pleasure of being with them again grew. Nevertheless, as she finished her dinner, she found herself yawning.

Richard ruffled her hair. 'It's been a long time since you just had fun, hasn't it? Let's get you to bed, Meg. We can all catch up tomorrow.'

'I don't tend to sleep this early. Night owl, you know?'

'I think I can do something about that,' Blake rumbled, getting to his feet. Megan's heart jerked up inside her, and pounded at her ribs. An ache burst back into life inside her, a raw need that had never been fulfilled. She glanced from Blake to Richard and then to Daniel.

'Whatever are you thinking, Megan?' Richard teased, his words undercut by a deeper affection than she remembered from all those years ago. 'Come on, girl. Have your bath and then Blake'll give you a massage that will make you sleep like a baby. Anyone would think we'd suggested an orgy.'

The bath felt divine, the perfect temperature mingled with scented oils. Used to the clinical neatness of her en-suite shower at home, Megan luxuriated in the claw-footed tub and closed her eyes until a knock sounded at the door.

'I'm setting up out here. Just come in when you're ready,' said Blake.

Seriously, a massage before bed? What were they up to? All this pampering was liable to go to her head. She sank back in the water, watching it lap the underside of her breasts. She sank lower, letting the warm water creep up around her nipples and work its insidious fingers between her legs.

'How did you end up doing massage?' she called out.

Blake laughed, the same slightly dirty, knowing laugh she remembered of old when she asked about a conquest or one of his affairs. 'It came in handy. Turns out I have a knack.'

'I bet you do,' she murmured to herself and ran splayed fingers over her stomach. Her skin had grown sensitive in the water. She shivered beneath her own touch.

She pulled on a baggy nightshirt before going out to face Blake. It wasn't stylish. It wasn't anything, but it covered her completely and that seemed important right now.

Blake stood over the bed. He didn't even look at her. 'You'll need to take that off and lie down.' She paused, uncomfortable with his brisk attitude, and he looked up. A smile tugged at the corners of his lips, not the sex smile she expected, but one of amusement and affection. 'Don't worry. Trust me.'

'A lot of women have fallen for that line, Blake,' she told him, trying to keep her tone light and wondering where the nervous edge had come from.

'And not one of them has regretted it,' he assured her. He spread a towel out on the bed and lifted another so he could cover her when she lay down. 'Come on, love. It's me. I promise.'

'Promise what?'

He laughed, a deep chuckle. 'I promise not to do anything you don't want. What's wrong? Chicken?'

She did trust him, despite the ten years and his un-diminished reputation. With a dramatic sigh, more for his benefit than hers, she pulled off the T-shirt and lay down. True to his word, his strong hands smoothed fragrant oils over her skin, working out the knots of tension in her shoulders and neck. Megan closed her eyes.

'You still have the most beautiful skin tone I've ever seen,' he murmured. He had told her that, hadn't he? Years ago. Not long after they first met. She should have snapped back with some witty retort about his having seen enough bare flesh to be a good judge, but she didn't. His hands worked their magic, soothing her towards much-needed sleep. He brushed his fingertips in circles at the small of her back, tracing the spine lower, but not so low that she tensed.

Deep inside her, another voice – not her own, surely – gave a groan of dismay when he moved back. Her pulse pounded in her groin and she squeezed her thighs together to quell the rising heat. Blake took one of her feet in his strong grip and worked his fingers into the arch. Breath sighed from Megan's lungs and the tension ebbed. He took a little longer on the other foot. 'You haven't been taking care of yourself, Meg,' he chided. 'Long hours, hunched over a desk. We'll have to see about that.'

Too tired to argue, she drifted on the scented breeze while he manipulated her muscles, forcing her to succumb to the rest she needed.

She almost went to sleep lying there. Though she didn't open her eyes, she could hear Blake packing up. And the door, opening slowly, a cooler breeze coming from the corridor outside.

'Is she asleep?' asked Daniel in a whisper. Blake must have nodded, for he gave no verbal reply. 'You OK?' A grunt this time. And then . . .

She heard the sound of two bodies coming together, the soft thud as one pulled the other hard against him. And a kiss. There was no mistaking the sound of their kiss. She opened her eyes a crack to see Blake holding Daniel, their mouths moving together. Daniel gripped Blake's shoulders, but to pull him closer rather than push him away, and Blake, always the stronger, ran his oil-scented hands up Daniel's torso, pulling the shirt out of his waistband so they could slip underneath.

Daniel broke the kiss, gasping for breath. 'Wait. If she wakes up . . .'

Blake glanced towards her, the hunger in his eyes disconcerting. Megan rolled as if in sleep, hiding her face from him, and fought to keep her breath even. 'All right. But you owe me, Dan. Remember that.'

'I do.' The new tone in Daniel's voice startled her. Completely submissive. 'Richard has it all planned, Blake. Let's not fuck it up by . . .'

'Fucking?' Blake laughed, that old cynicism weakened by the loss in his voice, the need. 'We should never have let her go in the first place. Richard's right. You should have seen her in that office. Like another woman. Not our Meg.'

Our Meg. She waited until they had left before rolling onto her back to gaze at the ceiling. Is that what they thought of her? As theirs? A possession? And what did Richard have 'all planned'?

She sat up, reaching for the T-shirt. The spell of the evening wore off suddenly. They were up to something. None of this was a coincidence. They weren't just planning a fun weekend of reminiscences for old times' sake. They wanted something from her. Suspicion prickled her conscience and she dug out her phone, staring at the screen. If she rang anyone about this, she wasn't sure she wanted the answers she might get. They were her friends. She wanted that friendship back. And yet ... if this was a scam, if they were planning something ...

Megan got the call she expected the following afternoon. Expected and dreaded because she knew it would lead to a showdown. And just for a little while, she had been able to forget about reality, forget about the world where people were only interested in the money, where they only looked out for themselves.

She woke long after breakfast and decided on a floral sundress a world away from her normal attire. Past noon. She hadn't slept so late in years. It felt positively decadent, or would have done if the information she had unearthed last night hadn't popped up to mock her whenever she started to unwind.

'Fancy a walk?' asked Richard when she appeared downstairs. Before she knew it, they were all wandering through the old walled garden of the manor house and down to the edge of the lake.

After graduation they had come here, Richard's father happy to let them party through the night and into the next day. She remembered lying here, feeling the grass tickle her bare feet when she kicked off the high heels. Richard had passed her the champagne bottle. And Blake had said something which made her laugh. She'd nearly drenched herself in the stuff. Daniel had helped her wipe it up and they had known it was the last time they would be together like that. She remembered the moon on the water, the fizz of bubbles on her skin, the undercurrent of pleasure, of love. It was the first time she had felt regret, knowing that she wanted each of them, and had never done anything about it.

As she sat in the long grass, the sun warmed her skin but couldn't penetrate the dread that filled her.

'What's wrong?' Daniel asked, rubbing her back gently, but she shook her head, staring at the water. 'You can tell us, you know.'

'You used to tell us everything.' Blake picked a long blade of grass and used it to tickle her ankle. She smiled thinly and moved out of his reach.

Richard just watched her, his eyes hooded. Megan refused to meet his gaze.

The jangling ring tone jolted her out of her reverie. 'I have to ring the office back,' she told them. She expected a flash of guilt, or interest, but Richard gave no reaction. 'Alone, guys. It's confidential.'

Blake made a face, but finally Richard nodded. 'We'll be in the library. I'll fix some afternoon drinks, OK? Come up when you're ready.'

She waited until they had walked away then flicked the phone open to hit redial. 'It's me.'

'You were right,' said Derek, the company lawyer. 'He's a shareholder. Not a major one, but he's involved.'

And the cold shell snapped shut around her heart. 'Thanks. Leave it with me, OK?'

'Do you want me to tell the board?'

'No, I'll deal with it.'

She watched the sun glinting off the water. This had been her favourite place, her favourite memory of the three of them together.

And Richard had brought her back here, made her remember it and hope, so he could manipulate a business deal.

Sudden anger burned inside her. More than anger. Rage. How dare he use her? How dare he use their past? And the other two had to be in on it, from what she had heard last night. The image flared back into her mind: Blake and Daniel, locked together, a kiss that was partly a wrestling match. The most erotic thing she could ever recall seeing. Anger and desire inflamed each other.

She shook the sensations rippling through her body aside. She didn't have time for this. Marching back across the lawn, she planned her next move. She would pack her things and head back to town. There was nothing for her here, not now.

In the window of the library, Richard watched her, his arms folded across his chest, a proprietary stance, a commanding gaze.

Right, Mr Lord of the Manor, she glared back and picked up her pace, *just wait until I tell you a thing or two.*

Megan burst into the library to find Richard pouring wine into delicate crystal glasses. Daniel sat by the fireplace, flicking through some huge leather-bound tome that might have outdated the house. And Blake lay across a chaise-longue, his eyes closed, like a great cat, not quite asleep. He looked up lazily at her dramatic entrance.

'Bad news?'

'Shut up, Blake,' she snapped, heading for Richard as if she were going to kiss him or punch him. And in that moment she didn't know which she wanted more. Instead, she slapped his face as hard as she could and shoved him back with her other hand. It felt like pushing against stone. 'Were you going to tell me? How were you going to ask? Just get me to fix a few figures? Just make sure that your shares didn't dip?'

Richard moved faster than she had imagined he could, grabbing her wrists and holding her back from him. 'What the hell are you talking about?'

'I have to spell it out for you, do I? Parker House. My project. You've done all this to manipulate me so you'll either profit from Parker House or ruin my company, haven't you?'

He looked bewildered, but he didn't let go of her wrists. 'I don't even know what Parker House is. Dad had shares in hundreds of companies, Megan. I have an accountant who keeps track of that.'

'Sure. Then why I am here? Why after ten years do you waltz back into my life, the three of you?'

'You really don't know?' asked Daniel. He closed the book and got slowly to his feet. 'Meg . . .' Her name fell so softly from his sensuous mouth that she flinched. She wanted to look at him, but Richard held her wrists tightly, refusing to let her go.

She tried to pull away, anger pulsing inside her, but his grip tightened, which just made it worse. Then he kissed her.

Not a chaste brush of lips, not a fraternal peck. Richard pulled her hard against his body and kissed her the way she had watched the other two kiss last night, his mouth devouring her, churning a rising current of need she didn't want to acknowledge, couldn't afford to acknowledge. She squirmed, trying to get away from him, trying to get closer. Wanting him. Wanting to kiss him, wanting to slap him again. Just wanting him.

Richard let go and her legs almost went beneath her. She stumbled back and Blake caught her against his broad chest. Her body heaved for breath. She blinked, trying to clear her head.

'And now do you know?' Richard asked.

'Wh– what?'

Blake steered her back to the chair Daniel had vacated. It was still warm from his body, cradling her as she sank into it. But the shock wasn't over. Blake's hands closed on her shoulders, caressing the knotted muscles, brushing against the most sensitive areas and threatening to make her brain shut down entirely. Daniel knelt at her feet, his fingertips playing with the sensitive skin of her wrist. They gathered around her, watching her.

Richard approached her. Megan sat like a startled rabbit in the headlights of his suggestion. Their suggestion. On either side of her, Daniel and Blake didn't move. They watched her, a new, hungry glint in their eyes. Dark eyes, always her weakness. Blake's darker than Daniel's – Americano coffee to Ecuadorian chocolate – with Richard's eyes a startling blue in comparison. Not one of the three had ever expressed an interest in her before this moment. Had they? She couldn't remember. Little side comments and half-jokes. Not seriously.

Richard stopped, towering over her. 'We agreed back then that if any one of us took it further with you, Meg, it wasn't fair on the other two. And we had no wish to compete.'

'No wish to . . .' she echoed, swallowing hard.

'Not at the expense of our friendships. And yours.' A somewhat mischievous twinkle entered Richard's eyes. 'Of course, we hadn't imagined the alternatives then. Life has . . . educated us all in ways we didn't expect.'

Megan's head lurched, bewildered by the closeness of three men she had fanatisised about for years. About all three of them.

But together?

Her stomach knotted in on itself. At the same time she felt a slow insistent warmth begin between her thighs, thrumming in time to her heartbeat and swelling with every breath. Liquid heat pooled in the core of her being.

'I'm not sure I . . . I don't really . . .'

'Understand?' Richard's laugh was deep and affectionate. It vibrated through her and made the growing ache even worse. 'I beg to differ, Meg. I think you do.'

'And it scares you,' Blake growled. Megan closed her eyes so tightly that lights sparkled behind her lids. *He* scared her. Always had, in some deep dark place. And that place, that secret place, longed for him.

Her pulse jumped beneath his caress. Blake trailed a fingertip along her jugular vein and her breath shuddered.

'We have wanted only you,' said Daniel, and brought her other hand to his lips. He kissed the centre of her palm. 'But you would never have picked just one of us, Meg. Would you?'

She shook her head, still too bewildered to form words.

'You gave me the idea,' Richard said. He leaned back against the table, gripping the edge.

'Me?' It was hard to think with Blake's wickedly dexterous hands on either side of her neck, and Daniel's lips pressed to her palm, his warm breath playing on her sensitive skin.

'It was that night after graduation, down by the lake, remember? You said you wished you had found just one man, one person to love for the rest of your life. I said you were a bit young to have given up on love.'

'I remember. But I didn't mean ...'

'You had not given up on love. I know that. I thought I could persuade you, make you see that I loved you, but I was just a boy, just a fool. I wanted you to myself, didn't I? And you loved them too.'

Yes. She couldn't get the word to come out. Daniel's hand slid up her calf. Testing, teasing. Daniel was always able to make her smile. Now he made her gasp.

'We would never harm you,' he said. 'You know that.'

And she did. She had always known that. None of them would ever harm or allow harm to come to her. Her protectors, her guardian angels.

Daniel's fingertips caressed the soft skin of her thigh. He looked up into her face, his eyes asking permission in a way Blake or Richard never would. But Daniel had neither Blake's domineering presence nor Richard's self-assured alpha nature.

So he asked, where the other two would not.

Megan's body answered for her and she nodded, closing her eyes.

Daniel shifted position, though his hand still stroked her thigh. He knelt between her legs and drew her to the edge of the seat. He pushed her knees out to either side and pushed her skirt up to bunch in her lap.

Megan trembled. 'Wait, I ...' It was too fast, too much.

Blake's hands covered her eyes. 'Better?'

She opened her mouth to answer, but Daniel's fingers skirted the edge of her panties, pushing them aside so one could edge inside her. Wet and more than ready, her body welcomed him. A groan escaped her lips.

Blake lifted his hands and she found herself looking up at him, just for an instant. 'Let go, Meg,' he told her. 'Trust me.'

'I do,' she tried to reply, but when Daniel pressed his tongue to her clit, she wasn't sure what words she formed. Fingers and mouth joined together in a tortuous combination and she rocked her hips forwards.

'Here,' said Richard. He was holding a scarf, a length of white silk, and Blake took it reverently. Meg gripped the arms of the chair, her nails digging into the leather.

Blake drew the makeshift blindfold over her eyes and the world slid away from the conscious, the rational, to a world of questing hands, of lips and tongues. Blake kissed her, cradling her head in his hands. Daniel grew more insistent, thrusting his fingers deep inside her, curling against the most sensitive spot and caressing her clit until her body began to quake.

'That's it, Meg,' Blake whispered against her lips.

Richard's hands joined their worship of her body, opening the bodice of the dress. His mouth closed on her right breast, the pressure he exerted on her nipple the final connection she needed before she came, crying out for them, her voice muffled by Blake's mouth.

She shivered as they stroked her body, casting aside clothes. Naked between them, Megan reached out, pulling one after the other to her, revelling in the feel of their hands, their kisses, the trail a tongue left down her spine, the sensation of being held and filled, and loved. Yes, this was what it meant to be loved.

Someone lifted her, Richard, she guessed, although she could not be entirely sure. It felt like Richard. He cradled her in strong arms and brought her to the chaise-longue, stretching her out on its lush velvet upholstery, raising her arms above her head and holding them there while two mouths claimed her breasts, each one determined and expert.

'Tell me it feels good,' Richard murmured.

'Yes,' she gasped. 'Oh yes.'

They rolled her this way and that, into whatever position would give them the access they desired. She lost track of the number of times the white-hot bliss of orgasm spiked through her, of joy in their voices matching hers. Time bled away in ecstasy.

Warm oil pooled in the small of her back. Blake ran his hands down her, over the globes of her ass, and the oil followed as he parted the cheeks, ran his fingertips over the rose of her anus. He pushed against it, just a fingertip, pressing resolutely until she admitted it, and the oil came too. It drizzled down the gap, over the sensitive skin, and Blake began to work it deep inside her, slow and insistent, patient. Megan arched her body, pressing her aching clit against the chaise-longue, and Daniel's mouth captured hers, his tongue meeting her demands.

Satisfied that she was ready, Blake lifted her hips up, holding her on her knees. She heard the sound of a condom wrapper tearing and Daniel settled himself on the chaise-longue beneath her parted legs, taking her hips and drawing her down. Blake guided them and Daniel's cock slid inside her. So slowly it was torture, he filled her, stretching her. On all fours above him, her hair trailed across his chest and Daniel shivered, deep inside her. Blake climbed up behind her, reaching around to toy with her clit while his cock nudged her slick anus. Daniel thrust gently, then withdrew, holding himself just inside her, poised. Richard's mouth claimed hers at the same moment that Blake's cock pressed inside her, forcing its way past the tight sphincter and deep inside.

Megan sucked in breath after breath, and Blake held himself still. She wished she could see him now and as if in answer to her thought, Richard tossed the blindfold aside. Her arms shook with the effort of holding herself up and in mute response Daniel seized her, taking control. He held himself rigid, still, waiting. Her eyes met Richard's, their blue dark with triumph.

Daniel thrust into her, as deep as Blake. She could feel both of them inside her, filling her beyond endurance. She sank her fingernails into Daniel's skin and he jerked, his eyes fluttering with pleasure and pain combined.

But something was missing. Something vital.

She looked for Richard. He stood at the end of the chaise-longue and smiled.

She marshalled words, the concentrated effort almost proving her undoing. 'You can't just watch. Much as you seem to enjoy it.'

'Let me savour the moment.'

'No, Richard. Now.'

She parted her lips, licking them. Richard stepped obediently closer and Megan claimed his cock, taking him deep in her mouth, her tongue caressing him, swallowing him down. He steadied himself against the chaise-longue as Blake and Daniel began to thrust in earnest.

Megan writhed between them. She felt Blake's tongue on her neck while his hands hugged her hips, buffering her against Daniel's thrusts. Daniel filled his hands with her breasts, teasing the hardened nipples, raising them to peaks. And Richard's hands came up to frame her face, fingertips brushing the sensitive skin of her jaw while she swallowed him down, unable to let him escape her. She would not let any of them escape her again. She had lost them through time, neglect and all those other petty reasons true love slips away. She had lost herself without them. Never again. She seized all they had to offer with relish. Within the confines of their love, lost between their moving bodies, Megan sank into a new world completely fulfilled for the first time in ten years. The one man she'd always wanted didn't exist, because he was three. Three aspects making one perfect whole. And she should have known that ten years ago when she called them her musketeers. All for one, and one for all.

It's Got to Be Perfect
Portia Da Costa

How to Seduce Yourself! Indulge in a Night of Total Fantasy with your Dream Guy!

Yeah, right. Like that would work.

But then again, what else was there to do? Slob on the settee in her sweats, watching reality TV?

Might as well do the self-indulgence thing, and not let the fact that she'd just been dumped bring her down.

Right. First things first. A good old-fashioned long, luxuriating perfumed bath.

Bit of a cliché, but who cared, it was still sexy.

Lucy tipped her best bottle of bath essence under the hot tap and kept it tipped. So what if she used the whole lot? It was her bath essence and her money she'd spent on it.

Dense white bubbles surged up immediately, and the surface of the tub looked as if a washing-up-liquid tanker had been dumped into a cyclone. The pungent scent of roses and exotic spices surged up too, a wall of fragrance that made her feel light-headed.

Tonight was a private festival of indulgence. Excess was everything. No scrimping. No half-measures. No holding back.

In the words of the advertisement, she was worth it.

Shucking off her old dressing gown, she bundled it into the cupboard out of sight, out of mind. No threadbare velour with cocoa stains tonight!

Naked, she padded over to the mirror to check out her bod.

Not perfect, but not bad either. Much better than that slag Linda. Simon had no taste. The man was a moron and Lucy didn't know why she'd ever even bothered with him.

That 'summer tan' body lotion was really working for her now, and – joy of joys – she'd lost a few pounds. None of which had gone from her breasts, thank God. There was still a couple of nice handfuls there, and she was going to fantasise about a worthwhile guy fondling them tonight. Some delicious hunk cupping and squeezing and caressing her, his hands tanned and strong, not pasty and slightly hairy like Simon's.

Mm ... who to choose?

Not too much of a debate, really. She had a huge crush on the big, gorgeous detective guy from her favourite cop show.

Right, Mr Tall and Yummy Detective ... it's your lucky night, you're my Dream Guy of Total Perfect Fantasy!

And he did have lovely hands. Large, elegant, and prone to evocative gestures. She could well imagine fingertips like that being accurate and sensitive. Perfect for her needs. Hugging herself, she imagined them gliding all over her body, floating over her belly, into the creases of her groin, and up the insides of her thighs.

Oh yeah ...

Not yet, idiot. It'll be much better if you save it for later.

Bunching her hands to keep from touching herself, she blew her imaginary suitor a kiss, then looked around, ticking items off her erotic nirvana checklist.

Bath, full of hot, silky water, topped with a thick mat of perfumed suds. Tick.

Tea lights arranged around the room in little porcelain holders, each imparting a sexy flickering radiance. Tick.

Wine in the glass cooler on the shelf, within easy reach of the bath. Champagne, the best she could afford, with more in the fridge for later if she wanted to get really wasted but in a classier way than usual. Tick.

A big bottle of her fragrance, silk and buttermilk body lotion, and a very posh moisturiser full of exotic rejuvenators for her face. Tick.

And instead of her hidden dressing gown, a set of La Perla lingerie and a sexy silk wrap. Ivory satin, very tasteful, not red or black like that slapper Linda would wear. Tick.

Soft music played in the background from her little hi-fi. A bit of Mozart. She was partial to Wolfgang Amadeus. She'd dismissed Barry White and Marvin Gaye in favour of the piano, light and floating, also very tasteful.

Time to begin the first stage. Lucy poured herself a glass of champers to get things started, and it fizzed and fluffed in the narrow crystal flute. Her best glassware, of course, not her everyday stuff from Tesco.

Gingerly, because the bath was over-filled, she slid into the water. There was just an inch of clearance between the foam top and the bath rim, so luckily it didn't whoosh over and slop onto the floor. But as she pushed her toes down to the bottom end of the bath, Lucy frowned.

The taps. Bugger. They reminded her . . .

An extraneous, non-perfect, non-romantic, non-erotic, non-self-indulgent thought plopped into her head and sat there like a dollop of mud.

When the hell are you coming to fix the pipe under the sink, you git?

Her landlord had been promising to mend a dripping leak under the kitchen sink for weeks. And weeks. She'd endured several cajoling assurances on the phone that he'd be here 'tomorrow', but so far he and his tools were a no-show.

Bastard! Fuck! Plonker!

And now her mind was filled with that scruffy creep when she should be focusing on her gorgeous detective. Her landlord was a clod, and the most ill-kempt creature she'd ever met. She'd never seen him yet in jeans or T-shirts that weren't streaked with paint or full of holes in dodgy places. He always seemed to be in the midst of some protracted DIY or renovation project or other. And yet he couldn't get his arse up to the flat of a prompt-paying tenant and do a simple plumbing job!

Dickhead!

Reaching for her wine, she closed her eyes and concentrated on the act of drinking. Anything to banish her grungy landlord from her mind and get back to her fantasies.

The wine was superb. Creamy, biscuity, redolent with fruit yet fine and sophisticated.

I should drink this all the time.

Rolling the fabulous fluid over her tongue, Lucy promised herself that even when she wasn't planning a fantasy self-seduction evening, she'd drink more champagne, and other good stuff, and less of the sweet, cheap Italian plonk she tended to swig down in front of the telly.

The sort of thing her landlord would probably bring if he was seducing a lady. Or a 'bird', as he'd probably call her.

No, get out, you! Fuck off! I don't want you in my head!

Swigging down more champagne without respect for its quality, Lucy sneezed as the bubbles went up her nose and the water level rocked dangerously.

But as it settled again, the wine started to have the desired effect. There was a sensation of golden effervescence as if the champagne were actually in her bloodstream and fizzing around her body, banishing all unwanted thoughts and restoring the integrity of her fantasy. Her lover-detective loomed large, sophisticated and refined in the centre of her dreamscape, making her skin tingle beneath the water and electricity flow to her sex and the tips of her breasts.

She drank more bubbly, rocking beneath the foam, aching with need for him.

Her pussy throbbed, and called like a siren to her fingers.

Not yet. Make yourself wait. Wind up the tension a bit.

Setting aside her glass, Lucy moaned. It was useless. She was so turned on. Waiting was agony.

With her eyes closed again, she let her imagination soar.

The door would fly back, and her 'lover' would stand there in the doorway, utterly magnificent. His body was an arc of dominance in his thousand-dollar suit and his tanned skin and his white teeth gleamed as he smiled at her. Dark and sultry, his eyes had the power to see straight through the scented lather to her body.

Ooh, he was magnificent. A prince of charisma. Utterly male. And when he came to her, she was a princess, and he'd treat her like one. Lavishing complete attention on her, superb lovemaking . . . and rampant orgasms.

'Oh God, yes . . .' she breathed, clenching her inner muscles, trying to believe she was clenching down on *him*. His cock . . . his fingers . . .

He'd think nothing of reaching into the water and drenching his designer jacket, just to play with her because *she* wanted him to. He'd find her clit without any hint of guidance.

Rolling her head against the folded-up towel she'd placed behind her neck, she submerged. Not into the water, but deep into the fantasy.

Her lover whipped off his jacket, rolled up his sleeves, and immersed his strong right arm beneath the foam. His fingertips settled against her breast, stroking lightly in a circle around her areola, flicking against the puckered little crest then alighting on the very tip of her nipple and rocking it gently. The caress was so slight, so delicate, yet somehow also huge. Raw lust fired her senses, making her gasp.

'Oh please . . . oh please . . .' she chanted, knowing she was his, and that he could do whatever he wanted with her.

Riding the silky water, his fingers slipped to her other breast.

Their touch was tantalising, barely perceptible, light and frustrating. She began to thrash again and lather slipped and slopped and surged.

'Please . . .' she breathed.

In her mind's eye she saw his eyes, as dark and compelling as they were on the television, but ten times as fiery.

Tell me what you want, he commanded silently. *Tell me, out aloud, no holding back*.

'I want you to touch me . . . I want you to touch my clit. I want to come.'

The ghost of a smile warmed his handsome face, adding humanity to its idealised perfection. His fingertips withdrew from her breast and she thought for a moment he might tease her, deny her the pleasure. But why would he? He was perfect . . .

She frowned, losing her grip.

A cold shudder rushed through her, along with a sense of dislocation and uncertainty. This was all silly. A bit sad and pathetic.

No! No! No!

Centring herself, she sipped more wine. And caught the thread again.

Easing herself down a little way beneath the water, she opened her legs wider.

Immediately, *his* hand found its clever way to exactly where she needed it to be.

Deft fingertips parted her pubic hair, and far, far back in the reaches of her mind, she made a note to wax next time. She imagined herself bare down there, with a neat, smooth-skinned cleft.

Even more perfect for the perfect seductive man.

But in this fantasy, tonight's fantasy, he played with her curls, neatly dividing them and slipping in to discover her clit. Then he settled upon it, just as delicately and ethereally as he'd stroked her nipples.

'Slowly, slowly, not too soon . . .'

Who was she talking to? To her lover . . . or to herself?

But he was clever and he maintained a perfect pace.

Circling, circling . . . gathering up the wetness within the wetness and anointing her with it. His touch was nurturing, but had authority. He was her master.

Lucy wriggled her bottom against the base of the bath, massaging her own nether cheeks as her lover massaged her clitoris.

Her imagined lover.

But the scented air and the champagne made him real to her, not just a fantasy. Everything was perfect, and idealised, just like him.

She pictured his face, his body, his arm in the water, his hand between her legs.

She felt his finger, rubbing her clit, and she came.

The delicious pulses of pleasure were overwhelming. She surged uncontrollably, rocking the mass of perfumed water and sending it over the edge as she soared on a bright, sweet wave. The bath mat suffered, but she didn't care, she only writhed and gasped and climaxed.

Oh lover, you're incredible. You're the man.

But as the orgasm faded, then came the anti-climax. The anti-orgasm. A sense of deflation and the wrench of loneliness and disappointment.

Lucy sat up in the water. She shook her head, flinging off dark thoughts. Bollocks to all that, the night was young. She could still have more fun.

The water was starting to cool now, but while it was still comfortable, she took another hefty swig from her champagne glass, then started to soap herself with a natural sponge and expensive soap. And while she did so, she imagined again that it was the detective washing her, his hands just as deft as when he'd played with her clit.

She was just getting into it again when her stomach rumbled.

Time to satisfy another appetite. There was a mouth-watering platter of gourmet cheese and biscuits with fruit and olives waiting for her. Everything was the best, from the supermarket's finest range. Primo products to match the perfect primo fantasy.

Pausing every moment or two to take a sip of champers, Lucy worked her way through her beautification routine, primping and creaming and fluffing and teasing. By the time she'd done, she was feeling slightly tipsy.

Crikey, I'm going to be pissed at this rate!

But what did it matter if she felt loose and freeform? Losing her inhibitions was good for her fantasies.

Right on the point of stepping into her new pair of beautiful but scandalously expensive panties, Lucy stopped dead.

What the hell was that banging noise? A heavy repeated thumping. She scowled and let fly a fruity oath.

There was someone at the door. Someone who didn't have to buzz up to be let in the building.

Oh no!

There were only four flats in the house. The tenants of two of them were away and the third flat was being renovated. Which only left ... sigh ...

Her fucking idiot clod of a landlord!

For a fifth of a second she considered ignoring him, but he'd be able to hear her Mozart playing throughout the flat. Bugger!

Abandoning her posh panties, she dragged her scraggly old dressing gown out of the cupboard and bundled herself into it again, belting it up tight. Too tight. She felt as if the sash were cutting her in two, and all her golden champagne-glow mellowness rapidly dissipated.

She was stone-cold sober again, her fantasy in rags.

Shoving her feet into her equally ratty old mules, she hesitated. *I could still ignore him. For all he knows, I really do have a man in here.*

But as the rapping on the door came again, it was obvious he wasn't going to go away until he got an answer, the stupid donkey.

She stamped to the door, teeth gritted, and even as she reached it, the panels rattled under another fusillade of blows.

'All right! All right! Keep your hair on!'

Wildly, she swung the door open, making it bounce on its hinges.

Steve, her landlord, grinned at her across the threshold. He was leaning on the door jamb, looking even more ill-kempt than usual if that were possible, with a battered canvas tool bag swinging from his hand. His shabby Southern Comfort T-shirt appeared to have been washed a thousand times and beaten on rocks by tribeswomen, and his jeans were in holes and worn white in strategic places.

Places Lucy really didn't want to be caught looking at but couldn't quite stop herself. There was obviously quite a good-sized tool in there too.

When she glanced up again, Steve had a wide, smug grin plastered across his cheeky, stubble-clad face.

'Hi, babe ... Didn't know whether you could hear me over the Mozart.' His blue eyes danced over her, settling on the V of her dressing gown, even though it was very snugly fastened and not revealing anything. 'I wouldn't have disturbed you, but I'm going up to town tomorrow for a few days, and I remembered I still hadn't fixed your pipes ... Is now a good time? It'll only take a moment.'

Scenarios from cheesy 70s porn films flitted through Lucy's mind. Plumbers and their wrenches. Electricians and their socket sets. It was a million miles away from her dreams of her television lover. The very antithesis of them ...

Here was Steve the randy landlord, not her perfect and sophisticated dream man. Although to his credit, he did at least recognise Mozart when he heard it, she accepted reluctantly.

Still, she sighed inside.

Why on earth did you have to turn up tonight of all times? Can't a girl have a bit of peace and quiet to have sex fantasies and masturbate?

'Come in . . . it's all right. I'd rather you fixed it now than wait much longer.' She *was* fed up with all the dripping and the wet towels and constantly replacing a bowl beneath the sink.

Sly dark eyes looked her up and down, as if searching for a chink in the tightly belted-up robe.

'Look, if you're busy, I can come back after I've been away.'

The louche expression on his swarthy face dared her not to refuse him. It was actually rather a nice face too, she realised, taking the time to look more closely for a change. You could even call him handsome in a rough-hewn sort of way.

And his body certainly wasn't bad either . . .

A big man, he seemed to displace quite a lot of air when she stepped back and ushered him past her into the flat.

'No, go right in . . . You might not come back for a month and I'm fed up with soggy towels under the sink.'

Steve laughed softly, as if tacitly and unapologetically acknowledging his erratic stewardship of his own property, while Lucy studied his broad back as he preceded her down the passage.

My God, he *was* big. Strapping, in fact, and seeming more massive than ever in the confines of the flat. Heavy of shoulder, his arms and chest and thighs were powerful in a way that reminded her of the detective, although her fantasy man had a refinement and grace about him that her lumbering oaf of a landlord sadly lacked.

Or did he? He was light enough on his feet as he strode towards the kitchen.

Once in there, he zeroed in straight away on the elegant platter of cheese and fruit that she'd laid out for herself.

'That looks nice ... Expecting someone?' The lift of his eyebrow seemed to speak volumes about his speculations on her sex life.

Words froze on Lucy's lips.

What could she say? How could she explain her fantasy night for one, with possible masturbation?

Steve's eyes narrowed, as if he'd sussed it out already.

'OK, love ... none of my business, obviously,' he said cheerily, squatting down before the cupboard under the sink and letting his bag of tools drop on the kitchen floor with a heavy clump. 'I'll get out of your hair as quick as I can.'

Lucy dragged in a deep breath, but kept it quiet, not obvious. She wished he hadn't turned up when he had, but still, somehow, there was a strange comfort in having him in the flat. He was a real man. Solid and living. Scruffy and a bit loutish but, in his own way, peculiarly appealing.

Something twisted in her heart, gouging and aching. She imagined a flickering, fluttering sound ... the card-house of her fantasies cascading to the carpet in disarray.

She couldn't tear her eyes away from his thighs, and the way they flexed as he crouched. They looked hard and packed with muscle. As did his bottom in his faded work jeans.

Fantasy and reality phased in and out of her imagination, making her giddy. Here was a real, very attractive man. Earthy, but desirable. What the hell was she doing with her life? If she turned her nose up at possibilities like this, she was letting Simon and that harpy Linda win.

What's the point in faffing about with fantasies, when I should be reaching out for the real ... and the available?

She hadn't seen Steve with a girlfriend lately.

'I'll have to turn the water off at the stop-cock,' he announced, straightening up. 'Just for a couple of minutes, though. I won't spoil your evening.' He snuck another glance at the cheese, and had the effrontery to lick his sexy lower lip.

'No problem.'

'But it isn't under the sink.' He gave her another provocative grin. 'It's a renovation, this flat . . . things were changed around. The stop-cock is actually in the bathroom. OK to go through?'

He nodded in the direction of her sybaritic haven. With its scented water, its solitary champagne glass, its flickering tea lights.

Titillating lingerie laid out for nobody to see. Expensive perfume to seduce a man who didn't know she even existed. Mortified, she wanted to grab Steve by the arm and stop him discovering her pathetic secrets, but he was too fast for her. Or maybe, somehow, she wanted him to find her out?

In the bathroom, she half-expected a mocking, laddish reaction, but he remained silent, his dark eyes flickering around, taking it all in, weighing it all up. Then his expression grew thoughtful when he paused to glance at her magazine, on the stool and wide open at the 'seduce yourself' article. But his reaction wasn't at all what she'd anticipated. He looked more wry and sympathetic than anything.

Still not speaking, he strode to the sink and opened the little cupboard underneath it. With swift efficiency, he reached in and turned off the stop-cock.

'Won't be a mo,' he said again, his eyes gentle. The kindness was so tangible that to her horror she felt tears well in her eyes, and she could only thank God that he turned away and left for the kitchen again almost immediately.

He felt sorry for her.

He thought she was a sad, frustrated, bloody spinster who couldn't get a real man and had to resort to fabricating faux dates on the advice of silly magazines, and indulging in solitary masturbation pretending a man off the telly fancied her.

Lucy sat down on the side of the bath and wept. Wept so hard that a few minutes later, she couldn't stop when Steve came back.

'Hey, love, what's the matter?'

In an instant, he was perched on the edge of the bath beside her, his big brawny arms around her shoulder. Pulling her to him, he pressed her face against his crook of his neck, and she smelt a whiff of some cologne he must have applied earlier in the day, all blended with healthy male sweat and something volatile like paint or thinners.

It wasn't Gucci or Dior, but it was still sexy, and it was real, not imagined.

'Come on, pet ... Don't cry. It may never happen.' It was nonsense talk, comfort talk, but his arms around her made every kind of sense. The blue meanies of despair started to retreat.

'You'll think I'm a totally sad bitch ... all this, it's just for pretend.' While she dragged in a calming breath, he pulled a handkerchief out of his pocket. It was old and well laundered but it looked reasonably clean and she let him blot her eyes with it. 'Girlie fantasy night in, and all that ...' She sniffed again. 'I've just been dumped and I felt like some self-indulgence ... know what I mean?'

The words had whooshed out of her like air, and she felt empty, at a loss. But the warm arm around her imparted a glow. Healing comfort. And more.

'Tell me about it, love,' he said in a strangely weary voice. 'It's a bloody cattle market out there. Sometimes, it's just easier to stay in, isn't it?' His other arm came around her, rubbing her arm, squeezing her as if she'd been out in the cold and needed warming up. Which she did. 'I've been working hard on renovations and stuff ... building up my business. Sometimes I'm too tired for anything more than a night in with Kylie or Madonna or Beyoncé on the box ...' He paused. 'A few cans of Stella, a takeout ... and ... well ... a bit of the old hand shandy, know what I mean? And some KY with it if I'm feeling sophisticated.'

What?

A feeling bubbled up. Like she'd drunk several more glasses of champagne, straight down, one after the other. Laughter gurgled up and she just couldn't keep it in. She simply guffawed.

'What? You as well?' she gasped eventually, in between hiccups of laughter. 'I mean, not Stella Artois or Beyoncé ... but the other thing?'

'I'm afraid so.' She drew back, looked at him, and saw the ruefulness in his expression. His big shoulders lifted in a shrug. 'Now who's a saddo?'

'You're not sad. And neither am I,' Lucy announced. More warmth rushed in, and light, and a feeling of conspiracy and companionship. And more of that other thing. The thing she'd never expected in a million years to feel for Steve. 'We're just busy people ... who ... um ... make a logical choice. Sort of ...'

She looked at him, suddenly really, really liking his shaggy hair and his solid body. He was disreputable and piratey-looking, but he had beautiful blue eyes, a strong, kind face, and the promise of a truly exceptional physique beneath his tatty, paint-stained work clothes.

It took less than a heartbeat to come to a decision.

'Look, I haven't got any Stella ... but I do have another bottle of champagne. Would you like some?'

The blue eyes, which were *really* beautiful, flared, hot and interested.

'Yeah, why not? I can go upmarket.'

Lucy stood up. She glanced quickly at her lingerie, and her sexy wrap, but Steve caught the look.

'Hey, you look great in what you've got on ... It's kind of subtle ... makes a man speculate ... and fantasise.' He cast another quick glance at the mag, 'That bloke, the one you split up with … he's a bloody idiot letting go of a hot woman like you, I can tell you. Come on, let's go and get some of that fizz.'

Lucy's heart thudded as he followed her into the kitchen. She liked the way he'd said 'you split up with' rather than 'dumped you', and his large presence behind her seemed to vibrate, give her energy. And confidence.

In the kitchen, she pulled the second bottle of wine from the fridge and it seemed natural and companionable to hand it to Steve, so he could do the man thing and open it while she got the everyday glasses from the cupboard.

With an encouragingly deft hand, he uncorked the champagne and poured it out.

'So what shall we drink to?' He handed her a glass, and waited.

Lucy's heart thumped. She looked him up and down. Bollocks to shitty exes, fantasy figures and elaborate idealised scenarios. This was here and now and real.

'How about … seduction?' She caught his eye, then clinked her glass to his, still holding his gaze. 'The real thing, not the imaginary kind.'

He laughed. He smirked. But she didn't mind. The rude twinkle in his eye made her laugh back at him, and she loved the way, when he sipped his wine, he went 'Mmm …', and smacked his lips, suggesting he had far more in his mind to taste than just champagne.

They drank in silence for a few moments, then Steve took her glass from her. 'We don't need this, do we, love?' He set both their glasses aside with a determined 'clomp'.

Moving closer, he looked down at her, that naughty glow in his expression even brighter. Lucy swallowed, her heart bashing in her chest, and hot blood careening around her body at a pace a fantasy lover could never have induced.

She was burning up. She wanted Steve. And she was going to get him – and far more than she'd ever get from sad dreams of a man off the telly.

OK, so his jeans and mucky T-shirt weren't a match for Armani and Hugo Boss. But he had a hot body, gorgeous eyes, and an imagination that was more than a match for hers.

She grabbed him by the T-shirt, hauled him close to her, then slid her hand behind his head and drew his mouth down to hers.

His lips were soft and full of potential. He tasted like wine, and his shaggy hair was far lusher and silkier to the touch than it looked. For a moment she hesitated, confidence wavering, but then he pushed his warm tongue gently but firmly into her mouth, and began to tease hers with little pokes and darts and strokes.

He didn't grab her, he just kissed, standing there, letting her control the seduction. But everything about his presence and the stance of his body said he liked it. And wanted more.

Which she gave him, standing on tiptoe, pressing her body against his, feeling his hard cock jut against her belly through their clothing. His answer was a sort of eloquent grunt, his breath in her mouth.

But still he didn't touch her. Infuriating man! But in a good way . . .

Wrenching open her robe, she tried again, pushing her naked breasts against his chest and her soft bush against the denim of his jeans.

Again, the grunt. Still he teased, making *her* make the running.

Lucy laughed, enjoying the challenge.

'You're really making me work for this, aren't you, you devil!' she gasped, breaking her mouth away from his.

'Seduction, babe,' he purred, his expression warm, teasing but amiable. 'Gimme some of it.'

'All right . . . you asked for it!'

Lucy assessed the situation, quickly and excitedly, her bare nipples tingling, her pussy starting to drip. This was so real, so wonderful, so raw. She didn't feel as if she could do anything wrong here. Hooking a finger into a little hole in his shabby T-shirt – from a burn or something – she ripped down and hard, and the ancient, over-washed cotton tore like tissue paper.

'Baby!' he exclaimed, his eyes surprised but darkening with delight and lust.

Ooh, his body was even better than she'd expected. A match, easily, for any fantasy man's. He was muscular, not deeply cut but just believably firm and tanned and strong-looking, with rough hair on his chest. Unable to stop herself, she leaned over and kissed his nipple, licking and biting it playfully.

'Oh, baby . . .' he gasped again, his control breaking as he buried his fingers in her hair.

Steve's skin was salty, a bit foxy, a bit sweaty. His odour was earthy too, but it made her mouth water around his tiny teat. He was all man, and his hips bucked against her.

She wanted more. All she could get. She started pulling at the belt on his jeans and more by main force than dexterity wrenched it open, still lapping and sucking on his nipple.

Belt negotiated, she as good as ripped open his jeans, cooing in her throat on discovering nakedness within. Hot nakedness. Hot, hard nakedness.

Hot, hard nakedness enrobed in silky, velvety skin and slippery with copious sticky fluid.

She had to see it. So with a last nip at his teat, she drew back, broke free of his grip, and looked down at the monster in her hand.

Now that *is what I call a tool! And much more fun than anything you've got in your bag, landlord mine!*

His cock was reddened with blood, fierce and hungry-looking. Ready to do the business, ready to fuck her.

Steve groaned as she stroked him lightly, loving the feel of him as much as she loved the sound.

Now this was where dream lovers would always fall short, and what vibrators, dildos and Magic Rabbits would never be able to replicate. Because they didn't come powered by strong backs, muscular buttocks and powerful thighs.

'Oh yeah ... oh yeah ...' he chanted, folding his big hand around hers and guiding the way she worked and rode him. 'That's it ... not too hard, I'll come too soon.'

There was pleasure in just touching him. Joy in handling him and feeling his response, his excitement. Power of her own in tugging him gently forwards and rubbing his tip against her bare belly.

He made sounds now that weren't words, just growls and deep throaty utterances of rough male appreciation. Slick fluid poured from the tip of his cock, wetting her fingers.

Lucy wondered how long he could last before coming. She wondered whether it might just be fun to make him come, to exert control over him in a real physical way that she'd never be able to do in her fantasies. But just as she was about to experiment, Steve stopped her, moving her hand away.

'Hey, sweetheart ... I'm getting all the good stuff here. We need to see to you too.'

With that he lifted her hand to his lips and kissed it. His wicked tongue shot out and licked up his own pre-come, and when she gasped in surprise, he just waggled his eyebrows and winked at her.

How incredibly horny ...

And then his hand was upon her, settling on her belly, curving delicately and in exploration at first, then moving more purposefully. Long, thick, workmanlike fingers parted her pubic hair, then the middle one dived in between her sex lips like a missile homing in on just the spot that craved it.

'That's better, isn't it?' He began to rock the pad of his fingertip across her clit.

Yes, it was. It was far, far better than solitary, imaginary fantasies with a man she'd never seduce. Oh, masturbation was fine and good, a treat, an indulgence, but not when done in sadness and a yearning for something mutual.

She wrapped her arms around his neck, riding his finger, loving his touch.

It didn't take long. It didn't take long for hot, golden pleasure to ball in the pit of her belly and roll and tighten to an intolerable pitch. It didn't take long for the ball to burst, in ineffable pleasure, making her howl and latch on to Steve like a limpet while she shuddered and climaxed.

She slumped against him, still clinging, her labia still divided by his finger, her chest heaving like a sprinter's.

'Was that nice?' His voice was an awestruck whisper.

'Fabulous,' she panted. 'I should get you to come up here and do odd jobs a lot more often.'

He laughed in a low rumble, delicately patting her clit, as if making sure it knew that there was plenty more of what it had just had available. As he touched her, he pressed his cock against the side of her hip. It was like an iron bar, streaming with pre-come all over again.

'Have you got a condom, love?'

His voice was soft but rough, as if he were trying hard to control himself and only just succeeding.

Oh no!

But . . . yes. Befuddled by pleasure, she visualised a box with a few in it in the bathroom cabinet. Left over from less lean times, sexually, and tucked away out of sight and mind.

'There're some in the bathroom cabinet . . . I'll get them.'

She made as if to move, but he held on to her.

'No need, babe . . . we'll go to them!'

With that he slid his arms around her, beneath her robe, and, scooping his hands under her buttocks, lifted her up. Lucy's thighs parted around him and her arms hooked round his neck, their movements co-ordinated.

Steve laughed and dropped a kiss on her face, then hoisted

her more comfortably before striding off in the direction of the bathroom. Still poking out of his flies, his cock bobbed tantalisingly against her bottom as he walked.

When they reached the softly lit room, with its still-flickering tea lights, he laid her down like a precious treasure on the thick, fluffy bath mat and stroked her hair. Then he stood up again, located the cabinet, and rummaged for the condoms.

'Catch!' he said, tossing the little packet to her, then sat down on the seat of the toilet to pull off his work boots.

Boots first, then socks, then jeans, then tattered T-shirt. All off. Only to reveal a body that was almost the stuff of her fantasies, but somehow more attractive and sexually alluring for *not* being quite perfect.

He was slightly chunkier naked than she imagined her dream guy to be, but she liked his solid, latent power. He was hairier too. The nice pelt on his chest and belly was matched by a rough, dark dusting on his legs. Mmm, primitive ... and good.

He was all man. Real man. Horny and honest. His cock seemed to yearn towards her, bold and pointing, craving her pussy. His smile was macho, pleased with himself, but his boyish self-confidence made her smile back at him.

This was all so easy. No striving to be perfect, to make everything perfect and idealised. It was OK to be a bit clumsy, and to giggle.

Which she did when he knelt down, pushing her thighs apart and shuffling in between them. The sight of his cock bouncing and swinging induced mirth, as well as lust.

'Well, don't muck about, love queen, stick a condom on me,' he urged cheerfully, jutting his hips forwards.

Lucy complied happily. She didn't care about being bossed about, because she knew it was all in fun. He wanted sex, but somehow he also cared. She ripped open a packet and reached for his delightful rod.

It was a fumble, a sticky fumble, with much groaning and wriggling and touching and more laughing as they squirmed about into position.

'Do you want a bit more fingering, love? I mean, I will ... but I'm dying to get into you.'

'You're a prince, landlord mine,' she replied, taking hold of his cock and gently dragging it towards its destination. 'But I think I'll manage ... I'm dying for *you* to get inside me.'

He pushed. She jerked with her hips. He slid in with a mighty thrust, his big organ stretching her.

She wrapped her arms around his torso, and her legs around his hips.

He leaned over and kissed her, his lips gentle in the moment before the action. The words, 'You feel beautiful, babe,' followed, exquisitely soft and full of meaning.

They rocked and bucked, they heaved and shoved, his pubic bone knocking hard against her clitoris as his delicious cock slid and pumped inside her.

It didn't take long until they achieved their goal together, and Lucy flew, her heart soaring on sweet waves of pulsing pleasure, then lifting again as she felt Steve lose it, and pulse inside her.

Later, after using almost all the condoms, and drinking all the champagne, Steve turned the water back on so they could make tea and use it to wash down enormous bacon sandwiches that they scoffed like famished kids. Replete then, they sat in silence, just smiling at each other across the table.

And Lucy realised something as Steve reached across and gave her hand a companionable squeeze.

There was silence from beneath the sink. No dripping leak. Another job well done.

She placed her other hand over Steve's, then winked, and nodded in the direction of the bedroom.

Grinning again, Steve was on his feet fast, reaching for her hand, his fingers warm and sure around hers.

There was still one condom left, so tonight was turning out to be perfect, after all.

As might other nights, Lucy hoped. She really hoped ...

Portia da Costa is the author of the Black Lace novels *Continuum*, *Entertaining Mr Stone*, *Gemini Heat*, *Gothic Blue*, *Hotbed*, *Shadowplay*, *Suite Seventeen*, *The Devil Inside*, *The Stranger*, *The Tutor* and *In Too Deep*. Her paranormal novellas are included in the Black Lace collections *Lust Bites* and *Magic and Desire*.

The Shopping List
Shayla Kersten

At five minutes to closing, Morin Lansing flipped off the OPEN sign and the display window lights then walked across the store to the dressing room. Paul would be here in half an hour to pick her up. Time to ask her customers to leave.

The man had insisted on being in the dressing room with his girlfriend ... wife ...

Whatever ...

The two of them had gone through at least twenty different dresses. Three of the last four were draped over the rod holding up the privacy curtain.

Morin opened her mouth to speak but stopped as a soft moan slipped through the thin curtain. She raised her hand to knock on the door frame but a breathy groan made her hesitate.

Peering through a tiny opening in the curtain revealed the woman – fair and curvy – her shoulders pressed against the wall with her hips pushed forwards. The woman's mouth hung open, her tongue skittering across her full lower lip.

Morin dropped her gaze, following the swell of the woman's breasts past the six-hundred dollar dress – not yet paid for – hiked around her waist, and found the dark-haired man with his face buried in the apex of the woman's thighs. His hands rustled under a swath of expensive silk near her ass.

Heat swirled in Morin's lower stomach. An ache of need reminded her of Paul's recent neglect in the bedroom.

'Jason ...' The woman breathed his name like a reverent prayer. 'We shouldn't ...'

Jason lifted his head. His lips glistened with her juices. 'Come on, baby ... You know the rules. If it's on your list, you have to go through with it.' The staid suit jacket was gone and his tie hung loose, dangling down over his open shirt.

'List?' Morin's lips mouthed the word. Her teeth caught her bottom lip, forcing silence. Curiosity kept her still, suppressing a shiver of desire.

'I know.' The woman's whisper was almost inaudible.

Jason's hands ran down her thighs and back up again. 'Hey, the list thing was your idea but we can stop if you want to.'

'No!' Her fingers ran through his hair. 'No ...' This time the word was gentler. She banged the back of her head against the wall with a soft thud. 'What if the salesgirl comes back?'

Standing, Jason planted a quick kiss on the woman's mouth. He sucked on her lower lip then murmured, 'Then we get caught. Wasn't that part of the excitement? Part of what got you so hot to begin with?'

A shudder swept through Morin from the base of her neck, down her spine and straight to her sex. Wet heat laced through her pussy.

'You're so sexy, standing there exposing yourself,' Jason mumbled between kisses. 'Sara, so hot ...'

Sara wrapped one leg around Jason's thigh. Her body undulated against her lover's crotch. A flush reddened her creamy breasts, rising up her throat to her face. 'Yes ...' Her whisper barely reached Morin's ears. 'Let's do it.'

Twining his fingers through Sara's hair, Jason ravaged her mouth with passion-filled kisses, hard and deep. He angled his head from one side to the other, revealing a flash of tangled tongues, as he devoured her mouth.

Morin pressed a hand to her lips as if she could feel the bruising assault. Her face flushed with heat. A thin sheen of sweat beaded her forehead.

Jason freed one hand from Sara's hair. Sliding down, he cupped a full breast. His thumb and forefinger tweaked a barely concealed nub into a plump knot.

Soft moans escaped from Sara, past Jason's lips. Her body ground against him with more and more frantic motions. Lifting her leg higher, she hooked her heel into his tight-muscled ass. Her fingers curled into his broad back.

Morin's rapid breath threatened to expand into a full-blown pant. Afraid they'd hear her, she cupped a hand over her mouth, forcing slower breaths through her nose. Her body trembled with fear of discovery and the delicious thrill of the forbidden.

Tugging the low-cut neckline of the expensive silk dress, Jason exposed one full breast. With a final hard kiss, he licked his way down Sara's long neck, leaving a shining trail of saliva.

Sara's head bumped against the dressing-room wall as she arched back, allowing him greater access. One hand moved from his back to his wavy dark hair. Long fingernails combed through the unruly curls then her fingers clutched several locks. Pulling his head lower, Sara gasped a long moan-filled sigh as his mouth clamped onto her nipple. 'God, yes . . .'

Morin trailed a hand across her breast. Fantasy moist heat surrounded her nipple. A rush of not-so-imaginary dampness lined her panties.

Jason's mouth freed the rosy nipple. Glistening with moisture, the areola pimpled from either cold or desire.

A shiver raced through Morin, shuddering its way down her spine. She squeezed her aching breast, letting her thoughts place her in the dressing room instead of Sara.

Large hands, strong and sure, moved past Sara's waist. Pushing between their bodies, Jason's movements hinted at his action. His arm slid up and down, cocking at the elbow with each stroke.

Morin resisted the temptation to mimic his actions. Her customers might not care about getting caught but she didn't want them to find her fingering herself ... while watching them. She should walk away. Leave them to their public seduction in private. But her body refused to obey her mind.

Instead, her thoughts drifted to Sara's 'list'. Morin's mind twisted through a dozen thoughts – public sex, obviously – but what else?

Morin had fought with Paul over their sex life. He wanted to spice things up a little ... try different things. Although public sex hadn't been on his list.

A small voice whispered in the recesses of her mind, 'Maybe it should be ...'

Desire forced a small gasp from her lips. Her heart froze, chest tight as she held her breath. When Sara and Jason didn't react, Morin took a long slow breath.

Her gaze riveted on Sara's pumping hips, Morin caught vague glimpses – or maybe her imagination supplied the view – of Jason's fingers, slick and shiny.

Clenching her thighs, Morin shuddered as a rush of pleasure pulsed through her cunt. Her teeth dug into her lip to silence a moan. The salty taste of blood teased her tongue. Even pain didn't dampen the heat burning through her.

Shit ...

The sharp stab of her tender lip seemed to heighten the sensuous tremors consuming her body. And a little pain was on Paul's list – not that he'd made one. A frown creased her forehead. At least she didn't think he had.

Paul had started out with subtle hints, little things. Watching a movie or pictures from the internet, he'd commented on how some things were hot. Forbidden things like tying up, spanking. Once or twice, he'd spanked her – just a few slaps to her ass while fucking her from behind. And she couldn't ignore his enthusiasm for holding her down, restraining her.

For the most part, she had ignored his suggestive comments and let him get away with certain activities. When he'd finally come out and asked about inviting another couple to join them in the bedroom, Sara had had to draw the line. The idea haunted her, both exciting and terrifying her. Afterwards, their sex life had grown cold. Paul had grown distant. She was losing him because of her own fears.

Her mind lost in the memory, she didn't hear the words Sara mouthed near Jason's ear. Or maybe she hadn't spoken loudly enough. Whatever she'd said, Jason's head popped up, a wide grin spread across his face.

'You really want to?' Even as he spoke, Jason tugged the tie from around his neck.

'Yes.' Sara rubbed her body against his. 'Do it.' She held her hands in front of her, wrists together, mouth crooked in a lopsided smile. 'In for a penny and all that . . .'

Jason twisted the tie into a noose then slipped the loop over Sara's hands. Tugging the tie tight, he pulled her hands above her head, tying the other end onto a hook meant to hang clothes, not experimenting lovers. Dropping to his knees, Jason pulled Sara's thighs apart. His tongue slipped between her folds.

Morin's knees went weak. She grabbed the door frame to keep from pitching through the curtain concealing her from the two lovers. Could they read her mind? Know what she was thinking?

Instinct screamed at her to run, get away from the scene unfolding in the dressing room, but her feet refused to co-operate. Images jumbled through her mind like a slide show – first Sara, restrained to the wall with Jason's face buried in her snatch. Next, Morin bound across a bed with Paul's hand reddening her ass. Paul fucking her hard with her tied tight, immobile, unable to resist.

'No,' Morin whispered. What would Paul think – really think of her – if she let him? *Why had he had to ask?* The thought ran through her mind for the thousandth time that month. If he'd acted instead of asked . . .

Clenching her thighs, Morin braced her hand against the door frame and closed her eyes as an orgasm washed through her. The harsh gasp of air rushed in her ears like a sonic boom. Flicking her eyes open, she glanced through the slit in the curtain.

Sara's stare met Morin's but she didn't speak or alert Jason to her presence. Instead, Sara's pink tongue ran a wet trail across her lower lip then she puckered her mouth in Morin's direction.

Freed from her frozen state, Morin stepped back away from the curtain. Her heart raced in her chest, echoing in her ears. Long hard breaths forced her close to hyperventilation. Leaning against the wall, Morin ran her hands through sweat-damp hair.

Sara's soft moans grew louder. Words mingled with the sound. 'Oh, yes, Jason. Feels so good.' The woman knew Morin was lurking outside the dressing room. Her volume must be for Morin's benefit.

Turning to face the wall, Morin pressed her flushed forehead against the cool wood. In spite of the need to run, Morin edged back along the wall until one eye met the opening in the curtain.

One of Sara's thighs rested on Jason's shoulder, her knee crooked around his back. Her gaze met Morin's again. Tilting her hip slightly, Sara revealed the small tuft of hair at the top of her hidden folds. Jason's dark bobbing head concealed the rest of her flesh from Morin's sight. 'Feels sooo good.' With her gaze locked on Morin's, the words weren't meant for the man kneeling at Sara's feet.

One of Jason's hands, fingers bright with Sara's juices, ran a trail from her waist to her exposed breast. He twirled one finger around her areola, just missing the swollen nipple.

Mesmerised, Morin couldn't drag her gaze away from the creamy flesh, the circling finger. Morin's heart raced as her fingers fumbled with the buttons on her blouse. Tugging her bra aside, Morin slipped her hand against her bare flesh.

She began to mimic Jason's actions. Her other hand reached for the curtain, fingers tugging the crack open a little wider.

Sara's gaze dipped to Morin's chest then her full lips curved in a wide smile. Jason's hand slid away from her ample flesh. Crawling up her chest, slowly up the long line of her neck, his fingers stopped at her mouth. Her tongue flashed out, circling his index finger several times, licking the slickness from his finger.

Morin's taste buds recalled the taste of her cream, sharp and sweet, from Paul's lips after he'd feasted on her pussy. Temptation slid her hand towards her waistband but fear stopped her.

Sara released Jason's fingers and her mouth formed a silent dare. 'Do it.' Nodding, she dipped her head towards her lover's long fingers then sucked the three middle ones deep into her mouth.

Morin's breath sounded loud and raucous. Her heart raced with an erratic beat, threatening to burst free of her chest. Her pussy ached with intense need in spite of one orgasm. She needed more than the pressure her closed thighs could provide.

Her hand resumed its motion towards her waistband. Sucking in her stomach, Morin pushed her hand into her skirt. Her gaze locked with Sara's, she didn't miss the woman's head shaking no.

Once again freeing Jason's fingers, Sara mouthed the words, 'Show me.'

Morin gasped but she obeyed the silent command. She clutched her skirt in her fingers and gathering the material in a slow creeping crawl, she raised the short skirt. Cool air breathed on the damp cloth between her legs as she exposed her crotch to a total stranger. A female stranger . . .

Sara nodded encouragement. Her hips pushed into Jason's ravenous tongue. The muscles of her thigh clenched as her calf pressed against the back of Jason's neck. Sara's moans grew louder, coarser.

Morin's fingers traced the edge of her thong. Hesitation kept her from making the final move. Morin had never been comfortable with masturbation, and here she was letting a total stranger watch? Something wasn't right with her. But then her excitement over Paul's suggestions had already proved that.

Sara's increased arousal was contagious. Her hands struggled against the tie, pulled the noose tighter, leaving reddened trails around her pale wrists. Moans and grunts from both of the lovers mingled in the air. 'God. Yes. Jase.' Harsh breath punctuated Sara's words. Her gaze locked once again with Morin's. 'Do it!'

Morin yanked her thong aside and obeyed the harsh command. Plunging her fingers into her aching cunt, already slick with cream, Morin bit her tender lip to stifle a shout of relief. Her palm pressed hard against her clit, rubbing the swollen flesh as her tight passage clenched around her fingers.

'Fuck me, Jase. Now.' Sara's body convulsed with tremors as Jason sprang from the floor.

His hands grabbed her hips, twirling her around to face the wall. His slacks bulged with a fierce erection. A dark stain marked the material with more evidence of his arousal. Fingers fumbled his fly open, revealing a long thick cock. The weeping crown was flared and almost purple with need.

'Gonna fuck you so hard.' Hiking up the back of Sara's dress, he guided his dick towards the apex of her thighs.

'Yes. Fuck me.' Sara pushed back towards Jason. Standing on her toes, she strained to meet his flesh.

Morin slid her fingers deeper, faster as Jason's engorged cock slid into Sara's willing hole. Her other hand caught the curtain, clenching the coarse material in her fist. Shuffling her feet farther apart, she worked her aching flesh harder. Lost in the pleasure, the need, she couldn't control her gasping breath, grunted moans.

Sara's head tilted towards her and then back, encouraging her forwards.

With her steps hampered by her own hand deep inside her dripping cunt, Morin shuffled forwards, into the doorway.

Jason sighed as he sheathed his flesh in Sara. As he pulled back, he glanced in Morin's direction. Instead of surprise, he flashed her a cheeky grin before slamming hard into Sara. 'Like what you see?' He slid back until the flared head slipped free of Sara. 'Want to see more?'

His fingers dug into Sara's hips as he impaled her again. Long hard strokes, bruising force.

Morin took one more timid step forwards, now inside the dressing room. Her fist still clutched at the curtain, a sheath of the material draped over her shoulder. Her other hand caught in a vice between her legs, her thumb rubbed against her clit.

Pleasure and fear fried her brain. She should run, hide. Her throat threatened to close, breath caught in her chest. Her body burned from lack of oxygen, from shame, from desire.

'Touch me.' Sara gasped the words as Jason continued to pillage her body. Her full breasts jiggled with each hard blow.

Morin tried to keep her hold on the curtain but her fingers, numb from her fierce grip, refused to obey. As she shuffled forwards, the material slid across her breast, her shoulder, then fell behind her. Standing so close, she could smell the tang of Sara's cream, heated with desire, and the friction of Jason's cock slamming into her.

Swallowing hard, Morin took one more step. Heat radiated off Sara's body, or was Morin's own temperature rising?

'Go ahead. Touch. Me.' Sara's breath caught in a moan. 'Now!'

Releasing her hold on her cunt, Morin took the final step to Sara's side. Her hand slid under Sara's restrained body. Grazing

225

a plump breast with her juice-slick hand, Morin drew a ragged breath.

'More.' Sara strained forwards until her flesh rested in Morin's hand.

The fullness, so different from Morin's small tits, fascinated her. She rolled the soft mass in the palm of her hand. The hard nipple teased her skin. *What would it feel like against her lips?* Morin tried to banish the thought from her mind but the words taunted her.

'More!' Sara struggled back and forth, her body flailing between her lover's cock and Morin's hand.

Something snapped in Morin's brain. Dropping to her knees, she crawled into the tight space between the wall and Sara's suspended body. Kissing the soft flesh of Sara's stomach, she licked a path up to the pale breast. Morin's thighs clamped closed on her overheated sex. As she wrapped her lips around Sara's nipple, her pussy clenched with a second orgasm. Waves of pleasure shot through her body as her mouth sucked hard on the captured tit.

Her hand slid up Sara's soft thigh. Her fingers plunged into the wet folds, bumping against Jason's pounding cock. Flicking her thumb across Sara's clit, she clung to her breast like a starving child. If she let go, she knew she'd be lost.

A scream of pleasure laced through the tiny dressing room. Sara's thighs clenched on Morin's hand. Warm liquid covered Morin's fingers. Sara's shuddering shook Morin's mouth loose.

As her mind screamed no, Morin licked a path down Sara's stomach. Reaching the juncture of her thighs, Morin leaned in. The tangy sweet scent of Sara's cream enticed her closer. Her tongue flicked against Sara's swollen clit then pierced between the folds.

Sara's body shuddered as she howled her ecstasy. Her hips flexed forwards, mashing her pussy against Morin's face.

Morin grabbed Sara's thighs near the V. Her hands steadied Sara's movements as her thumbs pulled the outer lips open.

Pink and rose flesh greeted Morin's hungry mouth. Delving into the wet heat, Morin's tongue caught Jason's cock as he stroked in and out of Sara's hot tunnel.

Sticky liquid coated Morin's face, dripping down her chin as her own pussy leaked down her inner thigh. Her fingers dug into Sara's flesh as she buried her face in the tantalising snatch. Her teeth raked against Sara's clit as her mouth covered the swollen flesh. Sucking hard elicited another scream from Sara.

'Enough!' Sara sobbed above Morin's head. 'Can't take any more ...'

With a sigh of regret, Morin backed away. She knew the feeling of being over-sensitive. Falling back against the wall, Morin fought to catch her breath. Her mind reeled with what she'd done. What would Paul say?

'Now it's your turn, Morin.'

Morin jerked her head towards the dressing-room door. Standing with the curtain pulled partially open, was Paul with a grin on his face.

'What the fuck ...' Morin scrambled to her feet, bumping Sara as she rose.

'I knew you wanted to play, to experiment.' Paul walked into the tiny dressing room, crowding her against the wall. 'I just wanted you to admit it.'

'How?' Morin couldn't deny his words. Not with Sara's cream coating her face, the taste still teasing her tongue.

'Because whether you admitted it or not, talking about it always got you wet. Then you started pushing me away so you could keep your secret.'

Morin's accusations died before she opened her mouth. She'd told herself Paul had grown cold but he was right. If she were too tired or too busy, she wouldn't have to think about his tantalising ideas and he'd never know how the thoughts affected her.

'And now ...' Paul ran his tongue across her lower lip. 'It's your turn.'

The ache in her pussy intensified as he licked Sara's juice from her lips. 'But Sara, Jason ...'

A soft chuckle vibrated against her mouth. 'Remember the friends I wanted you to meet?'

'Shit ...' Morin ducked her head around Paul's shoulder.

Sara winked at her as she rubbed her now-freed wrists. The soft silk dress covered her sex. 'Sweetie, you can eat me anytime. For a first-timer, you did a hell of a job.'

'Very hot,' Jason agreed. He wrapped his arm around his lover while his other hand stroked his still-erect length.

Morin took a long deep breath. 'So now what?'

Paul's hands ran down her arms until they circled her wrists. 'Now, we do this ...' He pulled her arms in front of her.

Jason stepped forwards then slipped his crinkled tie over her right wrist. Sara moved to the other side. A thin scarf, discarded in the earlier shopping spree, twisted around her left wrist.

Pulling her around towards the door, Paul reached up and yanked the three forgotten dresses from the stout wooden curtain rod.

'Wait ...' The door of the dressing room faced the store. If someone came in – she hadn't locked up for the night. What if a passer-by looked too hard in the window? 'Someone might see.' Morin's fear clutched at her stomach and tightened her throat.

'Then they'll see.' Paul planted a gentle kiss on her lips. 'Doesn't the idea make you wet? Someone watching you like you watched Sara?'

Morin's pussy clenched in agreement with his words but she couldn't catch her breath to speak.

Caressing her chin with his cupped hand, Paul lifted her face towards his. His gaze locked with hers then his lips crooked in a smile. He pulled her arms up as Sara and Jason bound her wrists to the crossbar.

A shiver of submission tickled down her back. Wet heat seared through her neglected pussy.

Paul's foot forced first one leg and then the other to opposite sides of the door. Her weight eased onto her wrists as her feet pressed against the wooden frame.

Being spread-eagled and vulnerable had the feared effect on Morin. Need raced through her. Desire threatened to turn to begging but she wasn't ready to admit she wanted this. Needed this . . .

Paul ran his hand inside her half-unbuttoned blouse. His fingers caressed the skin on her stomach before twisting under her bra. With a hard yank, the delicate front clasp popped under the strain. Her breasts exposed to Sara and Jason, instinct pulled against her restraints with an attempt to cover her flesh.

'Be still.' Paul's harsh whisper stopped her movements. 'You're not allowed to move –' he leaned close to her ear '– or I'll be forced to spank you.'

Sharp need stabbed through her body. The desire to obey warred with the idea of Paul's hand stinging her ass. An embarrassed rush of heat flooded her body. She wanted to tell him no, no to the spanking, no to the entire situation, but instead she bit her lip and held still.

'Good girl.' Paul caught her chin in his hand. His mouth covered hers. He nibbled her bottom lip free from her teeth. His tongue bathed her swollen lip before pressing for an opening.

With a whimper, Morin allowed him access. The sweet rush of familiar passion pulled at her stomach. Her sex demanded pressure her position wouldn't provide.

She closed her eyes as Paul's free hand slid down her side then lifted her skirt. He tucked the hem into her waist.

Cool hands with long sharp nails did the same to the other side, and then across the front and back until her skirt did nothing to cover her modesty. A shiver of desire coursed through her as the soft hands lingered on her skin, fingernails tracing a line across her stomach.

'Do you want to stop?' Paul breathed the words in her ear. 'You have to tell me, Morin. I won't force you to do something you don't want to do.'

Her eyes squeezed shut, Morin shook her head.

'Speak to me, baby. Tell me you want this.'

'Yes.'

Paul's five o'clock shadow rubbed against her cheek as he shook his head. 'Not good enough. Are you saying yes – stop or yes – keep going?'

Her lips pressed tight together, Morin drew ragged breaths through her nose. Sara's hand disappeared from her waist. Fingers tugged at her restraints.

'Keep going. Don't stop.' The words burst free with a rush of air. Her body craved the attention. She'd never been so hot, so much in need before. The idea of Paul ploughing her cunt as Jason had Sara – bound, helpless. Paul . . . or Jason.

'Oh, God.'

Three sets of hands caressed her, touched her skin, fondled her breasts. The softest pair slid low on her stomach. Sharp nails combed through the nest of hair surrounding her pussy.

A clean-shaven cheek teased her breast before a hot tongue lapped at her nipple. Jason . . . She resisted the temptation to open her eyes, confirm what she already knew. His mouth covered hers, sucking hard while his tongue licked her sensitive nipple.

Someone slipped between her body and the door frame. Kisses rained down her back, accompanied by the brush of day-old whiskers.

A long-nailed finger pulled her thong aside then raked across her clit, dipping between her folds. The rustle of silk floated away then soft lips teased her lower stomach. Cool air washed across her aching flesh as fingers prised her open, exposing her.

A tongue, soft and gentle, lapped at her slit. Sharp pleasure lanced through her as she pushed her hips forwards, seeking pressure.

A loud whack accompanied a stinging burn on her left ass cheek. Morin yelped in shock and pain.

'You weren't supposed to move,' Paul's voice whispered from behind her.

Another swat, equally hard but not as surprising, landed on her right cheek. The blow forced her forwards against Sara's mouth. Jason's teeth raked against her nipple but he didn't lose his hold on her breast.

'You like that, don't you, love?' Sara whispered. 'His hand on your ass while I lick your pussy.'

Morin once again bit her abused lip. She wouldn't answer. Couldn't answer.

'All you have to do to get more is move . . .' Sara ran her hand down Morin's inner thigh then back up again. 'Go on, baby. Move.'

Her heart racing, Morin did as Sara demanded and canted her hips forwards. Another resounding slap rewarded her as Sara wrapped her lips around Morin's clit. Struggling against her binding garnered another whack. And another. Each swat sent pleasure peaking through her body, coming to rest in her clit.

'Looks like I might need something more than my hand.' The jangle of Paul's belt buckle warned her of his meaning. The snap of leather as he jerked his belt free scared her. 'If you stand still, I won't have to use it.'

Rough leather slid over her burning ass as Morin stood frozen in place.

Jason kissed a path from her breast to her neck. 'I think she wants it.' His voice was a harsh whisper near her ear. 'Don't you. Have your ass burning from a good leather belt. Gets you hot thinking about it.'

Sara's soft licking turned to hard sucking as Jason pinched Morin's nipples.

'Do you want it, Morin?' Paul's breath teased her other ear. 'Say yes . . .'

'Yes!' Morin broke into a thousand pieces. 'Yes!' The hard leather slapped across both cheeks. 'Yes!' She strained forwards against the delirious pleasure of Sara's mouth. 'Yes!'

Her eyes flew open as Jason planted a hard kiss on her mouth. His hand twisted through her hair, pulling tight near the base of her skull. Another blow. Another kiss. Another lick. Another pinch. Her senses went into overload. This orgasm wasn't just her cunt. Her entire body rode a wave of intense ecstasy.

'More!' she moaned around Jason's tongue. Fighting her restraints with all the strength she could muster, she fell into the chasm of depravity she'd tried to avoid. She was putty in Paul's hands, to mould into whatever sexual situation he wanted.

Paul's insidious whisper invaded the furious pleasure storming across every nerve. 'Do you want me to fuck you now?'

'Yes . . .' she sobbed. She'd had too much but she needed more. 'Yes . . . please.'

'Or maybe you want Jason's cock up your hot tight cunt.'

Morin shivered from cold and heat, like a fever consuming her. The memory of Jason's cock, longer, thicker than Paul's, plunging into Sara forced the words from her tight chest. 'Yes . . .'

Paul chuckled an almost sinister laugh. 'Maybe we'll just take turns. Both have a chance.'

'Yes. Whatever you want.'

'No, baby.' Paul's tone lowered to a comforting whisper. 'It's whatever you want.'

'I want . . .' Morin gasped for air and swallowed hard. Her mind whispered, *To stop* . . . But her lips said, 'Both . . .'

Paul kissed the nape of her neck as his hands slid down her side. His fingers curled under the lacy strings of her thong. A hard yank snapped the delicate material. Her clit quivered at the shock as the material tugged tight.

Pulling the soggy remains of Morin's underwear away, Sara rose in front of her. 'Good girl,' the woman whispered before kissing Sara long and hard. The flavour of Morin's cream mingled with the aftertaste of Sara's. Then Sara slipped away, her curvy body replaced by Jason's tall muscular build.

His pants open, his thick cock waved in the air. Sara reached around him and slipped a condom over his erection.

Paul's arms tightened around Morin's waist, lifting her towards Jason. Grabbing hold of the wooden curtain rod, Morin relieved her wrists of her weight as she once again closed her eyes.

The cold tip of the condom brushed her heated flesh. A soft moan escaped her as the head of Jason's cock prodded her folds. The thick crown pressed against her opening.

'Be easy, Jase . . .' Paul's strong tone reassured her.

'Man, she's hot,' Jason murmured as he pushed inside.

Morin opened her eyes. Jason stared at her with a frightening intensity. His face was red, beaded with sweat, as his cock stroked inside her a couple of inches. He pulled back quickly then lunged forwards faster, but still didn't plumb her depths. His breath panted like a dog's on a hot summer day.

'Give me . . .' Morin whispered. Her gaze locked onto Jason's.

'Give you what, baby?' Paul spoke in her ear.

'All . . .' Morin leaned back against Paul's chest and wrapped her legs loosely around Jason's waist. Relaxing into Paul's embrace, she stared at Jason. 'Now . . .'

As if freed from invisible bonds, Jason surged forwards, slamming deep into Morin's channel. His fingers dug into her thighs, holding her steady as he reared back and ploughed into her again.

Another rush of pleasure shot through her. Turning her head towards Paul, she met his mouth, opening, demanding a kiss. Her lover ravaged her lips as Jason fucked her with long, hard strokes. Each plunge of Jason's cock matched Paul's delving tongue.

Soft hands massaged her breasts, teasing her nipples. A hot mouth caught one aching nub and held, sucking, taunting. Explosion after explosion of desire fired through Morin's synapses.

Jason's hips jerked against her cunt. 'Too much ...' He grunted his finish as he ground his pelvis into her clit.

'More ...' Morin's throat ached as she coughed out the hoarse whisper.

The thick cock slid free of her pussy. Her cream dribbled down the crack of her ass as Jason lifted her legs from around his waist. He kissed her, hard, full of teeth and tongue, while he lowered her legs to the floor.

Paul pulled her hips back, clutching her around the waist, then pressed his cock between her thighs.

Her lover's cock slid inside her stretched channel, fast and hard. His hand slapped her ass, refreshing the stinging blows from earlier. Her pussy clenched around his length. 'Yes!' she shouted into Jason's mouth.

Sara moved next to her then dropped to the floor. Morin didn't have to see what the woman was doing. She knew before the soft tongue lapped at her slit.

Yet another wave of pleasure launched Morin into a haze of brightness, light and floating. *Could someone die of orgasm?* The fleeting thought scared and amused her.

Paul's rough treatment didn't last long. His warm seed spread through her cunt as he bounced against her ass with a long groan. Sara's tongue continued to flicker against her slit even as Paul pulled out.

'Enough ...' Morin moaned, her body shuddering from over-stimulation. 'For now ... enough.'

Two sets of fingers fumbled with her restraints while Jason continued to hold her. Knees weak, she welcomed his strong grip but she was content when Paul wrapped his arms around her, freeing her from Jason.

'Are you OK, baby?' Soft kisses fluttered across her face.

'Uh-huh . . .' Morin didn't have the strength to do more than mumble.

'Not mad?'

'Huh-uh . . .'

'Want to do it again sometime?'

Morin nodded her head against Paul's face. 'Need a list . . .'

Twelve Steps

Shada Royce

A lot of couples go to sex therapy ... I just happen to go by myself. Why, you ask, would I bother going to a sex therapist alone? What good could this do for a twenty-something singleton with decent-enough looks who doesn't have a problem getting laid? The answer is obvious in its simplicity – I need to learn to enjoy sex. You heard me right, I didn't stutter. I've finally admitted my problem. Step one. Check.

So back to the sex therapist and my self-made, self-implemented twelve-step program to discover my 'inner' sex goddess.

Thinking back, I guess I came to realise I had a real problem sometime during my senior year in college. After a whopping total of four lovers in my life, I began to wonder why some women couldn't get enough sex. My best girlfriend used to go on and on about this thing her boyfriend could do with his tongue. Other friends discussed which sexual positions they enjoyed most, what types of foreplay, if they liked to be tied up or have their hair pulled. Tied up? Really? To my amazement, I realised women talked about sex and the big 'O' – a lot.

That was when it hit me, when I fully understood I had never had one of those mind-blowing, howling, clawing-your-own-skin kind of orgasms. Sure, sex had been pleasant enough but I didn't get antsy after going celibate for six months.

Although I never had problems finding a partner, most of the guys I slept with ended up being more of a buddy. Or worse, the guys I found really interesting would eventually say something to the effect of 'I don't want to ruin our friendship' even before the big dance.

Not only had I never experienced the seventh level of orgasmic enlightenment, but I came to understand how lousy I was at seducing a man into my bed. I mean, really getting a guy hot and bothered. Mind you, I know most college guys will screw anything with two legs and a pie-hole, but I wanted more. I wanted what my girlfriends chatted about and dreamed about. I wanted to make a man lose control, thereby making me lose control. So I embarked on a sexual journey to discover if I, like other women I knew, could become addicted to sex.

I began my path to discovery in the library. I know, you're thinking 'the library'? Did I fail to mention that my degree is in scientific research? Needless to say, the library was a natural place for me to begin. I researched everything I could find, from 'how to give a great blowjob' to the scientific evidence behind the elusive orgasm. I became obsessed with discovering who I was in the bedroom and what I really enjoyed. I wanted to know if there was any hope for me. Were men really immune to me or did I just need to learn the secrets of seduction?

Over the course of my research I developed a twelve-step program to aid my quest for sexual self-discovery. The steps resembled the Alcohol Anonymous program, but I guess you could say I was forming an addiction rather than fighting one. Don't laugh. I know it sounds ridiculous, but once I started following the steps I really started becoming more comfortable in my own skin.

So step one is, of course, admitting you need help and you have a problem. This was the easiest step: I figured since I was researching I had admitted I needed help. Steps two through eleven involved everything from buying decent lingerie from somewhere other than a cheap department store to going out in public with no knickers to learning how to pleasure myself with a sex toy. Anything I could think of that I would never tell another person, I did.

The final steps brought me to the library once again, but this time the step wouldn't involve research and books. Were the eleven previous steps enough to prepare me for the home stretch? The day I put the program to the test forever changed my perspective on seduction.

'Excuse me?'

The library attendant on duty turned around as I leaned across the counter. 'Can I help you?' He smiled, the small scar above his lip stretching with the action. My gaze focused on his firm, full lips. Flashes of how his hot, wet mouth would feel trailing a path down my shoulder made me dizzy. A wave of heat flashed over my skin as I considered what I was about to do, what I prayed I had the gumption to do.

A breeze drifted from the door to caress the length of my bare legs and flirt with the naked, heated flesh under my skirt. The cooling effect of the tendrils of the wind's breath reminded me of my state of undress. Knowing I didn't have knickers on brought a rush of fluttering sensations pulsing through my body, bringing goosebumps to my heated skin and tightening my over-sensitive nipples. I shifted over the counter, bringing my arms together so my breasts pushed against my hot pink tank top.

He glanced down at my cleavage then back to my face with little more than a blink.

I cleared my throat, a little unnerved by his nonchalant reaction to my display. Looking around, I leaned over before whispering my request. 'Do you have any books on oral sex?'

This time his eyebrows shot up into his hairline before snapping together in a tight V over his blue eyes. 'Is this some kind of joke?'

I leaned over further, giving him the full view down my shirt. 'No, I'm doing research.'

'On oral sex?' His lips tilted to the side and my heart fluttered against my breast. Steadying my resolve, I stuffed back the urge to look away. Instead, I pinned him with what I hoped was my steamiest come-hither look.

'Uh-huh,' I finally managed, and twisted my finger through a lock of my hair. The seconds between my question and his response stretched on. Would he tell me to get lost? Would he call security? My face bloomed with a rush of heat from the embarrassment tying a knot in my stomach.

'On giving or receiving?' he asked, breaking the unforgiving silence. The straight planes of his face revealed nothing behind his ice-blue eyes. I swallowed, fighting the urge to turn tail and run. Throwing caution to the wind, I glanced at him from beneath my lowered lashes.

'Receiving,' I managed in a low, sultry voice.

He snorted in a light, airy way, dismissing my request with a shrug. Pinning me with a look of disbelief, he finally turned to the computer and typed something in.

His chin-length sandy blond hair was tucked behind his ears and I took the opportunity to contemplate the ledge of his brooding brow, the straight edge of his nose, the turn of his top lip and the cut of his square jaw. The very profile I'd admired many times before. His sun-browned skin glowed copper in the morning light streaming in through the large picture windows. He cut his gaze at me without turning from the monitor. I didn't bother hiding the fact I'd been checking him out.

Either he didn't care to notice or he wanted me to leave, because he didn't even blink. 'You'll find what you're looking for on the second floor. At the top of the stairs, go right, all the way down, third row from the end.'

He granted me a crooked smile and turned as someone entered the library to drop off a load of books. The thin material of his light-blue polo stretched across his broad shoulders as he picked up the stack of books and moved them to a cart. I looked my fill of his cotton-encased back and his ass cupped to perfection in beige khakis. He turned and looked over his shoulder as my eyes travelled back up his body.

'You need help with something else?'

Yes, I need you to fuck me. I didn't say it, but I wanted to. Instead, I shook my head and turned towards the stairs, making sure my hips swayed enough so if he was watching, he'd know I was bare beneath.

I walked up the stairs, replanning and questioning all I had worked towards for the last few months. I'd been unable to seduce this particular stranger. Bloody hell, I couldn't even begin to tempt him. I headed to the location he'd described, figuring I could get in a little more research if nothing else.

Walking along the third aisle, I scanned the books. Women's fiction? Puzzled, I turned and travelled back up the aisle, reading the titles again. About midway down the aisle, a hand wrapped around my waist and clamped over my mouth. Stunned, I teetered between fighting the restraining hand and waiting to see who'd captured me. A man pulled me back against the length of his hard body and something inside me relaxed.

'Have you found what you needed yet?'

My mind whirled. It was him. I would have recognised the deep tones of his voice anywhere. His question vibrated through me, the baritone rumbling, sliding like a satin snake along every nerve in my body. He'd followed me and then he'd made the first move. All I could do was shake my head no.

He dropped his hand, skimming along my jaw, down my neck, trailing fingers along my collar-bone, to run a palm over my breast. My nipple swelled against the fabric of my shirt. He circled the tightening bud with the tips of his fingers. Dazed, I watched as if from a dream as my nipple peaked to life. The light dusting of blond hair on his knuckles glittered in the bright fluorescent lights, highlighting the tracing path of his hand. Those strong, tapered, long fingers teased me through my shirt, circling the point of my breast until the desire swirled in the pit of my stomach, in time with the rhythm of his hand.

From his hand over my mouth, I could taste and smell the heavy scent of his cologne. Citrus and evergreens wrapped around me, pulling my senses tighter to him. His body radiated heat, pressing along my back, to seep into my body and melt any resistance to his spell.

Moving my hair aside, he placed his lips to the curve of my neck. I moaned low in my throat. The wet path of his mouth left a burning line of sensual promise along my shoulder. Waves of pleasure pulsed through my body, bringing goosebumps to my skin. He continued his exploration of my skin with his mouth and tongue, the goosebumps retreating and then re-forming with each swipe of his mouth. Leaning back against his frame, I ran my hands down his legs, revelling in the iron-like muscles encased in soft fabric. His erection pressed into my lower back so I pushed up on tiptoe and ground my ass along the length of his cock.

'No.' He nipped my neck and jerked back on my hair. The sudden brutality of the action heightened my excitement and the place between my legs grew hotter, heavier and wetter. He traced his lips along my neck to my ear. I squirmed beneath the moist onslaught of his lapping, plunging tongue. The thumping accelerated in my stomach, radiating down to my pussy. Pressing against the restraining bond of his arm now around my waist, I stretched to touch myself, anything to ease the budding pressure. Unable to reach my clit, I dug my fingernails into his thighs, a silent plea for him to take it all the way.

A flush of hot breath fanned across my ear and cheek as he released my ear from his torturous tongue. 'Want me to stop?'

Too frenzied to form coherent words, I shook my head and ground against his dick. He jerked my hair again before running his hand down my stomach and along my hip bone to settle on my thigh, so close to my pussy the heat of his hands reached out to caress me. His fingers twitched on my leg, as if he fought them from reaching for me. I wanted to drop to my knees and beg, to have those fingers sneaking under my skirt to touch me at my core.

'That's not an answer. Say it,' he murmured into my ear.

Looking down the row between the aisles of books, I panicked at the thought of being caught. The panic morphed into heightened desire as my mind whirled into a fantasy of someone finding us then stepping back to watch the act unfold. The thought burned through me, soaking my body in a rush of lust-induced sweat. 'What if someone catches us?' I breathed, praying I wouldn't push him from me with the reality of the words, hoping he'd find the image as erotic as I did.

His erection jerked against my back and he tightened his fist in my hair. 'Good,' he ground out. 'Now say it. Do you want me to stop?'

I shook my head along his shoulder in answer to his demand, my thoughts disjointed and focused on where his fingers danced along my leg.

'Please don't stop.' My voice cracked with the soft-spoken whimper. I moved my hips towards his hand, hoping his fingers would slide to my clit and bump me enough to give me some relief.

'Uh-uh.' He moved his hands to my hips and pushed. 'Lean forwards and put your hands on the ladder there against the bookshelf.'

I didn't even question his command. All I could do was obey. I leaned forwards and he moved my feet apart. Spread-eagled against the ladder, I waited to see if he'd touch me. Then he did – a light feathering of his wet lips on the back of my knee. My legs threatened to buckle as his tongue travelled up my thigh before stopping at the hem of my skirt. He repeated the tease with the other leg, only his tongue and lips tasting my skin, leaving a warm tingling trail in his tongue's wake. His warm breath feathered across the back of my leg, sending shivers of quivering anticipation straight to my pussy.

He lapped at the back of my thigh, hot, bold strokes of his tongue so close to the crease beneath my ass. I nudged backwards, begging for his tongue between my legs, on my clit. My knees quivered when he stood and pressed into me from behind, grinding his hard body into mine.

'Whatever you do, don't move and don't make a sound.'

He pulled my hips out and up from the ladder and the bookshelf, so my ass jutted in the air. The position opened me, exposing my wet, throbbing pussy. Cool air brushed my naked ass when he lifted my skirt, exposing my body to his view. He ran a palm over my ass and the callused burn of his hand seared into my body as the movement laid a very blatant claim to me. He removed his hand as he moved near my pussy. I wanted to moan in disappointment, but before the thought left my mind his mouth was on me. First his tongue lashed out and traced along my slit, like a bird tasting the flower's nectar before devouring the sweetness within. Then he lapped along my clit with those same strong strokes of his tongue. In a slow, erotic motion he devoured me, tasted me with his chin and nose pressing against my skin as he buried his tongue inside me. He swirled his tongue in and out of me, teasing me with the symbolic motion.

A hot wave broke over my skin, bathing me in a light sweat. I couldn't catch my breath, my lungs locked as everything in my body stilled, a brief pause, like the quiet before the storm. Then he slid a finger inside my pussy, first one and then two, burying them to his knuckles. In long, smooth caresses he worked them in and out of my body in a slow, steady rhythm.

With one hand on my hip, he stilled my bucking, my begging for more.

Seconds spun out into minutes as he teased me with his fingers, building the fire until I thought I'd burst into flames, holding me to the edge of the peak with the practised groove of his hands. The space between my legs grew wetter and heavier, almost stinging with the budding of my coming release. I bit into my lip and closed my eyes, holding my breath and fighting the plea for him to hurry.

My eyes flew open when I heard a shuffle. Through the tops of the books I saw a figure move away from an aisle of books three rows over. I stilled, afraid to stop the man on his knees between my legs but fearful of being caught. Sensations rushed over me as the world seemed to freeze on a moment of indecision. First the buzz of the lights, then the musty smell of used books and dust invaded my over-sexed senses. Saturday mornings in the library were proving to be busy and over-crowded, at least in this section. Finally a faint mixture of sweet citrus-evergreen and hot sex invaded my practical brain and made the choice for me. I closed my eyes and dropped my head back so my long hair brushed the top of my ass, then I held on for the ride.

As if sensing the moment, his mouth moved to my clit and he drew the swollen bud between his teeth and gently sucked. Floods of ecstasy washed over me, breaking through me in wave after pounding wave, first retreating before rushing back like the tide, teasing my senses with the mind-numbing pleasure of the release. The orgasm broke over me in a burst of heat, radiating from the pit of my stomach and flashing out in a hot, molten tingle straight to the tips of my toes. My body bucked with the ferocity of it. He continued to suck on me, drinking my dew and prolonging the experience as I continued to come. I bit into my hand to keep from crying out, afraid he'd stop if I broke his rules.

When the tremors subsided, he scooted up my body, his hands running along the length of my legs and back up to my hips. With my skirt still riding up around my waist, he pressed his hard cock against my sensitised pussy.

'Please,' I begged, wanting nothing more than him buried to the hilt inside of me, using me for his own pleasure.

'Please what?' he breathed, his hands travelling around to the front of my body to cup my breasts. I could smell the sweetness of my come on his breath and my body pulsed in response. His question brushed the hair along my ear, sending tingling sensations down my nerves to the pulse point of my pleasure.

He squeezed my nipples and I drew in a broken breath, the light pain only serving to heighten the pleasure.

'Fuck me,' I moaned, grinding back against the length of him.

This time he turned me around to face him. My vision darted to the jut of his cock pressing against his pants and the wet evidence of my own pleasure smeared across the front. I pulled my mesmerised gaze back to the fire-blue depths of his eyes, wondering what he'd surprise me with next.

He glanced at my lips before moving in to kiss me. The first touch was tentative, a test, a tease to tempt me to take the next step. And I took the challenge because I wanted so much more.

I could taste my own come on his lips and smell myself heavy on his breath. Driving my tongue into his mouth, I pressed fully against him and tangled my hands through his hair. All at once, his hands were everywhere, touching every crevice he could. I could sense the hunger in him and the power of the raw need to claim and conquer. This was what I'd dreamed of. This was what I'd wanted. This was seduction.

We drank from each other's lips for a time, revelling in the newness of each other, the wonder of the first kiss. I nipped his lower lip and he moaned into my mouth. Then he drew my bottom lip between his and sucked. Wrapping a leg around his waist, I pressed against him, wanting to smooth my hands all over him all at once. I pulled at his shirt and ran my hands along his rippling abs and around to his back. His skin slid like satin beneath my greedy fingers, a glorious expanse of well-toned muscle encased in pure satin. I sighed, wondering what he looked like beneath his shirt. The inflaming need to see my hands on his body exploded inside of me. I wanted to see my pale fingers splayed across his chest. He didn't fight me when I tore at his shirt and as soon as the material cleared his head, he drew me back against him as he pushed up my tank top to expose my breasts.

The first touch of naked skin to naked skin ignited my desire like a match to paper. I wanted to cry, I wanted to sigh, I wanted to sink to my knees and thank him for touching me. I couldn't stop as my hands roamed along his torso, his back and his shoulders, to finally spear through his hair. The whole while he drank from my mouth and I gave all he wanted, and begged for him to take more.

He pushed against me and we moved backwards until I stopped against an ass-high table. Leaning me back, he lay over my bent body, pressing hot, open-mouth kisses down my chest to my breasts. I sucked in a breath as he drew one peaked nipple into his mouth. The other tip he rolled between his fingers as he sucked on first one breast then the other.

Rifling through the information tucked into the back of my mind, I dug for the lists of what to do I'd compiled from magazines and books. Men are visual creatures, I remembered that much. So I arched back and bucked against him, begging him with my body to give me sweet release once again. Telling him with my touch how much I wanted him to continue to fondle and play with me. Letting him know with my muted cries how much I appreciated his caresses. Eventually the only thought travelling through my head was, *Could he make me come like that again?*

I moved a hand to his cock and gripped his length through the fabric of his pants. Massaging him, I tried to remember all I knew about pleasuring the male body. He groaned with my nipple in his mouth. I pressed against his shoulder and he stood back, a little dazed. He fondled my breasts as I worked his belt free and dropped his pants to the floor. Taking his erection in my hand, I rubbed the length with one hand and circled the head with the other. Leaning in, I flicked my tongue over one of his nipples then the other. Looking up through my lashes, I locked his gaze to mine as I trailed a path down his torso, sinking to my knees.

His cock stood erect from his body, a good eight inches of hard, thick, silk-encased dick. I ran my hands up his legs and to the front of his body. Wrapping one hand around the base of his cock, I used the other to bring him to my mouth. I licked the pre-come from the tip, teasing the slit with my tongue. His fingers curled into my hair, flexing a little as I licked around the head of his cock. Then with slow deliberation, I looked up into his eyes and pressed him fully into my mouth. He watched me take him in before his eyelids dropped closed.

Moving him in and out of my mouth, I used my hands and tongue to swirl and suck his length. His fingers dug into my scalp, twitching each time I withdrew and relaxing each time he entered my mouth.

The tempo escalated and he pumped into my mouth as I continued to swirl my tongue along his cock. His musky scent blended with the richness of his cologne to form a heady aroma. I breathed in his scent as I took the length of his dick into my mouth. I pulled him free from my mouth but continued to work his manhood with my hands, then I drew one of his balls into my mouth. Sucking gently, I traced my tongue over the ball in my mouth. I squeezed my hand along his length as I nursed his nuts. Before I could suck and swirl my tongue around the ball any more, he pulled me up and sat me on the table.

My tank top rode around my neck and my skirt was bunched around my waist in a thick band of blue denim. He spread my legs and positioned himself between my thighs, the tip of his manhood kissing my entrance. The sight of the long, hard length of him poised to enter nearly had me coming again.

When he didn't slide into me, I met his intense glare. He gripped my hips and moved within an inch of my face. 'What do you want?' he asked, a cold, hard gleam cloaking his features.

For a moment, my heart thundered in panic. Would he stop if I asked? Did I really want to do this with a stranger? Someone who I knew nothing about?

I looked around me, taking in the secluded little corner at the back of the library. How many times had he played this game? And did I care? A heartbeat later I had the answer. But I wasn't ready to concede the battle.

I leaned back, positioning my body so my breast thrust high in the air. He looked from the pink tips back to my face. 'Answer me one question,' I demanded, tightening my legs around his waist.

His face shifted from desire to annoyance and back. I could almost see the questions swirling in the blue depths, so I jumped to the question.

'Why women's fiction?'

His eyebrows shot up in surprise and I knew I'd thrown him with the unexpected question. 'Huh?'

'Women's fiction.' I moved against his arms, brushing my breasts over the banded muscles. The hair braided against my sensitive skin, kicking my desire up another notch. 'Why did you send me to women's fiction, of all categories?'

He leaned forwards, his breath fluttering along my lips with his light laugh. 'Because I knew what you really wanted when you came to the counter. Women's fiction seemed appropriate for a woman wanting a fantasy.'

I smiled against his mouth. 'And you think all I wanted was a romantic fantasy?'

He didn't answer, but one light-brown eyebrow arched over his brow in an unasked question.

I shrugged. Let him think I wanted the sweet love-making of fantasies. Instead, I'd have to show him I wanted to be fucked good and hard.

'I want you inside me,' I whispered, and I moved forwards so the head of his cock pushed into me. 'I want to drive you crazy. Don't hold back. Tell me what you like.'

He pushed into me with one swift plunge of his hips. Under the cheap glare of the fluorescent lighting, I watched him enter me. His cock disappeared inside of me and I felt my body stretching to accommodate his length and width. His chest hair and the hair around his cock brushed against my skin, sending tickling little waves of pleasure cascading over my body. I put a hand on his shoulder and lifted myself off the table, enough to allow him to pull out and push back inside of me. I wanted to watch him fucking me, so I locked my legs around his waist and pulled him back to me. Again and again I worked his body, driving him against me, the tips of my breasts brushing his chest, my clit brushing the hair around his cock. Something about him allowing me to control the speed of the sex blew my mind, and the lines of restraint etched around his firm mouth told me all I needed to know.

'Fuck me,' I breathed, coming up against him again. This time, instead of pulling back I lay back and reached over my head to grip the edge of the table. Tightening my legs around his waist, I begged him again. 'Fuck me.'

His fingers dug into my thighs and he pumped into me, his brow creased, his gaze intent on the goal.

Moving a hand to where our bodies joined, I touched myself, rubbing my fingers along my clit. I could see the desire explode within him when I brought my coated fingers to my mouth and sucked my juices from them.

He heightened the pace and my body rubbed up and down the laminated surface. Sweat pooled at the base of my back, but I couldn't stop, even though my muscles screamed for me to rest. The table scratched along the carpeted floor, the sound like the sea washing over sand. Then the table bumped into the wall and rocked against the concrete block.

Our laboured breathing filled the small space of the corner. My legs tightened around his waist and my knees were in the folds of his arms. Without breaking pace he picked one leg up to his shoulder, then the other. Holding my legs to his chest with one arm, with his free hand he licked his fingers then traced the folds covering my clit. The position penetrated deep and his hands brought a new wave of sensations. All at once I wanted to scream, I wanted to moan, and I wanted to beg him to pound me harder.

As if reading my mind, his thrusts became fierce. I stuffed a fist in my mouth to keep from sobbing as he drove us higher and higher, the orgasmic sun burning our skin. Shock waves of pleasure pulsed from my toes and fingers to centre on my clit where his fingers circled and then the dam burst forth with a shattering, quaking force. I bucked against his body but his arm dug into my thighs to hold me against him as he pumped faster into me, while he gently feathered my swollen nub with his fingers. My pussy milked the length of his cock, pulling him towards his own release. The slapping of our bodies echoed around the corner, breaking through my pleasure-fogged mind. The sound brought a fresh wave of luxurious sensations. I came again, rocking into his body.

The force of my orgasm pushed him over the edge and he came into me with a writhing, pounding release. Broken, subdued cries broke the silence of our little space. His cock jerked inside of me, spilling deep against my womb. Then he collapsed on top of me, pinning me beneath the heat of his spent body. I didn't care. I lay beneath him, absorbing the mind-numbing effect of being ridden hard and liking it. Hell, I'd begged for it and all I knew was I wanted more. Lots more.

There was no after-sex caressing. Instead, we lay there, trying to catch our breath. My thoughts whirled around all I'd set out to accomplish and what I felt had been the achievement of my goal. He pulled back and stood, his cock still inside of me, looking down at me. Then he leaned forwards and pressed his lips to mine. I sighed into his mouth, and then pushed against his chest to rise.

I stood and righted my clothes as he pulled on his pants and shirt. I started to walk away, not knowing what to say or if there was anything to say, but he blocked my path.

'I've seen you before.'

I looked into his handsome face and my breath caught. My gaze travelled over his strong chin and full lips, all of which had been literally buried face-deep inside of me barely half an hour before. My knees weakened with the sexual image.

'I've been to the library quite a bit lately,' I replied before moving to step around him, and again he blocked me. His face was masked, but his eyes revealed a litany of unasked questions.

'No, you were in my biology class two semesters ago.'

'OK. So where are you going with this?' I didn't want to appear ungrateful or skittish, but I also knew never to have high expectations for a relationship after a quick roll in the hay.

'Nowhere. But why me?' He stood in front of me, hands on his hips.

Usually men ran in the opposite direction after sex but this one wanted a conversation. Maybe I'd done something right. I shrugged, lost and unbalanced with this new, unfamiliar turn of events. 'To be honest, I'm not really sure. I've been watching you since I first saw you here at the library, wondering how those lips would feel on my body, between my legs.'

'Hmm.' He chewed on the inside of his lower lip, an endearing little gesture I knew I could come to love.

He shook his head then looked down at the floor before bringing his gaze up to clash with mine, as if he'd made a decision on a whim.

'So, same time next Saturday morning, then?'

'What?' I laughed the question, unsure if I'd heard him right.

'Hey, if you don't –'

'No.' I looked around, knowing my voice had burst forth on the retort. Meet him here every Saturday for surprising, mind-blowing sex? I only had one answer.

'I mean, yes, I'll be here next Saturday.'

And that's how I seduced a pre-med student with aspirations of becoming a sex therapist into becoming my husband and, well . . . my sex therapist.

Visit the Black Lace website at
www.black-lace-books.com

LOOK OUT FOR THE ALL-NEW BLACK LACE BOOKS – AVAILABLE NOW!

All books priced £7.99 in the UK. Please note publication dates apply to the UK only. For other territories, please contact your retailer.

To be published in March 2009

THE CHOICE
Monica Belle
ISBN 9780352345127

Poppy Miller is an exceptionally bright and ambitious student at a top British university. Determined to make her mark in politics, she has her mind set on finding a husband with similar aspirations to herself. Stephen Mitchell, a second-year law student, seems to fit the profile and the young pair plan a future together. But then Dr James McLean, a rakish don, appears on the scene. Poppy can't help feeling drawn to the older man, and the campus stories about his colourful past and masterful character only increase her fascination. She knows that a liaison with the darkly seductive McLean will change the course of her life, but perhaps deep down that is what she wants after all. Poppy has to make a choice: should she go with her head or with her heart?

To be published in April 2009

THE APPRENTICE
Carrie Williams

Aspiring writer Genevieve Carter takes a job as a personal assistant, only to discover that the middle-aged woman she will be working for is none other than her literary heroine, Anne Tournier. However, her new employer expects rather more from her assistant than was implied in the advert and Genevieve gradually becomes enmeshed in a web of sexual intrigue and experimentation with younger and older men and women. Then, by accident, she learns that she has been cast as the heroine of an erotic novel that Anne is writing. Determined to get her own story out first, Genevieve starts a blog where she relates her sexual liaisons to a growing and appreciative readership. Lured by the prospect of a lucrative publishing deal, a competition ensues between mistress and apprentice, one which will push Genevieve to her artistic and erotic limits.

ALSO LOOK OUT FOR

THE NEW BLACK LACE BOOK OF WOMEN'S SEXUAL FANTASIES
Edited and compiled by Mitzi Szereto
ISBN 9780352341723

The second anthology of detailed sexual fantasies contributed by women from all over the world. The book is the result of a year's research by an expert on erotic writing and gives a fascinating insight into the rich diversity of the female sexual imagination.

Black Lace Booklist

Information is correct at time of printing. To avoid disappointment, check availability before ordering. Go to www.black-lace-books.com.
All books are priced £7.99 unless another price is given.

BLACK LACE BOOKS WITH A CONTEMPORARY SETTING

☐ AMANDA'S YOUNG MEN Madeline Moore   ISBN 978 0 352 34191 4
☐ THE ANGELS' SHARE Maya Hess   ISBN 978 0 352 34043 6
☐ ASKING FOR TROUBLE Kristina Lloyd   ISBN 978 0 352 33362 9
☐ BLACK ORCHID Roxanne Carr   ISBN 978 0 352 34188 4
☐ THE BLUE GUIDE Carrie Williams   ISBN 978 0 352 34132 7
☐ THE BOSS Monica Belle   ISBN 978 0 352 34088 7
☐ BOUND IN BLUE Monica Belle   ISBN 978 0 352 34012 2
☐ CAMPAIGN HEAT Gabrielle Marcola   ISBN 978 0 352 33941 6
☐ CASSANDRA'S CONFLICT Fredrica Alleyn   ISBN 978 0 352 34186 0
☐ CAT SCRATCH FEVER Sophie Mouette   ISBN 978 0 352 34021 4
☐ CHILLI HEAT Carrie Williams   ISBN 978 0 352 34178 5
☐ CIRCUS EXCITE Nikki Magennis   ISBN 978 0 352 34033 7
☐ CONFESSIONAL Judith Roycroft   ISBN 978 0 352 33421 3
☐ CONTINUUM Portia Da Costa   ISBN 978 0 352 33120 5
☐ DANGEROUS CONSEQUENCES Pamela Rochford   ISBN 978 0 352 33185 4
☐ DARK DESIGNS Madelynne Ellis   ISBN 978 0 352 34075 7
☐ THE DEVIL INSIDE Portia Da Costa   ISBN 978 0 352 32993 6
☐ EQUAL OPPORTUNITIES Mathilde Madden   ISBN 978 0 352 34070 2
☐ FIGHTING OVER YOU Laura Hamilton   ISBN 978 0 352 34174 7
☐ FIRE AND ICE Laura Hamilton   ISBN 978 0 352 33486 2
☐ FORBIDDEN FRUIT Susie Raymond   ISBN 978 0 352 34189 1
☐ GEMINI HEAT Portia Da Costa   ISBN 978 0 352 34187 7
☐ GONE WILD Maria Eppie   ISBN 978 0 352 34670 5
☐ HOTBED Portia Da Costa   ISBN 978 0 352 33614 9
☐ IN PURSUIT OF ANNA Natasha Rostova   ISBN 978 0 352 34060 3
☐ IN THE FLESH Emma Holly   ISBN 978 0 352 34117 4
☐ JULIET RISING Cleo Cordell   ISBN 978 0 352 34192 1
☐ LEARNING TO LOVE IT Alison Tyler   ISBN 978 0 352 33535 7

❏ DIVINE TORMENT Janine Ashbless	ISBN 978 0 352 33719 1
❏ FRENCH MANNERS Olivia Christie	ISBN 978 0 352 33214 1
❏ LORD WRAXALL'S FANCY Anna Lieff Saxby	ISBN 978 0 352 33080 2
❏ NICOLE'S REVENGE Lisette Allen	ISBN 978 0 352 32984 4
❏ THE SENSES BEJEWELLED Cleo Cordell	ISBN 978 0 352 32904 2 £6.99
❏ THE SOCIETY OF SIN Sian Lacey Taylder	ISBN 978 0 352 34080 1
❏ TEMPLAR PRIZE Deanna Ashford	ISBN 978 0 352 34137 2
❏ UNDRESSING THE DEVIL Angel Strand	ISBN 978 0 352 33938 6

BLACK LACE BOOKS WITH A PARANORMAL THEME

❏ BRIGHT FIRE Maya Hess	ISBN 978 0 352 34104 4
❏ BURNING BRIGHT Janine Ashbless	ISBN 978 0 352 34085 6
❏ CRUEL ENCHANTMENT Janine Ashbless	ISBN 978 0 352 33483 1
❏ ENCHANTED Various	ISBN 978 0 352 34195 2
❏ FLOOD Anna Clare	ISBN 978 0 352 34094 8
❏ GOTHIC BLUE Portia Da Costa	ISBN 978 0 352 33075 8
❏ PHANTASMAGORIA Madelynne Ellis	ISBN 978 0 352 34168 6
❏ THE PRIDE Edie Bingham	ISBN 978 0 352 33997 3
❏ THE SILVER CAGE Mathilde Madden	ISBN 978 0 352 34164 8
❏ THE SILVER COLLAR Mathilde Madden	ISBN 978 0 352 34141 9
❏ THE SILVER CROWN Mathilde Madden	ISBN 978 0 352 34157 0
❏ SOUTHERN SPIRITS Edie Bingham	ISBN 978 0 352 34180 8
❏ THE TEN VISIONS Olivia Knight	ISBN 978 0 352 34119 8
❏ WILD KINGDOM Deana Ashford	ISBN 978 0 352 34152 5
❏ WILDWOOD Janine Ashbless	ISBN 978 0 352 34194 5

BLACK LACE ANTHOLOGIES

❏ BLACK LACE QUICKIES 1 Various	ISBN 978 0 352 34126 6	£2.99
❏ BLACK LACE QUICKIES 2 Various	ISBN 978 0 352 34127 3	£2.99
❏ BLACK LACE QUICKIES 3 Various	ISBN 978 0 352 34128 0	£2.99
❏ BLACK LACE QUICKIES 4 Various	ISBN 978 0 352 34129 7	£2.99
❏ BLACK LACE QUICKIES 5 Various	ISBN 978 0 352 34130 3	£2.99
❏ BLACK LACE QUICKIES 6 Various	ISBN 978 0 352 34133 4	£2.99
❏ BLACK LACE QUICKIES 7 Various	ISBN 978 0 352 34146 4	£2.99
❏ BLACK LACE QUICKIES 8 Various	ISBN 978 0 352 34147 1	£2.99
❏ BLACK LACE QUICKIES 9 Various	ISBN 978 0 352 34155 6	£2.99
❏ MORE WICKED WORDS Various	ISBN 978 0 352 33487 9	£6.99
❏ WICKED WORDS 3 Various	ISBN 978 0 352 33522 7	£6.99

❏ WICKED WORDS 4 Various	ISBN 978 0 352 33603 3	£6.99
❏ WICKED WORDS 5 Various	ISBN 978 0 352 33642 2	£6.99
❏ WICKED WORDS 6 Various	ISBN 978 0 352 33690 3	£6.99
❏ WICKED WORDS 7 Various	ISBN 978 0 352 33743 6	£6.99
❏ WICKED WORDS 8 Various	ISBN 978 0 352 33787 0	£6.99
❏ WICKED WORDS 9 Various	ISBN 978 0 352 33860 0	
❏ WICKED WORDS 10 Various	ISBN 978 0 352 33893 8	
❏ THE BEST OF BLACK LACE 2 Various	ISBN 978 0 352 33718 4	
❏ WICKED WORDS: SEX IN THE OFFICE Various	ISBN 978 0 352 33944 7	
❏ WICKED WORDS: SEX AT THE SPORTS CLUB Various	ISBN 978 0 352 33991 1	
❏ WICKED WORDS: SEX ON HOLIDAY Various	ISBN 978 0 352 33961 4	
❏ WICKED WORDS: SEX IN UNIFORM Various	ISBN 978 0 352 34002 3	
❏ WICKED WORDS: SEX IN THE KITCHEN Various	ISBN 978 0 352 34018 4	
❏ WICKED WORDS: SEX ON THE MOVE Various	ISBN 978 0 352 34034 4	
❏ WICKED WORDS: SEX AND MUSIC Various	ISBN 978 0 352 34061 0	
❏ WICKED WORDS: SEX AND SHOPPING Various	ISBN 978 0 352 34076 4	
❏ SEX IN PUBLIC Various	ISBN 978 0 352 34089 4	
❏ SEX WITH STRANGERS Various	ISBN 978 0 352 34105 1	
❏ LOVE ON THE DARK SIDE Various	ISBN 978 0 352 34132 7	
❏ LUST BITES Various	ISBN 978 0 352 34153 2	
❏ MAGIC AND DESIRE Various	ISBN 978 0 352 34183 9	
❏ POSSESSION Various	ISBN 978 0 352 34164 8	

BLACK LACE NON-FICTION

❏ THE BLACK LACE BOOK OF WOMEN'S SEXUAL FANTASIES Edited by Kerri Sharp	ISBN 978 0 352 33793 1	£6.99
❏ THE NEW BLACK LACE BOOK OF WOMEN'S SEXUAL FANTASIES Edited by Mitzi Szereto	ISBN 978 0 352 34172 3	

To find out the latest information about Black Lace titles, check out the website: www.black-lace-books.com or send for a booklist with complete synopses by writing to:

Black Lace Booklist, Virgin Books Ltd
Virgin Books
Random House
20 Vauxhall Bridge Road
London SW1V 2SA

Please include an SAE of decent size. Please note only British stamps are valid.

Our privacy policy
We will not disclose information you supply us to any other parties. We will not disclose any information which identifies you personally to any person without your express consent.

From time to time we may send out information about Black Lace books and special offers. Please tick here if you do <u>not</u> wish to receive Black Lace information. ❏

Please send me the books I have ticked above.

Name ....

Address ....

....

....

....

Post Code ....

Send to: Cash Sales, Direct Mail Dept, the Book Service Ltd, Colchester Road, Frating, Colchester CO2 7DW.

US customers: for prices and details of how to order books for delivery by mail, call 888-330-8477.

Please enclose a cheque or postal order, made payable to Virgin Books Ltd, to the value of the books you have ordered plus postage and packing costs as follows:

UK and BFPO – £1.00 for the first book, 50p for each subsequent book.

Overseas (including Republic of Ireland) – £2.00 for the first book, £1.00 for each subsequent book.

If you would prefer to pay by VISA, ACCESS/MASTERCARD, DINERS CLUB, AMEX or SWITCH, please write your card number and expiry date here: ....

....

Signature ....

Please allow up to 28 days for delivery.